I0678056

WITCHFUL LINKING

MIDLIFE AT THE MAGNOLIA
BOOK TWO

JEN LASSALLE

MIGHTY OAK
PUBLISHING SERVICES

Copyright © 2025 by Mighty Oak Publishing Services, LLC in agreement with JB Lassalle and Jen Lassalle.

All rights reserved

This is a work of fiction. Names, characters, places, and incidents are products of the author's imagination or used fictitiously. Any resemblance to actual persons, living or dead, is purely coincidental. All products and brand names are registered trademarks of their respective holders/companies.

No part of this book may be reproduced in any form or by any electronic or mechanical means, including information storage and retrieval systems, without written permission from the author, except for the use of brief quotations in a book review.

Cover by: Maria Spada Designs

Editing by: Mighty Oak Publishing Services

CHAPTER
ONE

If the explosion had gone off an hour earlier, I would have been half-naked and fully screwed.

It had only been one week since I'd sat in the Magnolia's boardroom and laid claim to the magical inheritance left to me by my dearly departed childhood mentor Agatha. That same day, I'd signed divorce papers and ended a twenty-year marriage to a man who, at our best, was little more than a roommate.

That was a big day.

I was starting a new chapter at the ripe young age of forty-eight. In a mystical house that seemed to be thriving again. When I first arrived, the shutters needed paint, the gardens were filled with weeds and dead plants, and the exterior gave the appearance of a failing business.

But this afternoon, on my way upstairs after another long day of providing therapy to my inherited patients, I couldn't help but notice that the garden was in bloom again. The grounds were lush.

You'd never know it was July and not springtime. The house felt as refreshed and rejuvenated as I did.

And one of the drawers in the bureau of my bedroom, currently holding the title of favorite room in the house, had brand-spanking-new underwear in it.

I couldn't remember the last time I'd gotten new underwear. When I arrived here a little over a month ago with only the clothes on my back, this beautiful house had provided. Anything I needed from my old life sat in a trunk at the foot of my bed, transported by some power I didn't fully understand. Yet.

Everything else, old clothes and stale memories, stayed in New Orleans. The drawers at the Magnolia were filled with the best of the best. Soft, fitted clothing, both professional and casual. Luxurious toiletries that made me feel like a queen.

And underwear.

Not just any underwear: silky, vivid, age-appropriate underwear. No more granny panty married lady britches. No more worn elastic. Still full coverage, which was great because I both wanted and needed to protect the fanny. My butt was a peach, full on apple bottom as the song goes. I couldn't stand the idea, or sensation, of having a slim floss of fabric be the only thing protecting my most potent of creases.

After a particularly successful day in this beautiful space, I'd made a completely unsuccessful attempt to wear out the mystical hot water heater in my second favorite room, the bathroom, before getting dressed for bed.

And something about opening the drawers and seeing underwear lit a spark in me.

Satiny soft yet concealing. Sat just right on the hips. Felt like butter against my skin.

As I'd slid them on, I'd given in to the urge to bust-a-move in nothing but my undies. I'd let my tummy bounce and my boobies flap until I was out of breath.

I had other reasons to celebrate. Gabe was finishing up a summer internship then coming to visit. In a week, he'd be here, and we could have a real talk. Texts and magical letters were nice, but I wanted to hug my son. And apologize in person. And, hopefully, explain my new life in a way that wouldn't totally freak him out.

Finally, earlier in the day, I'd landed my first client at the Magnolia.

A patient who found *me* and came to *me* based on word of mouth, rather than being passed down from Agatha.

Don't get me wrong, I appreciated inheriting a business that was already nearly booked solid. And though it had been a rocky start, my patients and I were settling in to one another. I was making progress with them and hoped to phase a few of them out within a few months.

Not because I didn't want them, but because they didn't need me. Once they'd gotten used to my more modern methods—and an updated office that was probably my third-favorite room in the house—they'd relaxed into the idea of active recovery as opposed to talk therapy. They were engaged and aware and taking the tools I taught them in our sessions out into the world.

Sometimes, all someone needs is a change of scenery to break a pattern. I'd even gone a full week without a single panic attack.

Helping people made me feel good. Teaching them to help themselves? That made me feel great. And a person in need actually seeking little-ole-me out?

That made me want to dance.

As it turned out, my occasional attempts at running and very little else made for a woman pushing fifty with very little stamina. My dance party lasted a whopping ten minutes before I was gasping for air. Once my knee started making a weird popping sound, I gave up and threw on an oversized tee to sleep in.

I'd always been a full pajama sleeper in the past, but I was trying this new thing where I tried new things. So, with very little on but still feeling a little weird about it, I'd hauled my happy-but-still-getting-her-bearings booty to bed.

Where I'd immediately passed out, like I was a college student the morning after the big party. And I was sound asleep until the sound of the world ending set every nerve in my body on fire.

The walls rattled. Glass shattered as it rocketed off shelves, echoing across the room when it landed on the hardwood floor.

House groaned, the sound so booming I felt it in my gut. Pain shot through me as if my very bones had imploded. My feet tangled in my sheets on my way out of the bed, and I crashed to the floor. It was then the wrenching began. I turned in a quick circle on hands and knees, certain someone was pulling on my body.

It was just me and the house. But a force unseen surrounded me, digging claws sharp with power into my very being, and yanking some part of me I didn't recognize as if wanting it for its own.

"Shields up!" I screamed, both in agony and defiance, digging my fingers into the floor.

It vibrated against me, and my nails disappeared into the wood. I held tight, House and I clinging to one another, while a shroud of shadows roared.

"Hold on, House. I'm here with you." Its fear was my fear. Sweat stung my eyes, and a cold chill shivered across me, but I continued to grip my hands and fight. I couldn't be positive that if I let go, I'd be yanked out the window, but it certainly felt that way.

"Don't give up, House."

"I know this feels hard, but I'm with you."

"There's nothing you and I can't defeat together."

I was whispering words of affirmation to House like I was the content creator about to save its life with a well-timed meme. I still didn't understand my power well enough to fight back with words. I wasn't sure what the perfect expressions were. I only understood House needed me to fight back. So I sent House every pithy expression that lived rent free in my head.

"Hang in there."

"We're stronger together."

"Where you lead, I will follow."

Blood filled my mouth, a coppery reminder I was gnawing on the inside of my cheek. A chunk of plaster rocked loose from the ceiling, cracking the back of my neck on its way to the ground. If it weren't for the sensation of power, more intense than any I'd experienced in my admittedly short time around magic, I'd have believed Louisiana was experiencing its first earthquake.

The trembling may have only lasted a few minutes, but it felt like an eternity. I continued to whisper and shoot power through the floor, having no idea where it was going. Something in the Magnolia was very, very wrong. But since I couldn't reach it on time, I did what I could from here.

The pull grew stronger, as if I might be sucked down into the floor. It was then I realized that whatever was happening was on the floor below me. I yelled louder, my hand disappearing to the wrists. I had a quick vision of a gaping hole, a vortex inhaling all things mystical in its path, like a starving tornado.

I flexed my hands. The wood splintered against my fingers, but I ignored the sharp stings. Rather than grip onto House, I pushed against the storm. Something rested on my back, like I had support on my shoulders. Together, we fought back.

As abruptly as it started, it was over. The quaking ceased and the world around me stilled. A few clouds of dust settled. Then, it was quiet.

Too quiet. I was used to House being silent—it didn't creak like older houses sometimes did. There were no loose floorboards or cracks in the ceiling, no foundation that needed settling.

But this was a different quiet. This was the stillness of the dead. And it rocked me to my core.

My hands, now freed, rested on ripped floorboards. I dropped my forehead to them and sobbed.

CHAPTER

TWO

I didn't move. Even as a cacophony of sounds rocked the quiet, I remained still. The repetitive bangs of either feet or an object against the front door. The wail of its hinges as it flung open. A mixture of voices, some more familiar than others, growing ever closer.

I didn't want to move.

There was a small rush of air to my left, and my ears popped. The rumbling purr of my favorite cat soothed all the unsettled parts of me.

"She's in here." Gumbo lost his *I Can Haz* voice and spoke with an authority of ages he seemed to reserve for the most important situations. Despite his soothing, the wise voice did not ease my calm.

"You did good, Simone." He weaved through my arms, his soft fur and tail flitting against the exposed parts of my skin. The air around me cooled with his presence. "Everything is stabilized. Let's get you out of here."

I was in a daze, barely aware of what was going on. I'd rocketed from bursting with joyful energy to near coma to jeopardy fueled adrenaline. But I wasn't ready to leave. My fingers pressed into the floor.

"House needs me." My vision was a blur. Gumbo wasn't wearing a bow. Fatigue overwhelmed me. "I can't let go."

Voices grew louder as the bedroom filled with people. Murmurs of concern reached my ears, a few curses. I was trembling, unable to release my grip. Even Gumbo's power wasn't enough to reach me.

"House, are you okay?" I felt no answer, and that was even more terrifying than whatever we'd just gone through.

It was only the familiar tennis shoes edging into my vision that snapped me back into reality.

"Hey, Little Fox." Ethan kneeled low, cupping my chin with one large hand to lift my eyes. "House can take it from here. We need to get you downstairs."

Ethan's hand on my chin was all I needed to remember my seemingly bold, suddenly stupid, idea to try sleeping with no pants on. My full coverage undies were in plain sight of whoever was in the room at the moment, and from the sounds of it, I had a horde.

I mean sure, the house may have been through an earthquake, I had no idea if the foundation would hold us, and that was bad. But also ... my ass was hanging out.

My cheeks burned, despite the odd cold in the room. But at least the sensation of being yanked toward the floorboards had disappeared. I took a long, slow, exhale, giving my body permission to uncoil. Accepting Ethan's hand, I arose on shaky legs.

Yep. I was right. My room was full of people.

Most of whom I had only met in passing.

A few of The Eight—a term I'd accepted as describing the four women who ran the shops at Illusion Square and their men—looked at me with kind, albeit concerned, eyes. The women kept their expressions on my face, but would occasionally nod, as if speaking to one other. I'd seen the Twins do the same, a telepathy I didn't seem to possess.

The man with dark hair, I think his name was Rav, caught my eyes. With one arm around his lovely blond bride Amelie, he winked with a mischief I recognized. Rav had been caught with his pants down before, too. Despite my heated flush of embarrassment and ever-growing concern that the Wellness Center downstairs was not okay, a grin escaped.

The town's old sheriff stood behind them, Amelie's stepdad if I remembered correctly. He was retired, but another younger police officer stood behind him, despite being the one with the official badge.

Even farther behind them stood a woman with cropped black hair and the broadest shoulders I'd ever seen. She wore the company shirt of Lone Wolf Sentries, tight across her tree-trunk arms. Blood oozed from a gash on her forehead. When it hit her intense green eyes, she swiped at it like it was little more than a gnat.

More murmurs and talking travelled down from the hallway. So yeah. The town had come running.

"I need pants." I licked my lips, gagging at the chalky sensation of drywall that coated my skin. "And maybe some water."

"Here." My lost love from high school, Ray, emerged in the doorway, his own logoed black collared shirt tight across his chest. Anger radiated off him in waves I could almost see. He glared in my direction, making me wonder briefly if I'd caused the earthquake. Then I followed his eyes to the source of his ire: Ethan's hand, gripping tight to mine.

Without looking up, he extended a cold bottle of water. "Grabbed it on the way in. Thought you might need it."

9

I released Ethan's hand and took it with a mumbled thank you. Gumbo weaved through my legs.

Someone wrapped a large blanket around me, covering all my near-nude bits. The adrenaline was fading, and my desire to leave my favorite room nearly overtook me. I stepped forward—just in time to realize my legs would betray me.

At my buckle, Ray swooped forward. I was in his arms before my next breath.

"I got her," he said over my shoulder, his voice a tight warning no doubt aimed at Ethan. I didn't care. I didn't have it in me to deal with high school nonsense.

With another mumbled thank you, I let my eyes drift closed and dropped my head to his shoulder. The hum of his breath softened some part of me. The beat of his heart allowed my own rhythm to slow. What was it about this man that made me want to forget the world around me?

He carried me down the stairs and along the side to the front of the house. It was only when he lowered me, his breath quickening, that I remembered his injury.

"Sorry. Did carrying me hurt your bad leg?"

"Not even close, Spellbinder." He kept one arm under my elbow for support. A chuckle escaped, his eyes widening as if he hadn't expected to say it.

A fresh shiver zapped the moisture from my body. Spellbinder. The name he'd whispered to me during our nights under the stars at Bridge Island. *You must be a witch,* he'd joked, *binding me to you with every word you speak.*

Had he known then, what I didn't yet know? That I actually was a witch with power over words? Or had he only been lost in the flow of a passionate and reckless teenager? I didn't dare ask. I wasn't sure I wanted to know.

He opened the water for me, and I took slow sips, assessing the building. There was no sign of what happened from the front. The plant boxes still rested below the windows. The rockers were in place. No dust or debris littered the grounds. Even the sign I'd created as a first test of my abilities remained lit and in place.

"I don't get it." People I didn't recognize, most in fire or police uniforms, walked in then rushed out of the Magnolia, their heads shaking in disbelief. But something was wrong. It hung in the air like an ominous cloud. "Everything looks fine from out here."

"It must be inside." Brianne appeared at my right, clutching to her husband Nate, who was remarkably pale even for a vampire. Tears rimmed Brianne's lovely eyes, turning them red. Her hair was disheveled, and she still wore a button up pajama top and matching pants, pale yellow and decorated with pastries. She fiddled with the chocolate donut at the hem. "I can't bear to go see yet. Nate felt it, and the whole town heard it. What happened?"

"I don't know. Not exactly." I wanted to sit down. To wash off and recover. The house felt so far away, almost out of my reach.

And it was worse, seeing Brianne so shaken. She always looked like she could handle anything the world threw at her. But in that moment, Nate appeared to be all that held her up.

I closed my eyes and tried to connect with House. Lately, I'd discovered that we had a sort of bond. When I first arrived, it had been little more than a recognition of emotion. I sensed its joy when I used my magic, its frustration when I fought it.

But since the board meeting when I'd claimed my position, we'd grown close. Which was odd, because it was a house. Maybe it wasn't the house itself, maybe it was whatever entity created it. I still wasn't sure. It had a personality, though, an almost childlike response to me and the world around it. And since we hung out every day, I was protective of the space.

Its essence was still there, though faint. In my mind, it was a scared animal, hovering in a corner, frightened. It needed me to coax it out.

It needed me, and I was standing in the yard drinking water.

"The house is scared. I need to go in."

"Of course, CC. Let me make sure it's safe first." Ray's soft grip left my elbow, and he rushed forward.

I turned toward Brianne. Her gaze was eerily empty, her unblinking eyes fixed on our sign.

"Why don't you go home, Brianne? Try and get some rest and give me a chance to find out what's happened. Tomorrow is going to be a long day, one of us should be strong." It had been an attempt at a joke. She didn't even hear me.

"Bri? Honey?" At Nate's gentle nudge, her eyes flitted from whatever horror her mind had created to meet my face. It was the first time she took me in, wrapped in a blanket but no doubt pale and bruised. I could only imagine the state of my hair.

"You need to be checked out by medical!" Brianne extended her hand toward me, her fingers shaking. "My God, you're a bloody mess."

"I think I'm better than I look, hon." I took her hand in mine. It was odd, me being the one to comfort her. But as shaken as she was, the sensation that House needed me to be the strong one had bolstered me. My power surged through me, and I decided to trust it. "I need to go inside. I need to handle this, okay?"

I didn't think she could see me through the fresh tears falling, so I lifted my gaze to Nate.

"Brianne, go on home, friend. I've got this." Nate nodded toward me, wrapping her in his long arms and whispering reassurances in her ear. I took a moment to watch him guide her away, then turned on my heel and walked to the doorway.

I wasn't waiting for someone else to tell me it was safe. I wasn't going to stand in the yard like the damsel. I was the head. I'd accepted that responsibility.

I didn't care about my wobbling body any of the chaos. I just needed to be inside.

"I'm coming," I whispered to the house, and marched on my still naked legs to the front door.

CHAPTER

THREE

I nside, even more chaos greeted me. More people I'd never seen before, many of them wearing matching black shirts like Ray's. His security firm, charged with protecting us, no doubt trying to figure out how they'd failed to do their jobs.

Still hurried, but somehow graceful and taller, were scores of pale skinned beauties of all genders. Their hair flowed like the Twins', in varying colors of the rainbow. Pale, golden eyes landed on mine with looks of disdain before drifting away.

More fae.

The left side of the lobby seemed fine. The doors to Lauren's PT area and my office were intact. The floor pristine. Even the med spa, situated on my right by the entrance, was unmarred. Just like upstairs, there was nothing on the floors or walls that indicated anything unusual.

But at the far right of the room, a dry, cold breeze lifted the hairs on my arms and back.

The door to the salon stood upright and closed. Its ornate

markings were unchanged. The frame around the heavy wood was as solid and stalwart as ever.

But there was nothing behind the door. No walls on either side.

It was a doorway to nothing.

Well, not entirely.

A dark tunnel, like the inside of a tornado, swirled where the rest of the Magnolia used to be. It seemed to go on forever, endless and unyielding. A hollow wind swirled at a pitch that made my ears ache.

I hadn't yet been inside the salon, but somehow, I knew this wasn't what it used to look like.

The tunnel walls beckoned me forward. I stepped close, gasping when long fingers gripped my forearm and yanked me back.

"If you get too close, you'll be dead before you even realize what's happened." Lydia's sherbet eyes bore into mine. If I'd thought Ray seethed earlier, I had never seen anger. I could believe, standing next to her, that she might burst into flames at any moment.

At least, for the first time since I'd met her, the anger was not directed at me. I stepped back, really looking at Lydia for the first time. She hadn't exactly given me a warm welcome when I'd arrived. She and her sister Lyra had tested my magical abilities the first chance they got, putting some kind of charm spell on me that had felt both invasive and exciting.

Since then, Lydia and I had our tension, but I had to admit I respected her input. In the two board meetings I'd attended, even enthralled, she clearly knew what she was doing in the med spa. And her sister ran the salon with the same acumen. Though I was still far from truly understanding the financials of the Magnolia, I had the impression these two divisions made a lot of money.

What's more, Lydia was not afraid to tell me when I was screwing up. When I'd accidentally hexed Doug in our first therapy session, she'd been the one to call me out. And though she wasn't the best at reading my intentions, she was the reason I'd womanned up and embraced my abilities.

Looking at her picture-perfect beauty, I recognized the glamour she wore, even if I didn't understand who it benefited. Maybe she wanted to look beautiful for herself. Nothing wrong with that.

A muscle on her perfect jaw twitched, as if she were clenching her teeth. She repeatedly touched each finger on her left hand to her thumb. One foot tapped the floor in an amelodic rhythm.

Beyond the physical, though, her emotions threatened to burst through the wall she'd put between us. It was as if they were an actual wave, building to a crest that would crash if she let it. And I didn't blame her one bit. All I knew about the Twins was that they impeccably managed their divisions, kept to themselves, and were on a sort of work visa from another realm.

It didn't take all my smarts to ascertain that the realm in question lay just beyond the swirling vortex—the funnel cloud that seemed to inhale the salon. And there was no sign of Lyra amongst the ambling fae.

An extra weight of worry heaved itself onto my chest. What if something had happened to her? Could it have caused the black hole?

"Can I make you some tea, Lydia?" We may have had our differences, but we were in this together. The Magnolia had a chunk of it ripped apart, and though we weren't friends, or even particularly friendly—honestly, I'm not sure we even liked each other—we were business partners. "Come sit at the table, and I will get it for you."

She let me guide her to the break room, on the opposite wall from the salon and as far away as I could possibly get. She let me pull out a chair and took it seemingly without realizing she'd done so. Her hands weaved a basket of fear atop the table.

House still felt unsteady, so I rummaged through the cupboards and found a kettle. While it heated, I washed soot from my arms and face. I dropped the blanket, no longer caring that my body was mostly bare. It seemed like the least important thing in the world at the moment.

With two cups of tea and leftover cookies I'd found in the fridge, I returned to Lydia. She stared at the baked good I'd placed in front of her like it was an alien creature.

"Brianne always says the sugar helps." I broke it in half, pushing it closer to her. "I don't know if that's a magic thing or a Southern thing, but I'm willing to go on faith when it comes to Brianne's words."

"Still going along without asking questions of your own, I see." Lydia's words held no heat, so I decided to ignore them.

There was a racket by the salon door. I turned towards the yelling voices. A grown man and a cat screaming at one another. Ray glared down at Gumbo, now adorned with a cloudy gray bow. Gumbo glared right back up at him as Ray's hands made animated gestures.

It was an odd thing to see. A man and a cat having a spat.

Buried under the rubble of anxiety, I was surprised to find my goofball sense of humor still flared. A giggle escaped, earning a glare of my own from Lydia.

"Where's Lyra?" I kept my voice gentle, noting that she'd broken the cookie into a thousand crumbs but not taken a bite. She lifted her eyes to me. Tears shrouded them.

"In there. Somewhere." I had to admit my heart cracked a

bit at the fear in her voice. As strong as she was, just like Brianne, she was barely hanging on.

And much like it had in the yard with Brianne, a surge of power rushed through me. I closed my eyes and tapped into it. The mental image of House still frightened in the corner returned. A glow of light surrounded it, and a strange sense of peace overcame me.

"Lyra is safe. She will be back." Without opening my eyes, I reached for Lydia, found her strong hand, and wrapped it in both of mine. A comfortable warmth braided our hands together. I opened my eyes, finding hers on me. Her head was cocked to one side, as if I were under a microscope.

But the warmth grew, enveloping my body. My throat itched to speak, a sensation usually accompanied by cool. Not knowing what I was going to say, but realizing I was reciting a special form of magic, I opened my mouth.

"There is a tie here, a link between myself and the Magnolia. I won't give it up so easily."

Whoa. I didn't know what that meant, but it felt sinister and defiant. Agatha's last warning to me before I'd accepted my position rang in my head: *The chains of magic can bind, but the bonds of family can shatter even the strongest link.*

I felt vulnerable, suddenly, exposed and not just because I still wasn't wearing pants. Maybe Lydia was as tired as I was. Or maybe she was too worried about her sister. But she patted my hand before retrieving her own, offering me something that was almost a smile.

I left my hand on the table, rubbing it as if patting the head of a dog.

"I'm here with you, House. I've got you, and we will make this right."

Ray and Gumbo continued to rant at one another, and the house emptied as bystanders and officials wandered out. I drank the tea I'd made for myself. It tasted of blood and construction, a reminder I was still a damn mess. Ethan didn't return, and while the sheriff exchanged a few words with Ray, no one came to talk to me.

That irked me. Sure, Ray and Gumbo were in charge of security, but they'd clearly done a shitty job of it. And though I didn't fully understand the magic that engulfed me earlier, I was pretty sure I'd kept the giant swirly magic thingy from engulfing the entire house.

And I was the damn Supreme. I was Head of the Magnolia. I may be new, but I was in charge.

I excused myself, even though Lydia barely knew I was there, and decided to move closer to ground zero, and the bickering man-children.

CHAPTER

FOUR

H eeding Lydia's warning—because let's face it, if she's going to warn me about impending death, I should probably pay attention—I inched closer to what seemed to be ground zero. If there was one thing I'd learned in the past month or so, it was that magic manifested itself physically. So, for once, I paid attention to my body, and what happened with each step.

Step one. Normal. Step two. Normal. Step three ...

I must have looked like an idiot, sliding my feet across the floor as if a giant monster snake was going to come rushing out of the toilet and pull me in. But given that it was too-damn-early a.m., I was barely wearing clothes, and there was a gaping vortex in front of me. It didn't seem to matter whether or not my gait would get me an invite to the Ministry of Silly Walks.

I made it that way, step by step, just past Brianne's open office, using her desk as leverage in case a shadow hand reached out to grab my leg. My tired brain pictured myself upside down, dangling with my shirt around my neck, screaming as I was dragged to my doom. At least Ray would get to see my cute new panties.

It was after what felt like step nine thousand eighty-seven that the air around me finally changed. Almost similar to what I'd gone through upstairs, there was a tugging sensation to the space around me. As if my inner core longed to move forward, even if it meant leaving my body behind.

My breaths were growing shallower, the air around me thinning like I was nearing the top of the tallest mountain. My nose tingled, just the nostrils, but with my next step it intensified. A thousand pins and needles coursing their way through my sinuses. I sniffed, just to make sure my face was intact.

There were maybe twenty feet between me and the start of the mayhem. I risked extending one shaky arm, only to be met with an extreme cold. My fingertips burned in a way I imagined felt like frostbite. I glanced behind me, searching the top of Brianne's desk for a pen or sticky note, anything to mark the danger spot.

Her desk was spotless. I was covered in the remains of the debris that had showered me upstairs. But looking around down here, I realized it was as pristine as always. It was as if House had cleaned up, knowing Brianne would throw a fit if she started her morning with a mess.

Which she would. You know, if the tunnel to nowhere wasn't right next to where she sat.

She'd been a wreck when Nate guided her away. Not in her right mind. I couldn't risk her getting too close to this. I had limited magical powers, and I was struggling. Brianne was just an extraordinary human.

Oh, right. I had magic powers. I am a word witch. Duh.

"Hey, House, I know you're really shaken right now, but I'm here with you—and we'll get through this together. If I could pat you and soothe you, I would." The house made a small trilling noise, like a scared animal, and the space under my feet warmed. "There you are. Do we have enough energy to mark this spot? You know, create a do not pass line for humans and anyone else who, uh, doesn't want to get sucked in?"

At the sound of my voice and the rumble of the ground, Gumbo and Ray stopped talking, and Gumbo flicked two different-colored concerned eyes at me.

"What did you say?"

"Give me a sec." I held up one finger and closed my eyes. I couldn't explain it, but the warmth at the bottoms of my feet rose. My calves, then knees, then thighs were almost uncomfortably hot—and not in the fun someone-wants-to-rip-my-clothes-off kind of way.

It was almost as if I was being taken over. But it didn't feel invasive or vulnerable. In fact, it reminded me of my fifth month with Gabe, when he started kicking and being more active inside me.

I couldn't remember the last time I'd felt like a mother, but it was pleasant. For a short time, my body wasn't just mine, but that was okay. I was safe. I let House's entity move through me, smiling when it landed in my throat.

"Got it."

Just enough adrenaline had worn off for me to act, yet not so much that I was worn out. I was grateful for the chance to do something, even if I didn't have answers to any questions yet. And the sensation of being one with House, completely unfamiliar yet somehow right, gave me a feel for how much power we had when we acted together.

"Gumbo, Ray, you might want to move to the other side of the room." I waited as they exchanged befuddled glances, but they didn't move. "It's cool, guys. I get you're unaffected by the"—I waved my hands—"whatever that is. But not everyone has that going for them."

Their dumb little male mouths dropped open, then with a glance and a shrug, they joined Lydia at the table. With no one in the way, I got to work. Even though I was pretty sure House could see what I had pictured, I spelled it out.

"First, let's move Brianne's office away from the death hole. I don't think we have the energy to give her an entire new space, and she'll want to see people as they come in. Let's place her closer to the front door, between Lydia and Lauren's centers."

The air around Brianne's little space, complete with carpet and file cabinets, shimmered. Then it all disappeared and popped into the exact spot I'd imagined it. For a moment, my heart clenched. I hadn't realized it consciously, but I'd placed Brianne where my mother's desk used to sit. I understood why she'd moved farther back, but something about her desk there seemed ... right.

House caught on to my swell of emotions and shared them. But it was still overwhelmed and afraid.

"Good job, House. You're doing great." I rubbed at my throat, softening the muscles. "Okay, now let's put a barricade around Lyra's area, starting about where I'm standing." I took a step back. "And wrap it around to the wall on each side."

A giant, thick, forest green curtain billowed down from the ceiling, enveloping the area. It looked familiar, and it took me a moment to place it. With a laugh, I hummed the first few bars of "Defying Gravity." As if House read my mind, which it probably did, a sign appeared in front of me.

Renovations In Progress
Pay No Attention to the Man Behind the Curtain

"Good job, House," I said with a chuckle. It trilled again, a small animal happy to please its master, then the heat drained out of me and back through the floor.

"Well, that's a start." I turned toward Ray, Gumbo, and Lydia. They were all sitting at the breakroom table, each with their own version of an agape mouth. Gumbo's little pink tongue lolled to one side. Lydia's full lips gave a slight part. Ray's jaw could have been on the floor.

"What?" My throat felt like I'd swallowed sand, so I returned to them and drank deep from the full glass of water on the table. "There's a lot going on, but at least now I know no one will implode on my watch. When Brianne gets to the office, we can assess whether we need to shut down until this is resolved."

A pair of my most comfortable pants appeared, folded over the back of the remaining chair.

"Thanks, House." I slid them on and sat down.

They were still staring at me.

"What did I do?" Patting my hair, I pulled a chunk of ceiling out of my waves. "Is it because I look like I've been through an earthquake? Cuz I kind of have."

"It's because you're not acting like you've been through an earthquake." Lydia's voice sounded odd. Sure, she was shaken and worried about her sister, but there was something else in her tone I'd never heard from her before.

Respect.

In fact, looking at their faces now, I realized they were all shocked because I'd handled part of the problem. A small sliver of irritation ran through me. Had I been so incompetent the past five weeks that they thought I was useless? I mean it's not like I'd handled a shocking divorce, grasped a lifetime of magic I'd known nothing about, developed new powers, inherited a business, and recovered a lifetime of suppressed memories.

Oh, wait, I had.

Granted, I'd been whiny and clumsy about it. But I'd done it. And that had to count for something, right?

"Guys, I went through hell and back in the short span of one month, and I still managed to embrace my role here. I even brought a new client in on my own." I puffed my chest, enjoying the quick moment of pride then waved my hand toward the curtain. "I also went through whatever *that* was upstairs before all of you got here.

"Also, hello? I'm a therapist. I can deal with a crisis."

I turned away from them, focusing on the curtain I'd created and reveling in the power and sense of oneness House and I had shared. The goal was to keep people away from danger.

But I'd walked towards it. Carefully, and with a few missteps, but I'd faced it.

"I moved the bar."

"What's that, Simone?" Ray's deep timbre broke through my reverie. I turned back to the table.

"Oh, I didn't realize I'd said it out loud. I moved the bar."

Ray's eyes lit, and a soft smile played on his lips.

"You sure did."

He said it rough, and with more than a little pride. This time, the warmth that flooded my belly was the fun, someone-wants-to-rip-my-clothes-off kind of way. Not exactly a timely feeling, but hey, at least I knew I wasn't dead inside.

"For those of us not in the know, what the hell are you talking about?" Lydia tapped the table, a gesture uncharacteristically large for her. She wasn't used to being on the outside of things, and I had no doubt she was even less used to having to ask for something.

"Sorry, Lydia." I risked a pat of her hand, still on the table. "I don't know why that memory surfaced when it did. Probably because I'm so out of sorts." I paused to sip water. My throat still felt tender from speaking magic. Apparently, that was a muscle I'd have to build.

"Our senior year, Ray and I were both ... going through things." I paused, wondering why I'd bothered to cage it. After all, Ray knew, and Gumbo probably did too. If I wanted a chance at a relationship with Lydia, I should be more open with her. Maybe offering her a glimpse of my humanity might help her to appreciate my magic.

Or she'd just scoff at me.

"I was struggling to move past my mother's death. Ray was recovering from a serious injury."

"Career-ending injury," Ray put in. I risked the same pat of his hand, and he looped his fingers through mine, squeezing briefly. Hoo boy.

"We were eighteen, and everyone was asking us about our future, and we both felt stuck in the moment. Stuck in our pain." *The only thing we had was each other.* I almost said it aloud. I stopped myself.

"Anyway, one day I was reading one of Agatha's therapy magazines during a slow day in the office. She never bothered with them because they were 'too modern' for her liking." I used the opportunity for air quotes to retrieve my hand. I wasn't comfortable with the rise of sensation Ray's touch still brought me. And, again, I wondered where the heck Ethan had disappeared to after he helped me upstairs.

"I was reading about a concept called success dysphoria, where patients felt constantly dissatisfied no matter what they accomplished. Because they kept raising the bar of what being successful meant." I looked at Lydia, waiting to see if she caught on. Her face was as impassive as ever.

"It made me realize that both Ray and I were doing the same thing. We thought the only progress was on the other side of our grief. And whenever we felt a little bit better, we'd subconsciously push the bar to keep ourselves stuck in our trauma."

"And this has what to do with my missing sister and the disappearing branch of our business?" I couldn't help but wince at Lydia's pointed question. She was right, of course. I was trying to get her to understand me at the worst possible time.

"That's fair. But you tend to live in a black and white space, at least when it comes to me. I was realizing I'd started to believe you. That, because this big explosion happened, I had somehow failed. Again." I turned away to gesture at the curtains.

"But I handled it. I protected the rest of the space and helped House recover from its fear." I turned back in time to catch Gumbo's wide-eyed expression. It was gone in an instant. What had I said that caught him by surprise? I tapped his toe beans. "And Gumbo, you said upstairs I kept it from spreading."

I didn't wait for any of their validation. I didn't need it, and that was freaking amazing.

"Anyway, my point is I've made more progress than I realized. And knowing that makes me even more sure we can figure this out and put things to rights. So"—I leaned back, portraying a confidence I didn't totally feel, but I was circling it, and that had to be enough—"before the adrenaline totally leaves my body and I collapse, can my security handlers tell me what the heck happened?"

Ray and Gumbo resumed their glaring at one another, and I buckled up. Whatever their answers were, this was going to be an interesting ride.

CHAPTER
FIVE

"Ask your head of security." Gumbo didn't move his head, but he flicked his ears in Ray's direction, his voice laden with condemnation.

"Or ask your Mystical *Paw*tector." Ray's words were harsh, but they didn't have a lot of heat behind them. Even in this state, he knew that mocking Gumbo's *I Can Haz* voice was a bad idea. Because the other voice, the one that sounded like a thousand mighty lions roaring through the ages, was seriously intense.

Gumbo's glare would have been enough to glue me to my seat, but Ray glared right back. There was a long moment of silence, long enough for me to remember that Ray was a werewolf and I probably didn't want a cat vs. dog fight to erupt in my lobby. And the longer we sat here, the more the full extent of the chaos crept up on me. We needed to handle this. Now.

The sensation I'd come to recognize as my own power surged through me. My fingers and toes tingled with it. My heart skipped two beats, and when I spoke, my voice was enough to cut through their petulance.

"Hey, boys, I'm asking you both what happened. So ... you know ... tell me. Now."

Gumbo sat up straighter, and I had a moment to marvel that my word witchiness, however it worked, was powerful enough to kowtow a mystical being. He lifted one paw, feigning a lick to clean behind his ear, but his adorable fur stood on end.

I wanted to pet him, to soothe as he'd soothed me in the past. But I held my hands still.

"Ray can start." It wasn't quite a cute kitty voice, but it wasn't the scary ass lion sound either.

"We got an alert that there was an intruder in the house, but we were on the outer block." Ray did what I couldn't at the moment, stroking one finger along Gumbo's fur. Given how much they'd bickered, it was endearing.

I remembered that about Ray. He was an amalgam of soft, mushy spots covered in sharp barbs. When I was a teen, it was exciting as hell. Now?

I tucked that thought away. There were more important things to think about than my weirdly raging libido.

"What does outer block mean?"

"You're on single patrol." He held up one finger, as if I couldn't comprehend a number without a visual aid. "One guard covers the entire area, including this block and the three surrounding blocks." He lowered his hand, tapping the same finger on the table in thought. "Until now, it's always been enough."

"Who would dream of attacking a magic house protected by wolf shifters?" I asked. His expression was so laden with guilt I felt bad for him. I would have agreed it was enough.

"Well, that's just it." He gestured towards Gumbo. "Lone Wolf is primarily responsible for the mundane side. Treater's Way is a relatively safe town, but the odd robbery or teen vandalisms can occur. Our job is to deter trespassers, not much more."

I shuddered at the memory of Ray's wolf protecting me from a trespasser—who happened to be my now ex-husband—not that long ago.

"Okay, so your man was far away when the alarm went off, right?"

"A woman, actually. You remember Heidi?" Ray went on without waiting for my answer. "She was on the outer block rotation when our alert triggered. Still, she got to the house in less than a minute. Problem was, she couldn't get in. Something blocked her passage."

"Something? Something worse than a wolf?" A thousand chilly darts prickled my spine. I'd seen her upstairs, and though she looked familiar I couldn't place her. Other than the gash on her forehead, she was as stout as they come. I couldn't imagine a brick wall stopping her in wolf form.

"Not a creature." Ray reached across the table, as if to take my hand again. He pulled it back like he was on fire. "She said she hit some sort of armor. It knocked her a good hundred feet back and unconscious."

"Oh." Relief soothed the chill from me. Not a monster. Just an invisible wall. A wall that came from ...

"Oops," I said. "I had a superhero moment when things went crazy. House and I watched *The Avengers* last weekend. I think I placed a shield around us."

"You did that?" Gumbo had been quiet while Ray talked, but he piped in with his adorable voice intact. "How?"

"I asked." There wasn't another way to explain it, and to be honest I was annoyed at how shocked he was. Again, they thought I wasn't capable of anything. "I said *Shields Up*, and it happened."

They just stared at me.

"Like the Avengers," I said, as if that explained everything.

I couldn't blame them for their shock. I was a bit surprised at myself. Just how much power did I have? Anxiety coated my chest and throat. How much power *did* I have?

I didn't want to think about that. Yet. A Bayou Bliss appeared on the table in front of me. My mother's magic drink that always made me feel better as a child.

"Thanks, House. I needed that."

I took a sip while three sets of eyes stared at me. "House, do you feel strong enough to give everyone refreshments? They could probably use it. All I found was stale cookies."

A serving tray in Agatha's favorite shade of blue popped onto the table. Several slices of raw tuna were neatly arranged on Gumbo's side. In front of Ray sat a pile of french fries, so crispy-looking and salty my mouth watered at the sight of them. Lydia snatched at the delicate pastry before I could see what it was.

She shoved it into her mouth and hopped up from the table. Aside from a few questions, she'd been so quiet. It was odd not to sense her presence. With a lift of her chin to me, a gesture I decided to take as a show of respect or appreciation, she glided to the salon and disappeared inside.

"Guess she needs rest." I needed it to, but I fought the urge to let my head droop, opting instead to steal a few of Ray's french fries while I processed what he'd shared. Something wasn't adding up, and when it hit me what it was, I couldn't have swallowed another bite.

"If Heidi hit my shield, that means whatever triggered the alarm was already inside." I set my glass down and ran my finger along the rim. "So why didn't the alarm go off sooner? Like, before they got to House? When Jeff showed up, a freaking siren went off the moment he was in the yard. How did ... whatever ... get in and cause the explosion?"

Gumbo came close, his sweet purr vibrating the table. He ran his tail, so soft and silky, along my arm. It was meant to soothe me, but the fact that he believed I needed soothing only made me more tense.

"You're right, Simone. Whatever—or whoever—ever caused the explosion was already in the house. They broke the mystical barrier." He curled between my hands, lifting his chin for scritches. "That's where I come in. I protect the magical side of the Magnolia."

My weird-meter was at max capacity. Scratching a cute talking kitten's chin while he took blame for something magic causing my sentient house to blow up barely registered as bizarre anymore.

"Do you remember me telling you that the Twins are here on a sort of work visa from their realm?" He pushed his cute head into my palm, angling my fingers behind his one ear. "Right there." He purred. "I can never quite get that spot. Under the agreement, the Twins can move freely between our realms, and some of the more powerful fae can do so of their own accord. Granted they've been given permission by me."

He stretched and yawned, exposing a belly fat from the tuna. With a shake of my head, I rubbed at his soft fur.

"Why would they want to come here?" I asked.

"To shop. Or travel. They love Mardi Gras. They can sell jewels and baubles, and they just look like they are in costume." He rolled again, tucking his tail around his body. "And, of course, to seek the services of the Magnolia.

"If someone, or something, attempts to pass through Treater's Way without my permission or knowledge, or they aren't on the Magnolia's calendar, I'm alerted before they reach the barrier." Gumbo's voice was getting cuter and cuter, his eyes wider. He blinked at me, his sweet little whiskers drooping. "They must be granted access by the Mystical Pawtector."

He wasn't even trying to say it like a normal word. All his purrs and pets weren't to soothe me at all. Gumbo had been trying to distract me from what he was saying.

"You rascal." I poked his belly, then pushed him away. Sneaky little bastard. "You weren't at your post, were you?"

Gumbo, looking not-at-all ashamed, sat upright and curled his tail around him.

"I was at llaman. In Ireland."

"Ireland has llamas?" I scratched my own head, as if what he'd said would make sense if I tamed the itch.

"Not llamas. Llaman. You know? Lughnasadh."

"You're right. This is lunacy." I poked his chest. "Start making sense."

Gumbo heaved a giant sigh as if I were the most obtuse person on the planet.

"When Agatha died, and while you were transitioning, security went on high alert. Rumors were spreading that the Magnolia's power was threatened, and we weren't sure if you were going to accept. Plus, your husband seemed plenty mad you hexed him. It was a stressful time."

"Ex-husband." I didn't dare glance at Ray, but my ears and back of neck burned under his stare. I watched in fascination as Gumbo's giant bow turned kelly green. His nails matched the shade. I could have sworn I heard a fiddle playing a lively jig all around us.

"Okay. Ex. Since the board meeting, things have settled. You're finding your way." Gumbo's voice lifted an octave, becoming a pitiful whine. "But I missed Lughnasadh."

I wasn't getting it. It sounded like he was saying the word lunacy. Did he miss things being crazy and unsteady? What was wrong with him? I finally did look at Ray, hoping he could help me make sense.

"Lughnasadh is the midway point between solstice and equinox." As if he, too, couldn't resist, he ran his hand along Gumbo's back. Damn cat. "It's a Gaelic festival, lots of celebration, athletic competitions, alcohol ..."

"It's my favorite time of year. An annual vacation, if you will." Gumbo slithered away from Ray's hand, his body slinking as if he had no spine, and hopped onto a vacant chair. "So, now that things are calm, I popped back a few weeks to my favorite festival for a little R&R."

"Sure." I said it as matter-of-factly as I possibly could, but inside, my brain felt like I was ramming it against a wall repeatedly. Every time I felt like I understood everyone's abilities, I got thrown a curveball. And in just a few words, Gumbo had knocked me over like a dozen pins.

First, they were afraid the house would be under attack when I got here? From whom and why? I knew that some things were being run for me while I got my bearings, but I had no idea just how intricate that was. And I needed to understand that better if I were going to act as Supreme, not just head of the therapy division.

But the bigger source of my befuddlement was Gumbo's casual mention of popping back in time. What a rollercoaster. Every new piece of information slammed me around so badly I was mixing sports metaphors, as if I cared about anything other than American football.

"As soon as I felt an intrusion at the barrier, I came back. Of course, by then, the damage was done."

"Of course." Fatigue washed over me so suddenly I almost closed my eyes at the table. My skin itched from all the debris, and it didn't feel like we were any closer to an answer than we had been when this all started. "So, the million-dollar question is, are we safe right now?"

"The mundane side is." I snorted at Ray's accusing glare. He hadn't changed one bit in thirty years, which may not be a good thing. "We've amplified security and added a day shift. But since this wasn't on our side ..."

He lifted an eyebrow in Gumbo's direction. Gumbo, too, seemed suddenly tired. His fur looked dull and matted, like he was coated with a dark oil. The one eye that was usually so golden, had lost its gilding. It was as faded as the rest of him.

"Gumbo, you okay, bud?" I extended my hand, offering a bet that he declined by dropping to the floor.

"Time pops fatigue me." His voice was peak adorable, but even so it was laden with the same fatigue I felt. "And the vacuum you created pulled too hard."

He was fading, disappearing off to ... wherever Gumbo slept.

"Wait," I called out. "My what?"

But he was gone. I sat, staring open-mouthed at Ray, who only shrugged.

"Don't look at me. I don't understand your magic any more than I do his."

"Did I cause that?" I gestured toward the curtain, hoping he knew I meant the space behind it.

"Maybe." His voice was soft and reassuring, and even with my head turned I knew he'd shifted forward before he took my hand. "Hey."

When I turned, the force of Ray's deep, emerald eyes held me in place. My breath caught, and for just a moment, I was an eighteen-year-old girl, not a newly divorced grown-ass woman no longer controlled by hormones. "Lyra went across, and she'll come back with answers. Until then, try and get some rest. I will make sure you're safe."

It was a nice gesture, but I wasn't sure he could keep me safe. After all, he was a wolf shifter. It seemed like his specialty was brute force and strength, which I supposed had its advantages.

"Thanks, Ray. I do appreciate how quickly your team arrived. And I think we owe Heidi a free massage or something."

"We were doing our job, CC." He said the words lightly, but they felt heavy for some reason. As if he were doing more than his job. As if he'd been watching over me for longer. His swallow filled the silence between us.

"Listen, when things are settled, I'd love it if we could talk. You know, catch up."

"Yeah, that would be really nice actually." I stifled a yawn and stood up to stretch. My eyes were heavier than I'd expected. As if the same fatigue that came over Gumbo so suddenly had sapped him entirely and was coming for me. "Maybe we can hit Gino's one night? Sit in the corner and have a chat?"

I hadn't meant to mention Gino's corner. The old pizzeria's known make-out spot. But he chuckled, sliding one hand under my elbow and guiding me outside and up the stairs.

Once I stepped over the threshold, the door slammed shut behind me, leaving Ray on the other end.

"Oh, House, I could have at least said goodnight."

A feeling of protection washed over my body, an almost motherly hug, and I was guided to the shower already running. I scrubbed debris and muck off my body in a zoned-out, half-awake state.

Then, just as I'd done a few hours before the mayhem, I crawled into bed and passed out.

CHAPTER

SIX

Forced wakeups are the worst. My phone blasted the shrillest alarm I'd ever heard—so harsh and loud it yanked me from a lovely dream where I was dancing in the forest with a midnight-black wolf. Granted, I had no desire to analyze the dream, but I sure didn't mind the experience.

The thing is, I hadn't set an alarm. In the admittedly few weeks that I'd slept in this bed, I'd relied on House or my own internal body clock to wake me on time. When I'd needed an alarm or anxiety convinced me I should set one, I was careful to choose charming songbirds that beckoned me from slumber with their delightful and lyrical tweeting. Happy sounds that acknowledged that hey, waking up sucks, but at least we can do it pleasantly.

But no. This alarm was the blare a firehouse might hear when a four-alarm fire is raging. Given I'd woken up the night before to disaster, it pumped more adrenaline into me than I could ever manage with coffee. I bolted upright, splaying my hands out as if to protect myself from whatever created the cacophony, my heart thudding against my shirt.

The sound died as quickly as it erupted. I blinked for a full three minutes, trying to get my bearings. The room was dark, as if it were still nighttime. I fumbled for my phone and brought the numbers into focus.

Well, it was morning. But I wouldn't normally wake up for at least another ten minutes. The house could still be recovering from the hefty dose of magic. Or something else terrible was happening.

"You okay, House?"

The sensation that ran through me was unsettling. Until now, I hadn't realized just how much security House was providing me. This was the first uneasy morning I'd woken up to since I got here. And the first bad night's rest.

House was not okay. And neither was I.

"Do we need to check your foundation?" My bed trembled. "Um, I'm going to take that as a yes." I ran my hand along the bedspread, not that I could reach the foundation from here.

Feeling more than a little foolish but deciding to trust my gut, I dropped to the floor and patted the wood. Maybe it just needed a friend. When I've had a troubling session, I find sitting near someone whose energy soothes me is a good way to release the hard emotions. Brianne had already gotten used to me pulling a chair near her desk and hanging out later in the afternoons.

House had a personality. I may as well try it.

"I'm here, House. We'll figure this out."

I sat even as my hip began to ache and my knee throbbed. It was one of the few times I'd felt almost fifty since moving in. At first, my stomach tied itself in knots. Waves of anxiety and confusion drifted through me, as if I were working out a problem. I didn't know what to do or say, so I just held the emotions until they passed.

When I felt more secure, which probably meant House felt more secure, I got up to prep my day.

Brianne was already in the lobby by the time I came downstairs. She wasn't at her new office space, but instead in front of the curtain I'd put up last night. One shaky hand was lifted, fingers barely grazing the smooth velvet. Her back was to me, so lost in thought she didn't turn or acknowledge me.

"That sign isn't just for show, Bri." I thought my voice was soft enough, and I'd waited until I was close to speak, but Bri still jumped a foot high and squeaked like a mouse trapped by the fat cat. "I'm sorry!"

I wrapped my arms around her, bringing her in for a hug. Her body shuddered. My super-solid, only-known-her-a-month-but-it-feels-like-a-lifetime new bestie was crying.

Damn. House being shaken up was one thing. But Brianne, too?

Whatever happened last night had left an even bigger hole than I realized.

"I'm so sorry, friend." I rubbed my hand on her back, waiting until she gathered herself a bit. "It's going to be okay." A clinking of glass caught our attention. Waiting on the breakroom table was a tall iced sweet tea. Condensation ran down the sides in droplets.

I helped her sit and took the chair across from her, passing tissues in her direction each time her current one got oversaturated.

It turned out that I needed those extra morning minutes to support my people. And my house. Maybe its magic wasn't as broken as I feared.

Once she'd snuffled her last sniff, she shook her head, as if shaking the whole thing off.

"Thank you, Simone. I needed that."

As quickly as it had overwhelmed her, the despair was gone. She rose and grabbed the tissues and her tea, cleaning off the table and counters and mumbling her silent thanks to House.

"Well!" She clapped her hands together and rubbed, false brightness lifting her voice. "We've got quite a day ahead of us. We should make a plan."

Her short legs hurried to her new office location. I followed, feeling a bit whiplashed from her mood change.

"It was clever of Gumbo to move me over here and put up a curtain, though we'll need to make sure no one goes near it. That sensation is awful." She paused, running her hands over her bare arms.

"Actually, I did that." I tried, and failed, to keep my voice level. I know I hadn't exactly proven myself fully yet, but did I have to establish my worth to Brianne of all people? It stung that even she assumed I'd just sat and stared while everyone around me took care of things. "I put up the curtain and moved your office over here."

She paused her scribbling on a notepad and lifted her head to meet my eyes. Her usually bright complexion was faded, her expression soft. But there was something, a sudden shift of her foot and movement of her body that she couldn't quite hide from me. I'd surprised her, and that hurt.

"That was very thoughtful of you, Simone. When Nate and I left you were injured. I just assumed ..." she let her voice trail. "I shouldn't have assumed."

"No, I get it." I did get it, but that didn't stop it from sucking. Now that the dust was settling—metaphorically because there was still dust all over my bedroom—I was proud of the way I'd handled things the night before.

I was still trying to parse the big boom, but it seemed like I had connected to magic and fought against it before we all got swallowed. And I'd had the wherewithal to put up a shield to protect the neighborhood. What's more, I'd given Lydia support and thought about Brianne's needs.

I held my own last night. Even if no one acknowledged it. Still, I didn't want to be awkward with Brianne. Especially when she was in her feelings, too.

"I hope this new desk location will work for a while. I don't want you, or any humans for that matter, too close to the ... uh ..." I gestured toward the curtain.

"What's behind it?" A look of pure awe and terror darkened her eyes. She hugged herself closer. "How bad is it?"

"Oh, you know. It's a giant gaping hole that apparently leads to another realm or reality or something. And it sucks your soul out if you get too close." I kind of laughed, like everything was fine. "So, not great."

Her eyes welled again, and her lip gave a tremble that she bit down on.

"Well, nothing we can do about it at the moment. I trust Lyra is on the case?"

"She is—but just between us, Lydia seemed worried about her." I looked around as I said it, as if either of them would materialize and berate me for talking about them. "I know I have limited knowledge about them, but I've never seen her worried before." An involuntary shudder ran through me as I cast my eyes to the curtain. "Something really bad happened last night, and none of us know what it is."

"Do we think it's safe for clients?"

"I do." I didn't. In fact, I had no idea. But my voice had come through clear and loud and when that happened, I had to trust it. "I think we should focus on as much business as usual as we can today."

"Right." Brianne gripped her pen. "Give me a task list, I can handle it."

Sheer panic took over. Just a few minutes earlier, I was frustrated that no one took me seriously. I'd wanted nothing more than to be looked at as the one in charge. So here was Brianne giving me *you're the boss bitch* eyes.

I was frozen in place. My mind blanked. I cleared my throat, expecting words to magically rise. None did.

"Should we start with calling clients?" Brianne gave me a patient smile.

Right. Yes. Logic and order, Simone. You can do this.

"I guess we need to call Lyra's clients first and cancel her appointments. Maybe we should come up with a reason why that isn't, 'Hey, there's a big hole in the universe. Where you get your hair done?'"

"Got it." Brianne let a smirk slide as she jotted it down.

"Actually, we should call everyone who has an appointment this week, starting with today obviously, because some folks may want to reschedule or cancel just because." My stomach reeled. I'd finally gotten footing with my clients and now this. And Gabe would be here by the end of the week. I didn't want to stop him from coming.

"I don't remember seeing Lauren last night. Do you?"

"No." Brianne shook her head, then tapped her pen to her lip. "But I wasn't altogether myself."

"Okay, let's call them first and see what they want to do. They may not be up to seeing clients today."

Brianne was jotting down more than I was saying, a key indicator that she'd thought of things I hadn't begun to. I really needed to know more about the inner workings of the Magnolia. Did we have an appointment system? Some magical portal that lives in a literal cloud, perhaps? All I knew was who I was going to see and when. The rest was a mystery."

"I'll call my clients," I told her. "I want them to hear from me."

"I like that." Brianne crossed an item off her list with a smile.

We went over a few other tasks, and by the time we were done, Brianne seemed more like her old self. She set her pad down and grabbed me for a quick hug.

"Lists create their own magic, don't they?"

"They do," I agreed. "Even the creation of it puts you back in charge." Except, I wasn't in charge. Not really. This lovely woman in front of me was. And that was mostly fine, but I still needed to understand how this place worked.

After all, Brianne may run the show, but it was still my show. That's what being the Supreme was. Maybe.

"Bri, when things settle, can we have a sort of administrative meeting?"

Brianne put her pad down and turned to face me.

"Sure. About what?" Her voice was tight. "Am I doing something wrong?"

"Oh gosh, no, of course not!" I started to reach out to her but stopped myself. There was a strange, guarded sensation between us I'd never experienced. "I've been thinking the past week that I don't really know anything about running the Magnolia.

"I don't know what you do, what happens by magic, or what my—well, I guess you could call it job as Supreme—even is." She gnawed on her lip. "It's more about me than you. Though I also have a sneaking suspicion you aren't paid fairly for all the work you do."

I waited while she processed, hoping she'd thaw a little. What had I said that challenged her? When she didn't speak, I continued.

"When my mom was here, Agatha always said that no one

understood everything she did. That she was like an iceberg. You could see some of the ice on top of the water, but what was underneath was far more epic."

At that, Brianne did soften. A sweet chuckle escaped her.

"Agatha always said that to me, too."

"I believe it." I squeezed her hand, relieved when she squeezed back. "The Magnolia is four times as big as it was when Mom ran it. I want to know how to help. I don't want to be an added burden."

"I'll put it on the books," Brianne said. "When the curtain drops, so to speak."

She settled at her desk and began to make phone calls while I escaped to my office to call my clients. Things weren't right between us, and I had to hope it was because of the big hole in our house and not my big mouth.

I was eager for some normalcy and more than a little relieved that so few clients cancelled. Not only was it a sign they trusted me to control the magic in the building, but it gave me a day full of distraction.

And, despite a vague sense of unease lingering throughout the Magnolia, I was very excited to meet my new client. If, given the notes I'd taken during our phone consultation, I could actually see her.

CHAPTER

SEVEN

T couldn't actually see her.

Not at first.

"Sarah?" She'd been one of the first clients I called, and she'd confirmed with quick enthusiasm. But there was no sign of her in the waiting room.

"I'm here." I turned, following the direction of the voice. There was nothing.

"Sarah, I'm terribly sorry, but I can't see you." I heard her sigh, long and suffering.

"I was afraid of that."

"But I *want* to see you very much, Sarah." Taking a guess, I walked towards one of the plush chairs. If I squinted, I could make out the rough outline of a woman. It was like pulling an image from clouds. A curvy mist, hovering in the air. "Sarah, is that you?"

"It's me." Bless her mopey heart. Eeyore the donkey wasn't this sad.

I smiled at what I thought was probably her face.

"Hi, Sarah. I'm Simone. Is it okay if I shake your hand?" I

extended my hand and let her decide whether to take it or not. Not everyone liked physical touch, and I didn't want to assume anything—particularly in our first meeting.

There was still a voice in the back of my head, reminding me that this was the first patient who had found me and not one of Agatha's decades-long clients. This was an opportunity to really help someone. But I wanted to do it for her, not for my own selfish needs. That was the first mistake I'd made when I started treating Agatha's patients, and I wasn't eager to make it again.

A cool mist touched my fingers. As we shook hands, I held my gaze at the spot where her face probably was, and with each shake, Sarah's form materialized.

"It's so nice to see you, Sarah."

Heavy lids hovered over red-rimmed eyes the color of a muddy sea. They turned down at the edges, giving her the appearance of perpetual sadness.

She smiled at me with thinning lips that trembled as she lifted her cheeks. Her face was round. Her body plump. She wore a loose-knit dress the color of a stormy sky. It flowed over her curves, stopping just above her sensible brown shoes.

"It's nice to be seen." Sarah's voice was soft, like water lapping on the edges of the shore. And there was a kindness to her that undercut her lackluster demeanor. Sweet, lovely Sarah —she was troubled. But deep down, she was a good person.

Well, I didn't know if she was a person. That might have to be something I added to the intake form.

"Let's get inside and get started." I led the way to my office, where Gumbo had taken up residence in my chair. "Shoo, Gumbo."

He opened one eye. Pretending he'd been asleep, and we'd interrupted a lovely dream where he drank from a never-ending cream bowl. He yawned and stretched with a mock-glare on his cute little face. One his way out the door, he let his tail glide along Sarah's calf, offering her a short meow. That half-instance of recognizing her was enough to let her know we could see her.

What a good kitty.

She perched at the edge of the chair, fully materialized. With ankles crossed, shoulders slightly hunched, and hands folded neatly in her lap, it was almost like she was asking permission just to take up space.

I took out my notepad, leaving her folder to the side. I wanted to maintain eye contact with her, to make sure she felt heard and seen in the space. There was no direct way to ask whether she was human or not. With the pearlescent undertone to her skin, and long, thin hair that might have once been blond but still looked wet, I had to guess I was treating some sort of water creature.

"Sarah, I know we've spoken on the phone, but would you like to talk about what brought you here?"

I thought her lip had trembled before, but what happened now was almost seismic. A full-on lip quake. The tremble grew, tears filled her eyes, and within moments, she was wailing like Alice in Wonderland. I half expected the office to flood.

I handed her a box of tissues and waited.

This wasn't the first time someone cried in my office. It was part of therapy. Granted, they usually managed to get a word out first. Then again, it had been a long time since I'd seen a brand-new patient I knew nothing about. Even with Agatha's clients, I had scores of files to catch me up.

House still felt unsteady to me, so I walked to the water cooler and poured two glasses. I placed one on a coaster in front of her.

"Would you like some water, Sarah?"

"Would I like water?" Her voice still flowed like a wave. It

49

was captivating, until she blew her nose like an elephant with a stuffed-up trunk. "All I am is water."

She was disappearing again, though now that I was seeing it up close that wasn't an accurate description for what was happening. It was more like an evaporation, as if her solid form was giving way to mist.

"Sarah, can you stay with me?"

"I'm sorry." She dabbed at her eyes with a new tissue. "It's always worse when I cry. I try to schedule it between two and three p.m. every day. Sometimes it just sneaks up on me."

"How is that working for you?" I asked. "Scheduling your cries."

"Not great," she admitted. "I hold it in until two. But by three, I don't wanna stop. My throat is so sore, my eyes hurt, and half the time I feel like a dam about to burst." She held up her hand. The fingers were already gone. "Then this shit happens."

The innocent little cuss word horrified her. As soon as she covered her mouth and widened her eyes, though, she was here again. Interesting.

"Sarah, you're allowed to cuss in here. You can say any damn thing you want." I smiled and gestured toward her hand. "Did you notice you were able to materialize when you let your frustrations show?"

She held her arm in front of her, turning it as if seeing a body part for the first time.

"May I ask why you think crying from two to three p.m. will help you?"

"Oh, you know." She shrugged her shoulders. "For control."

"What are you trying to control?"

"Everything." Her answer came after a long pause, during which she faded in and out of view. "Or maybe just me. I don't know."

"Do you know when you started to schedule your tears?"

"About two years ago." Her eyes drifted to the picture window behind me, a vast reflection of the open water beyond Bridge Island. "It started when my periods became erratic. For years, I was like clockwork. Then bam! I was bleeding every three weeks, then two, then six."

"I see." I was going to use that phrase with her a lot. "Did you see your doctor about it?"

"Yup. Hormones."

"Hormones." With a scoff, I shook my head. "They like to dismiss it, don't they?"

"Over time, I realized I didn't feel like 'me' anymore." Tears threatened to fall again. She bit her bottom lip until they receded. "When my periods stopped completely, I began to fade."

"You have children, right?" I risked a quick glance at her file. "Four. That's quite a happy brood."

"My youngest is five." She leaned forward, dropping her voice to a whisper. "A little vacation souvenir."

The grin that flashed across her face was wicked and fun. A brief glimpse into the Sarah her family must know. I made a few notes.

"You enjoy having children?"

"I love it. I was born to be a momma." This time, the tears that flowed were happy ones.

She listed each child, filling me in on their likes and dislikes until I felt like I knew them. I listened, shoving aside my own emotions. Gabe would be here soon. I'd be able to connect with my boy again.

Until then, I had to focus on Sarah.

What I found most interesting was the way her body responded. Her skin changed hue. She glowed as she told me about her kids. Literally. I almost put on sunglasses. After ten minutes or so, she realized she'd been rambling.

"Sorry." At that simple word, she began to fade again. "My children give me life."

"Did you and your husband discuss having more?"

"No." Her voice had a wistful, bitter edge that reflected on her face. Her nose was sharper, her lips thinner. "I'm fifty now. It's too late."

"Sarah, can we say the m-word?" At her lifted eyebrow, I dove in. "Menopause."

I had theories, based on the twenty minutes I'd spent with her, but I always found it better for the patient to be led towards a diagnosis, rather than be told. I hoped I could help Sarah see what was so obvious to me.

Then again, it's always more obvious from the outside.

"Yeah, I'm moving into menopause." She was more vibrant than ever now, and darker. Anger radiated off her. Even her hair moved like she was swimming against a current. "I'm no longer a woman."

"What makes you say that?"

"I can't have babies, can I? I'm old now. Withered. Dried up." I had to wonder if she knew she was crying, or how her body was responding to her outburst. Behind me, the sky in the window darkened. Storm clouds gathered.

Ooh, cool. I'd never seen it do that before.

"That's interesting." I turned to the window. With the darker sky, her reflection was more prominent. "Have you always tied your identity to your ability to have children?"

"Well, I've been a momma for twenty-five years."

"Sure." I swiveled back towards her. "But what were you before you were momma? And, assuming you have at least another twenty-five years, what do you think you'll be?"

She flopped into her chair, though I'd never seen her stand. The cushion was damp and flat.

"I'm curious about that." I smiled at her, maintaining eye contact. "Can I ask you to be curious about that, too?"

Sarah wrinkled her nose. She shrugged.

"Here, let's start with this." I reached into my bottom drawer for the stack of notebooks I kept in there. Flipping through them, I found one with a picturesque water scene on the cover. I grabbed a matching blue pen and passed them across the desk.

"You don't have to use the notebook. If you'd prefer to make voice notes or type into your phone, that's perfectly fine. We're going to try a little exercise."

For the remainder of the session, we worked through my idea. Sarah was going to spend a week documenting the times she felt like she was disappearing. What happened before and where her thoughts led her.

I wanted Sarah to see how she'd tied her identity to being a mother. It was a beautiful sentiment, but as they grew and her body entered a new phase of life, she was losing her sense of purpose.

I made a few notes for our next session. Sarah was going on a journey of self-discovery. I set goals for our therapy sessions. To help her embrace womanhood, even as her definition of a woman changed. To develop and practice grounding techniques to call herself back when she faded.

"You're not withered," I told Sarah as we walked to the waiting room. "You're just blooming into something different. Sometimes, we need time for it to take root."

I watched her go, a trail of wet footprints following in her wake. They faded, leaving no trace she'd been here. A chill shot through me. It was so easy for the house to forget who'd passed through it.

Would it forget me in the same way when my time here was over?

EIGHT

I had three more sessions immediately after Sarah's. By the time it was lunch, my mind and my body were exhausted. I hadn't slept much the night before, and the house was still on edge.

"We're going to have to start staggering my appointments," I moaned to Brianne. I dropped into one of the break-room chairs with a dramatic sigh. "I know Agatha's method was to meet them all at once, but it's making for very full days, and I don't feel like I'm getting enough time to prepare or recover from each one."

"We can handle that." She joined me at the break room table with two salads in hand. I took one with a grumble. She went to the kitchen and returned with a third salad, placing it in front of one of the empty chairs.

"Lauren is in?"

"You know, now that you mention it, I never saw her come in." She stared down at the salad for a moment, then back at the curtain. "I might have missed it."

"What did her clients say when you called them?" I moved

lettuce around on my plate, pretending it was food. "Has she missed any appointments?"

"I, uh ..." She blinked at me, her lips forming words, but no sounds came out. A crinkle drew her eyebrows low. "I don't think I called anyone. I think I went to my desk and ..."

She let her voice trail, turning her gaze back to the curtain. The air around me turned bitterly cold. Had she spent the morning staring at it? What if the boundary was wrong or it was expanding? Or what if her lack of powers meant it had a deeper effect on her I hadn't anticipated?

And where the heck was Lauren?

Unease replaced the hunger in my belly. I pushed my plate away.

"Bri? Honey? Do you want to go home for the day?"

Longing darkened the bright green of her eyes. She gripped her chair as if it were holding her in place, as if her body might run to the door and escape at any moment. Then the determination I knew her for took over. She firmed her lips and sat down. Not for the first time, I thought how apt her last name was—Brianne Steele was made of the toughest metals on earth.

"No. The Magnolia needs me." She fisted her fork and attacked her salad, inhaling it as if it were pasta or an amazing slice of pizza and not a bunch of stuff that grew in the dirt. "I need to be here this afternoon."

If I hadn't already lost my appetite, that strange statement would have done it. Maybe I should have talked her into leaving or asked Gumbo how the terrifying void behind the curtain would affect a mundane.

I didn't want to ask what was going to happen this afternoon. If something was telling Brianne to stay, I had to trust it. And hope it was the house and not some other force that had taken over the lobby while I was locked in my office.

"The Magnolia does need you, Bri. It always will."

She continued to eat like I hadn't spoken. And Lauren's absence still made me queasy. Our daily lunches had become a ritual we all enjoyed. Already, I felt more comfortable in Lauren's presence and was enjoying our gradual transition into true friendship. I still held hopes that the Twins would join us one day. And if Brianne hadn't called her clients, she must have.

"I'm going to go check on her."

It was the first time I'd gone into the physical therapy division. My hands clenched over the doorknob. The last time I'd gone into a clinic, it was to support Jeff while he met to discuss his treatment. I'd liked his therapist a lot. She'd been professional and detail-oriented, eager to include me in his recovery plan.

I still didn't know when they'd started sleeping together.

A knot formed in my throat and a surprising well of tears formed in my eyes. I pushed them down. There was no way I was gonna cry over my ex-husband's infidelity. I was done mourning his betrayal.

I'd been given a second chance.

I wasn't about to spend it dwelling on past pain.

Opening the door, I found an unexpectedly warm space. I shouldn't have been so surprised it was so different from the visual I'd kept in my head. Rather than the wide-open space I was used to, where people suffering through various treatments were on full display, a large wall blocked the majority of the space. In front of it was a check-in station, currently abandoned.

The room gave off an aura of calm and peace. The walls were a soft, natural color. Ash gray wooden beams ran the length of the ceiling. The furniture and desk were accented with mossy greens and wispy blue-gray. It was bathed in natural light, which technically shouldn't have been possible given its position in the house. Sun rays filtered through soft shades on the windows blanketing each side of me.

"Lauren?" I slipped past the wall to the area behind it. A large treatment room greeted me. Treadmills lined one wall, massage tables the other, similar to what I'd expected. In the center were several weight benches, as well as racks supporting medicine balls and dumbbells.

There were also things I'd never seen before. A notice on the wall displayed directions for using something called a wing harness. I'd seen foam rollers before, but the ones piled in the corner were adorned with sharp looking crystals, each of them glowing in different colors.

Unable to resist, I plucked one of the tiny gold spheres floating above a black shelf. A deep blue light emanated in my palm. It was delightfully warm. The muscles in my head and arm instantly relaxed. My breath came softer. I switched hands to balance the sensations, then put it back on the shelf.

I wanted to take a bath in those suckers.

But no one used the machines. Nothing rested on the massage table. There wasn't a person, or creature, or being in sight. A wide hall to my left led to a series of doors. I knocked on each, opening when there was no answer. The last door opened to an office that screamed *this is Lauren's*.

A cute green sweater I recognized as hers was draped over one of those cool office chairs you could sit cross-legged on or swivel to prop your leg up. The chair was pushed against the desk in front of a closed laptop.

There was nothing to indicate Lauren had come to work yet. No half-full coffee cup. No scribbled notes or pens tossed on the tabletop.

There was no one in the clinic. And no sign of Lauren.

I returned to the main lobby to find Brianne still sitting at the breakroom table. Her salad was half-eaten, her back to it as she fixated on the curtain. That was it. Brianne definitely needed to get away from that.

"Hey," I said softly. She jumped at my touch, pushing my arm away without looking in my direction. "Brianne." I said her name sharp and loud. When she still didn't respond, I clapped my hands in front of her. Her head tilted, just a nudge as if she thought she'd turned. Her mouth dropped open and her unfocused eyes remained on the curtain.

Fear gripped me, instantly seizing the muscles I'd softened in the therapy room. Placing my hands under her shoulders, I lifted her tiny frame and guided her to the desk. She walked along in a trance, neck turning to stare at the curtain.

Grabbing her purse and keys, I pulled her outside. On the front porch, she inched closer to the front door. I took her hand and yanked her down the stairs and sidewalk, only stopping when we were outside the tiny gate that welcomed patients to the Magnolia.

I released her hand when she squeaked, clamping her hand over her mouth in horror.

"What—" She looked around as if in a foreign country. "How?"

"I dragged you out here." I gave her a quick hug, even though I suspected it was for me and not her. "That was scary."

"What was?" Her voice was muffled against my shoulder. I stepped back, searching her face for signs of activity. She looked just like Brianne.

"The curtain. Well, not the curtain, the thing behind it. It had you in some kind of weird trance." Though I'd considered using my word magic to make sure she left, I didn't trust how shaky and unsettled I sounded. "I think you should stay home until we figure out what is happening."

"I thought you said that the Magnolia would always need me." There was an odd defensiveness to her voice. One nostril flared with sudden anger. "You think you can run this place on your own?"

"Not at all!" I reached for her hands, my heart squeezing like a vise when she took a deliberate step away from me. "No, that's not what I meant Brianne. I'm worried that the house isn't safe for you right now."

"Why? Because I'm not special like you?" A derisive sneer accented the heavy sarcasm lacing her words. "Because you're the Supreme? YOU?"

My mouth hung open. I had no idea how to respond. She crossed her arms, glaring at me like a sworn enemy. My throat tightened and tears burned. I'd never seen Brianne look at anyone this way. Logically, I could reason that it was the vortex. Still, it felt real. As if the vortex was giving her power to say what she'd always wanted to.

I let the tears fall.

"Everything okay, ladies?" Ethan's hand was at the small of my back. I hadn't even heard him walk up. He pressed it into me, a small show of support. Brianne's glare shifted from me to him, and I had to admit I was grateful for her change of ire.

Her words wiped away my gratitude.

"Ask the *boss*." She turned and stomped down the road. I felt rooted to the sidewalk, unable to follow her.

"What was that about, CC?"

"I'm not sure, to be honest." I swiped at my tears. Why was I always either crying or just finished crying when I saw him? "What's going on with you? Are you okay?"

"Well," he sighed, deep and long. "We should go inside. I'm afraid I have more bad news."

CHAPTER
NINE

My nerves were shot. The lobby was eerily silent, even more abandoned now that Brianne had gone home. My anxiety over a missing fae wasn't helped by a missing witch. I should have called an emergency board meeting last night, the second the explosion was over. There I was congratulating myself on handling a tense situation, and I hadn't even checked in on all of my people.

Some coven leader I was.

Were we even a coven if we had two fae and a mundane in our midst? Maybe I was the leader of nothing but a ragtag group of people.

I dug my fingernails into my palms to jolt me back into the moment. Those were thoughts I could entertain later.

Ethan followed behind, seemingly willing to go wherever I led. Even though the halls were empty, I couldn't comfortably have a conversation with him in the breakroom. Whatever bad news faced me, I'd rather deal with it in private for once.

At least I had pants on this time.

I led him to the conference room and shut the door behind him, turning to find him barely a foot away from me.

He was dressed oddly casual for a Monday in a short-sleeved New Orleans Saints T-shirt and dark, fitted jeans. Lord. The man still had tree trunks for thighs. I could practically see his muscles flexing through the denim.

Lust fluttered through me, brief but intense. Ethan had been handsome in high school, no doubt about that. But age had taken him straight from handsome to hot. Little threads of silver were weaved into his tight curls. His face glowed like he was a model for the latest in anti-aging skincare. There wasn't a wrinkle to be found.

Either he'd read my mind or I'd licked my lips. I couldn't be sure. Ethan grinned like a dog in heat. Mischief and desire darkened his lovely oak eyes. I definitely licked my lips.

I might have considered leaping on him then and there. The table seemed sturdy enough.

I pushed the impulse from my fried brain. What was wrong with me? Things were seriously wrong in the Magnolia and here I was distracted by hot guys and errant thoughts.

"Give it to me straight, counselor." I took my seat at the end of the table and gestured for him to join me. "What's the bad news?"

"Well. Bad may be a strong word." Ethan shuffled to his seat. "Maybe awkward is a better word."

"Everything is awkward these days," I said. It was meant to be a joke, a weak attempt to clear the air, but my voice was tight and harsh. I swallowed. "Is it a legal matter?"

"Unfortunately." Ethan hauled his briefcase to the table. Funny, I never saw him carrying it and yet he always seemed to have it. He pulled out a manila folder and opened it. "These are your divorce papers. Do you remember them?"

What a strange question.

"Yes, of course I remember my divorce papers. I signed them right over there." I pointed to the chair at the far end. "You were next to me."

We almost kissed. I bit my tongue before it slipped out. My voice was even higher, my throat tight. Heat stung my cheeks. Great. I was just adorable when I blushed.

"Right. You signed them." Ethan shuffled to the last page. "I saw you sign them. Brianne validated the signatures. All right here in this office." He started to rise, ready to pace. When Ethan paced, it meant he was nervous. I clamped my hand on his forearm to keep him in his chair.

"Spit it out, Ethan. I can handle ... whatever this is." I wasn't sure I could handle it, though. I checked my watch. I had yet another series of back-to-back sessions starting soon, and I'd missed lunch to check on Lauren.

Ethan tapped the page.

"Don't you see?"

I scanned the last page, reading through sentences that were vaguely familiar but mostly gibberish. I'd trusted my lawyer, the hot guy sitting next to me, to understand what it said. He'd pointed and I'd signed. Right at the bottom.

Except my signature was no longer on the page.

"What the what?"

"That's what I said." Ethan tapped the paper again, as if he could force the signature to reappear. "I went to the city and filed them. Everything was normal. This morning, I got a phone call informing me your signature was missing on one page."

He stood then, letting the pent-up energy loose.

"It can happen, though I was sure we hadn't missed anything. I went to the courthouse to get them." He stopped, running his hands through his hair. "Simone, every one of your signature lines was blank. All of them."

I lifted a page toward the wall, letting the light from the sconces show through. I don't know what I was looking for, maybe an impression or faded ink.

Jeff's signature was there. Even the date I'd signed the papers was there.

"How?" I rifled through them all, holding them up to the light, bringing them close to my face. "What? How?"

"These are all excellent questions." My anxiety seemed to soothe Ethan. He returned to his seat. "Could it have been a magic pen? Maybe one of the Twins stashed it in here to mess with me."

"Maybe." Ethan patted his chest, where there was no pocket. "I thought I pulled a pen out of here. It's hazy now."

An adorable little blush darkened his amber skin. Was it hazy because I'd distracted him with my tears and lips? I wanted to believe that.

Still. Ten minutes ago, I'd been divorced. Now I wasn't.

"Well, let's use one of your pens now." I reached into his briefcase and pulled one from its band.

"Hold on, we'll need another witness."

"There's nobody else here." I dropped my head into my hands. My chest was suddenly heavy. My breath short like my bra was too tight.

"What do you mean?" Ethan pushed back the chair and opened the door, as if he could see the entire house and not just the hallway. "I thought you re-opened today."

"I thought so too." I joined him at the door. I needed to be close to someone, anyone. The weirder this day got, the more isolated it made me feel. "Lauren's clinic is empty, I checked earlier. I haven't seen Lydia all day. Lyra is in the great beyond."

I walked out and into the lobby, Ethan close behind me. I pointed at Brianne's desk.

"And I sent her home." When I turned, he stepped back, creating space between us. That was fair, even though it hurt. After all, apparently, I was still married.

"It's okay, Simone." He reached out to squeeze my hand, releasing it quicker than I would have liked. "I'll come back in the morning."

"Like it'll be normal by then." The curtain billowed against a wind I didn't feel. Still, I shuddered, the air suddenly cold. "Where'd you go last night?"

"Huh?" Ethan blinked against my abrupt change of subject. "I was here."

"No, I mean after. You helped me up, I stumbled forward, then never saw you again."

"You forgot the part where Ray swept you into his arms and carried you away from me." His bottom lip puffed out. "I didn't think I was needed once he had you."

"Seriously?" Whatever wisps of attraction I'd felt disintegrated. "Are we back in high school?"

"Well." The pout deepened. He folded his arms and shuffled his feet like a damn child in the principal's office. "You dropped your head on his shoulder."

"I was exhausted!" I flailed my arms, stalking back to the board room to collect his shit. "I'd just been pulled into some sort of mystical battle. Everyone was staring at me in my underwear. I could barely walk."

I shoved the unsigned divorce papers in his briefcase and slammed it shut. He grabbed it, lifting it like a trophy.

"I'm not off base here, Simone. It's not just Ray. Your divorce papers ..." He sighed. "You're clearly not ready for this."

"Of course I'm not." I closed my eyes, fighting the welling frustration. "Even if there was a signature on those papers, it would have been a week old. I was married for twenty years to a man I'd dated for ten years prior to that. You don't just get over that."

Whoa. As soon as I said it, a cooling feeling ran through my throat. It was true. And I hadn't even realized it.

But I had patients to see and a house to repair and missing people to find.

My own angst was going to have to wait.

"I can't do this right now, Ethan. I'm sorry." I led him to the lobby. "I shouldn't have moved in on you the way I did that day. But there are more pressing matters right now. And—"

And I'm hurt you didn't check on me.

He stood silent, waiting for me to finish my sentence. He would wait, I realized. He'd be patient and let me come to him and be thoughtful while I processed.

But he wouldn't come to me. Not unless I asked outright.

"I have a patient." And, as if I'd materialized him, Doug Holloway strolled through the door. He stopped short at Brianne's empty desk, then took in the curtain, and Ethan and I staring awkwardly at each other.

"Bad day?" He asked.

I couldn't lie to Doug. He'd know. But that didn't mean I needed to overshare.

"Something like that." I ran a hand through my hair, suddenly feeling like it was mussed for no reason at all. "Come on in, Doug. I'm ready for you."

I gave Ethan a small, weird wave goodbye and hurried to my office, mentally prepping myself for a very long afternoon.

CHAPTER
TEN

I was giving my last patient of the day a few minutes to exit the Magnolia before I left my office. It was a habit that protected both myself and my clients.

And ... I was hiding.

I didn't want to go back to the lobby.

I didn't want to face another empty space. Or the now-intense level of stress that had settled deep into my bones. Or the nagging doubt that I'd finally put the past behind me and could move forward.

I took a moment, enjoying the live view of the basin surrounding Bridge Island. The waters were still. An occasional mosquito buzzed past. I watched a dragonfly skitter across the surface, dancing with fish I couldn't see. It was a peaceful scene, yet it brought me no peace.

Gathering my resolve, I cleared my desk and stood. Gumbo popped into the patient chair so suddenly I let out a squeak. This was a new habit I wasn't exactly proud of. I sat back in my chair, rolling it toward the window with an exaggerated clutch of my chest like Fred Sanford yelling to Elizabeth.

"Stop with the drama, Simone." Gumbo was full on *I Can Haz* voice, so his words held very little punch. "Lyra's back."

"She is? That's great!" I scurried out without hearing anything else, opening the door in time to see Lyra emerge from behind the curtain. I ran towards her without thinking, shocking both of us by wrapping her in a single-sided hug. Her arms held tight to her side, and I had about three breaths to think about how awkward it was before I finally let go.

"Sorry." I stepped away. "Actually, I'm not. Damn, it's good to see you. Does your sister know you're back? I can go tell her." I wasn't thinking clearly. Lyra's slightly lifted eyebrow told me she thought the same.

Given her wan appearance, I didn't care. There was a strange yellowish undertone to her skin, and her usually lustrous mint green hair was dull and unkempt.

But her eyes concerned me the most. I'd grown used to the strange orange creamsicle shade of them, but it was pale now, so pale they almost faded into the whites, like an elderly dog with cataracts. It was like she was present but ... wasn't. A drained version of her old self.

If I hadn't just hugged her deceptively strong body, I'd think I was looking at an illusion.

In sharp contrast was the woman who emerged from the curtain behind her.

She was as vibrant as a sunny day after a stormy night. Movie-star beautiful, with honey hair that showered down her back like red carpet magic, and a smart pantsuit designed to accentuate her height and curves. She had plenty of both.

She offered me a broad lipped smile, placing one hand at Lyra's back. Lyra flinched. This woman made a powerful fae flinch. My throat closed on sight.

"Of course, Lydia knows she's here, Simone. They are familially linked, after all." Her wide honey eyes—weirdly almost the same shade as her hair—lifted with her grin. She left Lyra's side to take one of my hands in both of hers.

"It's so lovely to see you again." She dipped her head to meet my eyes, reminding me she towered over me. "It's been, what, thirty plus years? My goodness, the times have been good to you."

This was all wrong. Her smile was forced. The way Lyra deferred to her was eerie. The completely polished look of her, despite having emerged from the vortex.

Warning signals pricked up and down my spine, a thousand tiny needles relentlessly hammering my body. The saliva drained from my mouth. I tried to swallow but couldn't.

It's so lovely to see you again. Of course.

Because we knew each other.

Yet another blast from the past.

"Julia? Is that you?" I knew it was her. I knew because the feeling of dread and discomfort reminded me I'd always felt that way in her presence. "It has been a long time. You left town when my mother died."

"Yes, it was right around then." That broad smile of hers thinned, as if I'd farted. "It was tragic I missed the funeral."

Yeah. Because that was the tragic part.

Julia and I had never been close, but she'd been a constant presence. A cousin from my father's side, if Agatha was to be believed. My mother had treated her with a kindness I'd never understood, inviting her to weekend dinners and including her in family events.

Just another mystery in my paternal ancestry. A mystery who'd left town so fast she couldn't be bothered to mourn the only woman in town who'd treated her like she wasn't a pariah.

I tried to shake that off. Why was everything about high school these days? I'd had Agatha. I'd moved on. I'd cursed myself away. No need to think about the past. Although there was one other thing I did remember about Julia ...

"... Ray?" She was talking, and I was lost in thought.

"I'm sorry, what was that?" I asked.

"I said, how's Ray? I understand he's back in town." She winked in a knowing way that made me cringe. "I'm sure you two have caught up."

Riiiight. Julia had been Ray's girlfriend. For years. It struck me how much of the storm of events in my youth happened at once. My mother died. Julia disappeared. Ray was injured. He had a falling out with his best friend Ethan. Then he and I ...

No wonder what we had was so passionate. It was shrouded in angst.

"I believe he's well. And I'd love to catch up, but perhaps later?"

Julia's appearance from behind the curtain was jarring, but I was way more concerned about Lyra. She swayed on her feet, speechless and vacant.

"Let's head to the breakroom, Lyra." I risked my own hand at her back. My fingers itched from the contact, but I gave her a gentle nudge. "I can get you something with sugar. When you're ready, we'll have a board meeting and discuss—"

"I can take her from here." Lydia brushed past me, disengaging Lyra and murmuring in her ear. I hadn't seen Lydia come in, but there she was, and her sister almost instantly brightened up.

"It was ..."

"I know." Lydia glared over Lyra's head at me, still standing at the curtain by Julia. She was usually brusque with me, but I thought we'd made some progress the day before. Apparently, I'd been wrong.

She opened her palm, and a small morsel appeared. It might have been chocolate, perfectly round and smooth, with a shade of brown so pure my mouth watered. Whatever it was, Lyra snatched it and put it on her tongue, closing her eyes and mouth simultaneously.

Within seconds, her shoulders relaxed, and the strange undertone of her skin disappeared. She opened her eyes, though, and they were still abnormal. She blinked at Julia, her delicate features drooping, then turned to her sister.

"What are you doing here?" It was Lydia who asked the question, though Lyra's expression told me she wanted to do the same. Which was odd, considering they'd both come in through the curtain.

"Isn't it obvious?" The falsely warm way she'd spoken to me was gone. She didn't like Lydia, and it oozed from every word. I had to admit, I admired the ovaries it took to speak to an all-powerful fae that way.

"I'm here to take my rightful place as Supreme."

Her words hit me like an icy shockwave, snatching the breath from my lungs and freezing every thought mid-spin. A cold, electric pulse surged through my veins, numbing my limbs until they felt too heavy to lift, as though gravity had suddenly tripled. My stomach twisted painfully, nausea clawing its way up my throat. My vision narrowed into a dizzying tunnel, leaving me stranded with nothing but the frantic, deafening drumbeat of my heart—too loud, too fast, drowning everything else out.

It should have been a ridiculous, over-the-top reaction to a ridiculous, over-the-top statement.

But it wasn't. It was a threat. And, somehow, I knew it was real.

House trembled.

Glass clinked and scooted along shelving in the kitchen. The breakroom table inched sideways, then wobbled in a tight circle that the Twins backed away from.

It wasn't the same as the night before, but it was similar. That pull from deep inside me. That wrenching feeling of someone or something reaching deep inside, yanking my soul out.

"Hey, House, you're going to be okay." I braced the table to still its trembling. I sat in a chair, though it shook beneath me. My arm muscles twitched, but I held still. "I'm here with you. We can fix this. Let's take a breath together. Not that you ... breathe. I think."

My words were low and careful. I was trying to soothe the pull away.

"Oh, for heaven's sake." Julia sighed and flipped her hair. "House, that's enough. Look, everything is well." Her voice was booming, so loud I almost covered my ears. She'd never need a megaphone, that was for sure.

Gumbo popped onto his table, his wide eyes a shade of blue that would rival the summer sky at noon. His nails and bows matched. He gazed at Julia with an alarming sense of awe.

She waved her arms dramatically, a conductor orchestrating a symphony of magic. Sparks of blue lights, little bolts of lightning, danced through the air as she waved her hands. She hummed a tune, not exactly on pitch but lovely nonetheless. A strange tune. Our high school fight song.

She looked ridiculous, but it was effective. The curtain disappeared. The sign I'd put there in half-jest went with it. Lyra's salon door was in its same spot, with walls actually connected to it.

Brianne's office space returned to its usual location. The aura of emptiness that haunted the Magnolia all morning evaporated. Poof. Everything felt normal.

"See? No sweat." Julia grinned at me like a leopard about to eat a face. It wasn't nearly as warm or welcoming as our first greeting. It was smug as hell and very punch-inducing. She dusted her hands together.

"As I've said, I've come to claim my birthright. I will be Supreme of the Magnolia."

That's when it hit me, and I wanted to kick myself for being so slow. She'd come through the door with Lyra. She'd faced Lydia without a hint of fear.

She'd come from the realm I couldn't even walk close to and wielded intense magic.

Julia wasn't human. And she was far more powerful than I was.

She was a legitimate witch.

House stilled. The glasses that had fallen and shattered returned to their shelves. I gaped at Julia, lifting my eyes as a series of words scribbled themselves onto the far wall.

Just over her head. Meant for me.

You Do Not Belong Here.

CHAPTER

ELEVEN

"Y ou can't do that." I barely stammered the words out before the message above Julia's head disappeared. "Yes, I do. I do belong here." I said the second part under my breath, probably looking slightly insane, but not necessarily caring. I wasn't trying to convince them. I was hoping to believe it myself.

A rush of heat built from my core, rising into my chest, and I couldn't control how my fingers trembled. It felt like the sides of my head were on fire. I couldn't see Lydia's or Lyra's reactions to Julia's statement. All I could see was her.

"You don't get to walk in and take what's rightfully mine." My inner voice warned me that saying anything angry in this moment was a mistake. The last thing I wanted to do was create a hex that complicated the situation. I drew a shaky breath. I needed to handle this calmly, if I could.

"Agatha left the house and the Magnolia to me in her will. I have staked my claim within the allotted period and become Supreme. House has accepted me."

My voice faltered at the last sentence, which was even

more frightening. There was a strange popping sensation in my ears. It reminded me of the feeling when a plane takes off, but it was the opposite—we were landing, hitting the runway with a jolt that left my stomach and body in different places.

Julia was nearly six feet tall. She towered over me. But I stood toe to toe with her, even though it meant tilting my head all the way backwards to meet her scoffs. Did it make me feel even smaller? Like I was being sucked into the ground? Sure.

But I wasn't going down without a fight.

"Yes." She patted my shoulder like I was a distraught child. "It's inconvenient that I wasn't here a week ago to claim it before the legalities, but all of that can be straightened out." She pulled out a chair and sat at the table as if she belonged there—as if I hadn't been eating lunch there every day, joined by my friends Lauren and Brianne.

Lauren! Brianne! The memory of one of our lunches appeared before me like a fog clearing. I'd told them something was coming. We'd had a private talk, shrouded in a magic bubble I'd created. What had I done? I remembered scarring the table and fixing it afterwards.

I snapped my fingers a few times, like flicking a lighter to create flame. My palms itched, the skin on my hands was strangely red, but no magic came out.

And if it had ... what then? Was I going to set the woman on fire?

None of that mattered at this moment, though. They'd promised to support me when the time came, and this had to be that time.

But I'd sent Brianne home, and I still didn't know where Lauren was.

"Look, you can have the Therapy division. I'm not a monster." Julia's eyes told a different story. One that made my stomach curl. "I'm also not a qualified therapist, and I hear you're ... efficient ... in that area. It's a clear division, as far as I'm concerned."

Rage still had a hold on me. Part of me wanted to stammer and yammer and flail my arms. As calm as I told myself to be, I was headed toward an adult temper tantrum of epic proportions. My fingernails dug into my palms with a death grip that made me sure I'd see blood when I looked. The fact that she was so cool and collected against my ire only served to tick me off more.

This wasn't right. It wasn't fair. I'd had enough upheaval. I'd earned my place here.

But that thought halted me. Had I earned my place here? Or had it been handed to me?

I took the last seat at the table. A Bayou Bliss appeared in front of me. At least House had my back, even if it just told me I didn't belong there.

I sent a silent thought to House:

I know you're still tired, I can sense it, but can you find Lauren? Or bring Brianne back if she's okay? I don't know if you have that ability. There's a magic-free toilet scrubbing in it for you.

House hated cleaning the toilets, and I didn't blame it one bit. What an absurd waste of magic—to run a brush over a place someone just peed. Or more.

Julia was watching me, her grin so smug I felt punchy. Her silent enjoyment of my obvious torment reminded me how much I'd disliked her growing up. It was always that way, and it irked me no one else could see it.

She was always scheming. Conniving to get her way. Everyone else seemed to trust her, but I never had. And I sure didn't now.

My inner voice was right. This wasn't the time for screaming or ranting or raving. I could do that later, when I was alone. The support I needed was my magic, not the offer of a scrubbing toilet.

"Okay, Julia, I can see you believe you have a rightful claim. I can respect that." I was using my therapist voice, digging deep to find my magic, which seemed to be failing me. "Can you tell me more about your claim?"

"Oh, it's very simple. As your elder, and a direct descendant of our magical line, I am more powerful than you and therefore the rightful heir to the coven." She tucked her hand under her chin and propped her elbow on the table. "Agatha didn't believe I'd return. You were her last resort. So legally, yes, you are the Supreme. But by rights, the position is mine."

A soft chime told me the front door had opened and closed. A pair of female voices, speaking in hushed tones, drifted towards us. As they got louder, Julia waggled her fingers in an odd wave.

"You're a direct descendant of the magical line?" I didn't turn to greet the voices, which were probably Brianne and Lauren. *Thank you, House, I will do the scrubbing for a full week.*

"Of course, I am. You didn't think your mother was a witch, did you?" She giggled. It was gross. "Your father passed some of his power onto you, but it's diluted of course. *My* father followed the proper protocol and married a sorceress."

Well, that was one mystery solved. I'd suspected my father was the reason I was a witch. It hadn't occurred to me that there would be others in my family. Except for Julia, no one from his side had made any effort to make contact with my mother and me. I'd never even met Julia's father, and he was my uncle.

Was it because my mother was mundane? Had they disowned my father for having a child with her? And if so, what had happened to him?

Lauren and Brianne rounded the table. They were standing

offsides from me, directly across from Julia. Brianne was still pale, but she looked ready to fight. My shoulders softened at the sight of them. Lydia and Lyra may not be willing to back me up, but my new besties would.

At least I wasn't alone in this.

"Lauren, it's so good to see you!" Julia lifted her voice an octave, sounding more like a stereotypical sorority sister than an all-powerful Supreme. Not that I had room to talk. "Why don't you tell Simone I'm the rightful Supreme, then you and I can go get drinks and catch up!"

Had they been friends in high school? I had a vague recollection of that. Julia wasn't a cheerleader, but if she'd been dating Ray and Lauren was with Ethan, it made sense they would have hung out.

My heartbeat suddenly sped up. How close had they been? Lauren had said she was on my side when the threat came. Surely this was the threat?

As soon as Lauren's eyes dropped to the floor, I knew I was screwed. It was her tell. When she was ashamed of something she'd done or was about to do, she averted her gaze. I'd seen it enough to recognize it.

Despite her promise to me, she was about to side with Julia.

The increase in my pulse became a loud thud in my chest.

"Magical powers are usually stronger when they're passed down from the mother's side. Julia's mother was very powerful, and yours wasn't. Even though you have distant abilities, Julia would, I guess technically, what I mean is ..."

I couldn't remember confident, boisterous Lauren being at a loss for words.

"Go ahead and say it." Julia leaned forward, an undercurrent of warning threading her words. "Tell Simone I'm the rightful Supreme."

"She is the rightful Supreme, Simone."

I swallowed the bile that rose in my throat. Tears filled my eyes, and I let them shed. I hadn't wanted to look weak, but it didn't matter. There was no way for me to control the way my body shook and my stomach knotted.

Because it wasn't Lauren who'd told me what I already knew.

It was Brianne who'd spoken.

The chains of magic can bind, but the bonds of family can shatter even the strongest link.

Sure, my link with Brianne was new. But I'd sure thought it was stronger than this.

Julia smiled at her, a full-toothed, award-winning smile that would have knocked my socks off if I wasn't already in shock.

"You must be Brianne! I've heard all about you, and what a gem you are." Julia stood and rounded the table as if I wasn't lost in tears. She put an arm around Brianne's shoulders. Brianne shrunk but didn't dodge her. "And we all know you're the one who keeps this place running."

And because that part was true, everything hurt even more. I scratched at the back of my hands, my skin burning.

"I'm sorry, Simone." I tried to meet Brianne's eyes but failed. She didn't sound sorry. "The family chain cannot be broken."

The house shuddered again, trembling like an earthquake had found its way to Louisiana. The table disappeared from between us, the glasses and plates residing on it shattering to the floor. Gumbo was gone. I had no idea when he'd left, but his absence made me feel even more abandoned.

Like hastily sprayed graffiti on the side of a bridge, a message appeared in blood red on the floor. Agatha's final warning to me.

The chains of magic can bind, but the bonds of family can shatter even the strongest link.

I'd just thought about it before. It had been little more than a vague threat. Seeing it take form was gutting.

The buildup of pressure in my ears popped. Like a cork, I ran out of air. I had no fight left in me.

I rose from my chair and left without another word.

CHAPTER

TWELVE

But I didn't leave. Not really. I didn't want to leave House alone with Julia.

And I had nowhere else to go. The deja vu was nauseating.

By the time I reached my front door, my grownup temper tantrum was in full storm mode.

House swung the door open for me, slamming it shut on my behalf. It was time for a proper tizzy, as my mother used to say, and it was nice to know House wanted one, too.

"What nerve! Can you believe her? She can't do this." I was pacing the carpet like I wanted to create a running track right in the middle of my living room. "There's no way she can do this."

This new sensation, this overwhelming anger, was foreign to me. I'd always considered myself pretty passive. Or anxious. Just one short month ago, I would have huddled in the corner and succumbed to a monster of a panic attack. And there was one waiting for me, I could practically feel it lurking just under my rage.

"Gumbo, where the hell are you?" I didn't know where he'd gone when the melee started, and I didn't care at the moment. All my emotions were out of control, and he'd always been able to talk me down.

There was nothing. The air didn't stir. My skin didn't tingle. None of the things I'd gotten used to happening before Gumbo arrived—things I was only just realizing—happened. It was just me.

Well, me and House.

"I don't suppose you know where Gumbo is? Or why he's avoiding me?"

House didn't respond. Not that I expected it to talk.

Cool. Cool cool cool. I was gonna have to field this one on my own. I squeezed my eyes shut, trying to gather hold of my completely off-the-rails emotions. The itching that had started on my hand was spreading up my arm. I clawed at my skin, digging my nails in harder than necessary, as if there were a poison inside me I needed to expel.

A series of red dots freckled my palm. When did I get a rash? I didn't recall touching anything poisonous or toxic. Maybe Lyra had infected me as punishment for hugging her. As if I needed the Twins to do more damage right now.

Three sharp raps on the front door broke through my self-pitying rant. I was somewhat grateful. Even to my own brain, I sounded whiny.

But what if it was Julia, and she had decided to evict me without notice. Crap. I needed to find my voice and fight back. I swung the door open, prepared to beg for a night to pack what little actually belonged to me.

Ray's form filled the doorway. He leaned deceptively casually on the jamb, his hand so close to the entrance I could make out the run of veins where his wolf shifter blood pulsed. Because his arm was lifted, the edge of his shirt was too, and a taut stomach peaked out where his jeans kissed his waist.

The closest we'd been since I returned home was across the table the night before. And I'd been too distracted to see just how good he looked.

Up close, I could be annoyed by how well he'd aged. Streaks of charcoal grey threaded through his black hair like silk weaved into a braid. A few days' worth of stubble covered his jaw, except for the slight cleft I wanted to touch. Even his beard was peppered with gray, and I didn't mind that look one bit. His jade eyes were hard and intense, just as I remembered —piercing, like he was looking through me. The outline of his biceps flexed under his company shirt. Were those damn shirts designed to allure?

Like a rubber band stretched too thin, my emotions snapped in the opposite direction. Heat burned my cheeks. A pool of lust tickled the undersides of my belly. I fought the urge to fidget, clinging to the residual anger I still felt.

"I take it you heard your girlfriend's back in town."

I stalked back to the living room to pace without inviting him in.

"I ... what?" He shut the door, taking my spot on my favorite red couch. He looked at home there, crossing one ankle over his knee like he'd sat there a million times. On my couch.

Only it wasn't my couch. House had provided it. And House would provide whatever Julia wanted when she moved in.

"Dear cousin Julia just popped in from the gaping hole that was once our salon with Lyra in tow. Oh! And then she closed it in a big ole showy show of big stupid magic. So yeah, everything's fine downstairs now, and there's a new boss in town or something."

I could say many things about Ray, but he was not a stupid man. He planted both feet on the floor and leaned forward, talking to me in the slow, soft tone a hostage negotiator uses to calm a crazy person.

"Simone, can you take a breath and tell me what on earth you are talking about?"

"Your ex! Julia!" I flailed my arms, scratching my hand mid-air. It burned like the dickens. I felt raw, like my skin had been replaced by layers of fire and ice. "She and Lyra returned from the void, and she repaired it then casually told me she's rightful Supreme and I need to get the f—"

I paused, my voice on the edge of hysteria. My throat closed up. I tried to continue talking, only to emit a tiny squeak. Closing my eyes, I fought for calm. Whatever I'd been about to say, I either stopped myself or some external force had stopped me.

Either way, it was a good reminder that my words had power. I swallowed a few times, breathing in through my nose and out of my mouth, pretending I was in a yoga class where I didn't hate the perky instructor.

When I felt somewhat more grounded, I looked at Ray. He was still leaning forward, his eyebrows drawn so low he had to squint up at me. His mouth was open, just an inch.

"I can tell by the look on your face you have no idea what I'm talking about," I said.

"Glad you can still read me." There was a hint of an edge to his tone, but the humor in his voice softened me the rest of the way. "What's going on with your skin?"

"Just some weird rash on my palm." I held my palm up to show him. But the rash was no longer just on my palm. It had spread all the way to my elbows, covering my arms in an intricate pattern of red and maroon splotches.

"Holy shit." Ray disappeared into the kitchen, returning with a warm washcloth. He took my arm in his hands and laid it on. The relief was immediate. "Stop itching, it'll only make it worse."

"House would have done that, you know."

Ray chuckled, his breath landing on my skin like a kiss.

"I know. But we don't need magic for everything."

He was too close. My stomach danced a jig as I caught his scent. He smelled of the woods. Soothing, and just a touch wild.

"Why are you here if it isn't because of Julia?"

He held my eyes, matching his breath to mine, helping me to find balance. Or perhaps he wasn't ready to answer. After a moment, he nodded—Ray, in his Ray way, understanding I'd calmed down. He returned to the couch, feeling a hundred million miles away.

"I was worried about you." He rubbed at his chin with the back of his thumb. My mouth went dry. "Last night was hard all around, and you handled it like a pro. But I thought you might want to talk."

This was a side of Ray I'd never seen. Ray had been caring and passionate when we were young, and our conversations always tended to run deep. But I couldn't remember him ever proactively checking on me. Maybe he'd been selfish. Or maybe I'd seemed stronger than I felt.

This was a stronger, more mature, version of the boy I'd left behind.

"You know what, Ray? I do need to talk." I rolled my shoulders. "Just let me change out of my work clothes first."

I walked down the hall, eager to slip into something more comfortable, pretending that didn't mean anything. But when I reached the bedroom, the door was missing. It was all wall, except for a yellow caution sign.

WARNING: LEFTOVERS NEVER TASTE AS GOOD

THE SECOND TIME AROUND.

"Oh, you're funny. Can I get into my bedroom, please?" I crossed my arms and waited. The sign changed.

BEWARE OF OLD FLAMES AND FRESH REGRETS.
CONTENTS MAY HAVE SHIFTED DURING LIFE TRAVELS.

"I wasn't going to put on lingerie or anything." I bit my tongue to keep from laughing. "I just want more comfortable pants." Nothing happened. "Okay look, yes, he's still giving me ... feelings. But so is Ethan. And things are way too complicated right now for ... that."

The door didn't reappear, but a stack of folded clothes landed on the carpet.

CAUTION:
OBJECTS IN MEMORY ARE HOTTER THAN THEY APPEAR.

"You're hilarious." I held up the shirt. It had faded from whatever color it originally was to a grubby looking gray. It had the texture of a cheap hotel towel, and it was covered in stains I couldn't define. And at least three sizes too big for me.

"You know this won't stop him, right? He'd just see it as a challenge." The air around me turned frigid. "I'm kidding. Just let me be comfy, okay? Nothing is going to happen. He's right. I need a friend."

The sting of Brianne's betrayal hit me all over again. I thought I'd had a friend. A good one. I squashed the pain down.

After a moment, the shirt popped out of my hands, and a new one appeared. My old high school logo adorned the chest. It was still too big, but buttery soft from years of wear. I was glad to see it had found its way over from my house in New Orleans. This was my go-to bedtime shirt in college.

Not very flattering, but comfortable, just the same.

"Thank you. I promise to be good."

The bedroom door emerged and opened. I went inside, changing into leggings and throwing the shirt on. Despite what I'd promised House, I ran a brush through my hair. Ray would know if I brushed my teeth. It would give him ideas.

I licked my lips. A little swish of mouthwash wouldn't hurt.

Maybe a swipe of mascara. And a dab of lip gloss. Just because.

CHAPTER

THIRTEEN

G umbo was in the living room when I came back, folded like a potato on the arm of the couch next to Ray. Their conversation was anything but chill, and yet Ray's finger stroked Gumbo's back with a leisurely pace that, quite frankly, made me want that finger to stroke me.

They stopped talking when they heard me clear my throat. Ray's eyes met mine, the laugh wrinkles at the edges deepening just a touch. Like he knew what I was thinking. My damn face. It had subtitles.

"Simone." Gumbo hopped off the couch and weaved himself around my legs. "You nearly panicked earlier, I'm sorry I couldn't arrive in time. I was ... detained."

"Detained? You disappeared in the middle of a crisis, dude." I tore my gaze from Ray to glare down at Gumbo, no longer weaving but instead perched on his back paws, his front two curled under his chin and his adorable, mismatched eyes wide.

"I can haz cream?"

I couldn't help but laugh. The all-powerful cat, who could

go back in time and appear from nowhere, needed help getting something to drink?

"House, could you ...?" I gestured toward the kitchen. A clinking sound followed.

"Go drink it on the tile, you messy beast." Gumbo skittered away, his kitten tummy swinging with each step. "And when you return, I want to know what detained means!"

I shook my head, turning back towards the living room. Ray was still staring at me. Hard.

"What is it?" I rubbed my nose. Did I have a booger? Had the rash spread? "What's wrong with me?"

"That was my shirt." His voice was thick with an emotion I didn't understand. Gruff like he was angry, but the words weren't harsh. It was like joy and sadness blended together and swirled around him.

Right. That's why I'd worn the shirt through college. My damn self-hex had given me just enough hurt to want a piece of him without remembering why. I hadn't put it together when I saw it. Now, I could picture him wearing it —and me, slipping it on in the mornings at Bridge House, tiptoeing to the kitchen while he was still asleep, and begging coffee from Sam, the house chef. I had to admit, House had jokes.

"Oh, sorry. I guess I kept it when I left." I came into the living room, intending to sit on the couch. But it was too close to him, and I didn't want to think about how to angle my body or where to put my legs. I didn't want to crane my head sideways and make my chin look funny.

It was all too much to think about. I opted for the reading chair I'd put where Agatha's rocker used to be so I could stare at him straight on. Although looking directly at him was also dangerous.

Maybe Ray's wasn't the ear I needed. But it was the ear

being offered. And I didn't want us to tiptoe around the past. I wanted it behind me, once and for all.

"There's probably a lot for you and me to discuss, Ray. Thirty years of catchup." I heaved an involuntary sigh. Just as suddenly as I'd been angry, then turned on, I was exhausted. Bone weary.

"Simone, we can save that discussion for another time. Neither of us are going anywhere." Ray lifted his hand, as if he could have reached for me, or close the distance between us. The air around his arm shimmered, a tuft of fur running along his skin. For a second, I thought I might have a giant wolf in my living room.

An involuntary growl escaped me. Yes, please.

He lowered his arm and closed his eyes, exhaling breath in the same way I had earlier. Interesting. Ray was using calming techniques to control his beast, something I didn't seem to be able to do currently.

The shimmer faded. The fur disappeared. I bit my lip to hold back my pout.

"Yeah, of course. Now's not the time." My voice cracked. I felt like a weird little goblin child riding a roller coaster. Or a ping-pong ball, knocked about by an emotional paddle. I needed to focus on the most pressing issue, not my raging libido.

"Actually, I'd like to talk about Julia while you're here."

"Okay." Ray reclined, and his lovely thick eyebrows drew low again. "I didn't know she was back, if that's what you're asking."

"It's not," I replied. "You proved that when I was ranting about her."

His features relaxed into a rare smile.

"What can I tell you? You knew her then, too. She's your family."

JEN LASSALLE

"True. But there's family and there's, you know, family." Ethan had told me things about Ray's past. He hadn't gone too deep, not wanting to betray the man who seemed to still hate him. I'd needed some backstory, though, to put puzzle pieces into place.

Ray's family pack had demanded he sacrifice his professional football career to become the alpha. They were forcing him into a world where he didn't belong, and he'd turned his back on them to pursue his dream. A dream that died on the field when he was injured.

But those were things Ray hadn't shared when we were together because he'd thought I was mundane. We'd both been in mourning, and I'd assumed he only lost the game. I didn't know what he'd done to recover, or what he'd done before he returned.

I had no idea what happened after I left. When he, and everything else I loved, became a distant memory.

There wasn't a way to broach that subject, though, without betraying Ethan's confidence. I didn't want to give them more reason to hate each other. Honestly, it seemed a bit ridiculous that a misunderstanding could lead to such a long-standing feud. Had they really not sat down over a coffee or gone for a walk and talked things out? How very alpha male of them both.

This was too small of a town for them to avoid each other. And what a petty waste of time. Maybe they just needed a mediator. Someone to listen to both sides. Someone who saw the good in them both and could sit between them to hash things out.

Yum. I wouldn't mind being in the middle of that sandwich.

The thought came on so suddenly I had to squeeze my thighs together, shocked by the flood of lust that stiffened the

94

tips of a certain part of my body he would be able to see, as I hadn't considered putting on a bra.

What the hell was wrong with me?

"I just mean Julia and I weren't close," I said, hoping to distract him from my boobs. "Mom always had her around, but we barely talked. You dated her." I leaned forward, propping my elbows on my knees. "Did you know she was a witch? I mean back then?"

"I promise you I didn't." Ray mimicked my position, meeting my eyes. "I knew Treater's Way was special, and I knew about Ethan and a few others. But Julia?" He sat back up and crossed his legs. "She never indicated she was magic. And that's something she would have shared with me."

"What do you mean?"

"Well, Julia liked to be special." He tapped the edge of the couch to the beat of our high school fight song. Why was everyone so obsessed with that stupid tune? "The truth is, she was only with me because she wanted to be popular. The center of attention."

"And yet you dated her for like three years." I rolled my eyes at him. Ray didn't seem like the kind of man who would put up with being used, and yet he was all but admitting he had. "And you only broke up because she left town."

"We broke up for other reasons." Ray shifted his gaze toward the window. I waited while he parsed his thoughts. There was so much we had to say to each other. One day. "We were young, Simone. She was pretty and charming, and I was the quarterback. It was just expected."

"I suppose it doesn't matter." I stood up to pace again. Going back to high school wasn't getting us anywhere. "If you didn't know she was a witch then, there's no way to know what her powers are. Or if she's even a witch and not something worse."

I shuddered, picturing her waltz through the void like it was nothing. Lyra had looked like death warmed over. But Julia didn't even have a hair out of place. She'd claimed her mother was a sorceress.

How powerful was she?

"Gumbo would know." Ray put his hands on my shoulders to stop my pacing. I hadn't noticed he'd gotten off the couch.

"Gumbo's avoiding me. Unless he wants cream." A lump formed in my throat—not the I'm-about-to-do-weird-magic kind. "They all avoided me, Ray. They stood there and let her claim my house. Even Brianne sided with her."

Shoot. Once I said it out loud, I couldn't keep the tears from flowing. Ray pulled me close, wrapping his big arms around me. I angled my head, pressing my ear to his chest. How many times had I done this same thing over our summer together? Dozens.

Listening to the steady rhythm of his heart, safe in his embrace, I let myself cry. This time last night, had I really been dancing around in my underwear, feeling hopeful and confident? It seemed like a million years ago.

Julia's words echoed in my head. She'd spoken my most intimate fears aloud.

"What if she's right?" My words muffled against Ray, I brought it to the surface. "What if I don't deserve this position, and she does?"

Ray made a noise, guttural and angry. He pulled away from me to grab my chin and lift my face to his.

"Simone, you are so powerful that you accidentally placed a curse that lasted thirty years. That even Agatha couldn't break." His eyes were intense on mine, rooting me in place. "You were always meant to be here. This is your home."

Then, his lips were on mine. Crushing against me, sudden and fierce.

And over before I could decide whether to reciprocate or not.

He pulled away, leaving me wide-eyed. His thumb stroked a lazy path along my chin, tender in contrast to the bruising kiss. I couldn't find my breath. My heart thudded into my ears. I was both frozen and burning, and there was nowhere else I wanted to go.

"You staked your claim. Now defend it," Ray said, his voice little more than a whisper. "Fight, Simone."

FOURTEEN

I was never more grateful for House than I was at that moment. It was minutes later, when Ray was long gone, that I was able to find my feet. I stumbled to bed and crashed atop it. The next morning, I awoke with my covers tucked around me cocoon-style. I'd expected fitful sleep, but somehow House had given me the opposite.

I didn't remember dreaming. I barely remembered falling asleep. Still, I didn't feel unsettled any longer. Ray was right. Maybe the person I was six weeks ago when I'd caught my husband cheating might have cried and whined and hidden in a corner. But I wasn't that Simone any longer.

I'd learned to use my voice with purpose. It was time I accepted that my roots were here, and this home was mine. The past was exactly that, little more than a series of events that shaped me but didn't define me.

Maybe Julia had an ancestral claim. But I had a legal one. And if it came down to a fight, I was willing to get in the ring. Even if I got my ass beat, at least I'd know I'd gone down on my own terms.

At least, that's what I told myself in the bathroom mirror. After I scrubbed the toilet. As promised.

Ethan was in my waiting room when I went downstairs to start my day. I'd hurried through the lobby and passed the breakroom, eager to avoid Brianne, or anyone else for that matter. My days were still booked solid. And, for the first time since I arrived, I'd be eating lunch alone.

Sleep still hung heavy around his eyes, and he'd skipped his morning shave. My fingers twitched to scrape my nails across the stubble, and a guilty pang in my gut reminded me that, just last night, I'd been ready to jump Ray.

Not that it mattered. The expression on his face was anything but inviting.

"I only have a few minutes," he said by way of greeting. "I'm due in court in New Orleans in an hour." He showed me his briefcase. "We've got a problem."

My stomach sank. "The divorce papers?"

"I'm afraid so." He followed me to the coffee bar in the corner, which I did not remember being there yesterday but was very happy to see, already pulling them out of the manila folder. "What's going on, Simone?"

"What do you mean?" I held out a cup in invitation, shrugging when he shook his head and pouring my own. "Thank you, House."

"I mean, why don't you want to be divorced?" He shook the papers in my direction.

Something like horror pinched me in the chest, twisting my stomach until the thought of drinking this amazing brew felt like swallowing vinegar.

Immediately following it was rage. Red hot and bright white around my eyes. I set the cup on my desk to keep from flinging it at Ethan. How dare he suggest that I didn't want to be divorced?! From the man who'd subtly put me down for years, controlling my decisions and relying on me to nurse him back to health only to screw another woman in my own bed? Why would I want to be married to that piece of excrement?

I didn't realize I was squeezing the mug until it shattered in my hand. Burning hot coffee and shards of glass dug into my skin, still tender from the strange rash the night before. A thousand tiny fire ants crawling the length of my fingers would have been less painful.

The divorce papers floated to the floor in a soft rustle when Ethan rushed to me. The accusation in his eyes only moments ago evaporated. A stack of towels appeared on the coffee cart. He grabbed one, gently removing glass and wrapping my arm.

"Geez, Simone, what is going on with you?" Those dark brown eyes—so deep I wanted to swim in them—lasered onto me like I was the only thing in the world.

Damn. Damn damn damn.

"I wish I knew." It was the clearest my throat had been for days, and it was oddly validating to have my magic back me up. "Give me a moment."

I stepped away, opening the towel to survey the damage. Though the blotches from the night before were fading, my skin was tight and shined pink. My fingers were swollen and cracked. Pain radiated up my elbow.

Every ounce of my being screamed to cancel my day. This burn needed treatment. Already, blisters were forming on my fingertips. Angry bubbles that throbbed to touch. Were you supposed to pop blisters to make them heal or not? I couldn't remember.

One thing I knew for certain, though, was that eventually they were going to pop. All the gunk under the surface was going to come out, whether I wanted it to or not. I could wait, and let it fester on its own.

Only yesterday, I'd told Sarah she had permission to take

control of her life, to build a new identity, no matter the cost. I could do the same.

"I want nothing more than to move on, Ethan." There was a sense of weightlessness within my chest, a new and odd sensation that I didn't actually mind. "Jeff hurt me. He betrayed me. But the worst part? I hurt myself. I became passive and meek and ignored my inner voice. I lashed out at my son, the person I love most in this world. We're still working to recover from the pain I caused him."

Ethan's mouth opened. Maybe he didn't trust himself to speak, or maybe he was speechless. I hadn't told him about Gabe. Maybe he knew I had a son, but I'd only told Brianne about our rift. He would be here in a few days.

But how could I repair our relationship when the one I had with myself was still so shaky? How could I convince my son to love me when I barely believed in myself?

Why was I still acting like a meek human when I was a witch? It was time I integrated my magic self to my human self, Supreme or not. I'd become a better therapist by taking steps forward to trust in my abilities. I was a woman nearing fifty, newly single and handed the keys to a pretty amazing kingdom.

Maybe it was the throb of the burn that put it all into perspective, or maybe it was because hormonally, I felt like a teenager all over again.

Whatever the reason, I was so over this ish.

"It's time I let myself heal." I held my hand up, waggling the fingers. "Starting here."

The pain was intense. Maybe I'd expected the wounds to disappear—or to recede—since magic was doing the work. Instead, my body went through the full process. The blisters grew. My skin darkened until it was almost maroon. The skin pulled taut and smooth.

The healing was gradual, and I felt every moment of it. I let myself breathe, soft and slow. I murmured words of encouragement to myself. I forgot Ethan was there, and I focused on myself. It sucked.

After a few moments, the swelling stopped. Then, it did recede. A touch of heat lingered, even after the rash disappeared, but that was to be expected.

The deepest wounds rarely heal entirely.

"Give me the papers."

They'd scattered on the ground. While Ethan bent to pick them up and reorder them, I turned to the coffee bar.

"I love this," I told the house. "Let's fix the mess I made, please." The cup I'd shattered popped onto the surface. There were still cracks in it. I ran my fingers on them. I'd read about a Japanese tradition of repairing things with gold, filling the holes to highlight the imperfections rather than conceal them.

That seemed fun.

"Fill these with gold." I had to admit, it was beautiful. Jagged lines of shining metal gave this simple white cup a touch of lagniappe. That little something extra, born from experience.

I refilled the cup and went to my office to get a pen. Ethan followed, spreading the papers on my desk.

"All I need you to do is sign here." He grinned, and for a second, I could see his wolf form. "And, you know, mean it."

I took a pen from my top drawer and let my hand hover over the signature line. I didn't want to sign with the same enthusiasm I had two times before. Like it or not, Ethan was right. Something inside me wasn't wholeheartedly into the idea of divorcing Jeff.

That seemed reasonable though, right? After all, he'd been my husband for twenty years. He was still the father of my child. I still had just enough fond memories of him to not hate him entirely.

And I still held guilt for hexing him.

More than that, though, I was hurt. Deeply hurt. No matter what the state of our relationship, Jeff had betrayed my trust. And because of how abruptly I'd transitioned from that life to this new one, maybe I hadn't taken the time to process that.

But I could still feel all those things and want to move on. I could hold two seemingly opposing emotions in the same space. Hadn't I just yesterday told a client the same thing?

"I want to divorce Jeff." My throat wasn't tight, not really, but a nagging doubt in my mind told me Ethan would be back. I slid the papers across to him with what I hoped was a confident smile and not a weird, toothy lear.

"There is something else I'd like to talk to you about, Ethan." He put away the papers, making a show of checking his watch.

"Look." I pointed at the clock on the far wall. I enjoyed the smirk that came naturally as he frowned at the clock, realized it wasn't moving, and checked his watch again.

"It's the same time as when I first got here."

"Pretty cool trick, right?"

"Very." He took one of my patient chairs, leaning back and crossing his foot over the opposite knee in his usual way. It accented the muscles in his thighs, tightening his pants around his crotch.

Looking at his snake—because I couldn't tear my eyes away even if I wanted to—my own desire slithered through me and struck my core. I wrenched my eyes to his face. There it was again. The damn wolf.

And here I'd thought I was a cat person.

"Um." I swallowed a gulp of coffee, forgetting it was full until it ran down my chin. I swiped at it casually, like I'd meant to spill it. Again. "Did you hear that Julia came back? Yesterday?"

"Julia Bardot? Ray's ex?"

"My cousin Julia." I ignored the ex part. "Skipped town when my mom died, then showed up yesterday claiming she's a witch."

"What?" His foot dropped, and he leaned forward. No small part of me was disappointed at the change in view.

"Yeah, she fixed House then declared herself the rightful Supreme." I didn't bother to keep the bitterness out of my voice. "It was an eventful day."

Ethan sprang from his chair, catching it just before it fell to the floor behind him. His thinking pace. The man could not sit still for long.

"Is she even a therapist?" He flailed his arms as he said that to me. "Why would she want your position?"

"She doesn't," I said. "She specifically said she doesn't want to head the therapy division. She just wants to be Supreme." My throat clogged again. "Both Brianne and Lauren agreed she has a claim because she's older than me and has paternal and maternal blood magic."

The way Ethan stopped in his tracks stilled my pulse.

"She has maternal blood magic?"

"Allegedly?" I lifted my own hands, palms up. "I don't know what that means, though I'm going to ask Gumbo. Last night—"

I stopped myself. I didn't need to make things more complicated by telling Ethan that Ray had come over the night before, or that he'd put thirty years of pent-up emotion into a kiss I was still thinking about.

Or that I'd wanted to pounce on him like a puppy and hump his leg.

"Um, I got some advice that I should challenge her, to go

after my claim, but I'm not sure how to do that." I took another sip of coffee and waited a beat. "I was hoping my lawyer might have some advice."

Ethan watched the floor as he paced it. His lips moved and his brow furrowed. I drank and waited, letting him problem-solve.

"I can verify her lineage and check the older versions of the will—see what I can find. Legally, you are airtight. Magically?" He gave my hand a squeeze, then released it. "Don't do anything rash, Simone. Give me some time to do research before you challenge her."

I didn't like that answer. However well-meaning he was—and it felt great to have Ethan on my side—I wasn't about to sit back and wait for a man to solve this problem for me.

It struck me how fundamentally different Ray and Ethan were. Ray was all fire and lightning. Ethan was foundation and strategy. Both had their allure. But me?

I needed information to make a decision. I also needed my emotions to guide me. And my emotions were a mess.

He'd said not to challenge her, but I didn't even know how. There was someone who did know, I was sure of that.

It was time for my cat to stop avoiding me.

FIFTEEN

"Gumbo, a word?"

Nothing happened. Irritation bubbled up.

"Stop being a coward and get your cute little furry tail over here." When the air didn't stir, I let out a sigh. "Now, or no more cream. Ever."

A sort of haze formed, Gumbo's chartreuse toenails the first to step out, then he followed, tripping over his comically large matching bow just as he reached my desk. I stifled the giggle at his almost meow sounding grunt. He gave a full-body shake then hopped soundlessly to the desktop.

"Simone." There was no cute kitty in his tone. It was formal in a way that shook me. Was the sweet voice reserved for Supremes or potential Supremes? Or had he lost respect for me when Julia fixed the house before I could? He hadn't used that tone the night before. Then again, he'd been thirsty.

Fear gnawed a hole in my chest. I needed information, but I needed connection as well. Gumbo had been a staple in my life since I was a young girl. We were pals.

He was my kitteh.

"Lord Gumboton of the Cajun Clan." I scritched behind his ear, calling him by the silly name I'd given him as a child.

Gumbo's purr vibrated up my arm and covered me. I wanted to sink into it, to allow him to calm every nerve ending the way he did when I had a panic attack. I'd not experienced one in weeks, but I could feel it brimming. Between the explosion, Julia's challenge, the rising tension between me and Ethan AND Ray, and the disappearing ink on my divorce papers, the past two days had left me on edge.

Gabe would be here in a few days. And I had a job to do. But I couldn't handle any of it without information.

"Sweet boy, I have some questions." I pulled my hand back.

"Aww, so soon?" There was a hint of cuteness in his voice again. Phew.

"Sorry, pet. I only have a minute and need to make the most of it."

Gumbo scoffed. I wasn't aware that cats could make such a human sound.

"Dearest Simone, you paused time." He dipped the earless side of his head toward the clock on the wall then butted his head against my hand. "Get to scritching."

With a laugh, I obeyed. I had to admit, I needed to give the pets as much as he needed to receive them. After what was probably a few minutes of pets and rubs, I felt more calm than I had for a while. I consciously dropped my shoulders and shifted my hips in my seat.

"I hadn't realized how much tension I was carrying," I said, giving him a final pat on the head. "Thank you."

"Thank *you*, friend." My heart warmed at both the tone and the term. Gumbo sat up straight, curling his tail around his paws. The bow shrank to a manageable size. "Now then, you have questions?"

"Many, actually." I took a sip of coffee, unsure where to start. "I guess my first is, what the hell is happening to me?"

Gumbo tilted his head. His one ear rotated, opening to me. Curiosity filled his eyes.

"Explain."

"My emotions seem to be ... erratic." I tapped my fingers on my desk, instantly annoying myself. "One moment I'm happy as a clam, an expression I've never understood, the next I'm breathing fire. Not literally," I added as he opened his mouth, internally horrified I had to clarify.

"Yes, there's a lot being thrown at me, but I've never been this off kilter. I'm like a randy goat." The heat of a blush crept up my neck and burned my ears. "I'm equal parts irritated and horny at all times. I feel like a teenager."

"A moment, please." Gumbo stood and paced my desktop. His gold eye expanded, past his cute snout. He stopped and scanned me with it. I stood perfectly still. Just in case it was a laser.

"How old are you?" He sat and wrapped his tail around his body.

"Forty-eight." I groaned. "Are you saying this is a menopause thing? Because if you are saying this is a menopause thing—"

"There's not a thing wrong with going through menopause, Simone." Gumbo held up his paw, cutting me off. "Aging is a natural and beautiful part of the experience of living. I myself am no longer the spry kitten I used to be. Agatha frequently said her second fifty years far surpassed her first."

"Maybe." I gnawed on my lip, annoyed to have my own words repeated to me. Why was it so much easier giving someone else advice? "That doesn't mean I'm ready for it to happen. Besides, I've had perimenopausal symptoms for years now, this is different. It's like I'm changing overnight."

Gumbo scanned me again, this time with the green eye, which stayed in its socket. The way an eye should. Thank the gods.

"You're correct, there is a mystical element to this. There's something ... off ... about your magic aura. It's cloudy. Like it's been polluted. Are you fighting it?"

"I don't know." The frustration took over. "I barely know how to use it. We haven't had a lesson in weeks. I've been so busy trying to get the therapy clinic boosted I haven't even thought about my magic. And things are so crazy half the time I forget I'm a witch."

I was glad Gumbo wasn't a dog. The pitch of my voice would have sent him over the edge.

"You are not using your magic in sessions?" At what I assume was the blankest of stares I gave him, Gumbo sighed. "Simone, a word witch can use her voice to put people at ease. Your gift can allow them to relax enough to get to their core issues and gently guide them to release trauma without as much pain and regression as a mundane session."

I sat back in my chair, feeling defeated and exhausted. It had felt so good to be a normal therapist again that I'd forgotten I wasn't a normal therapist.

"Surely you haven't been treating supernatural clients with mundane methods?" I didn't like the judgment in Gumbo's tone, not one bit. But I had to admit I understood it.

"Maybe," I mumbled, crossing my arms over my chest. "I tried magic, a few times. It didn't go so well." Poor Doug had been the victim of my first terrible attempts to weave magic into my therapy sessions. I'd forced him too far beyond his boundaries, and his response was an anger that almost cost me the entire practice. I wasn't eager to go back to that.

"Well, that explains quite a bit. You have stunted your magical gift, my dear, and created internal conflict. You see"— Gumbo stopped to lick his paw, dragging it behind his ear— "your magic is still young, given that you discovered it later in life. Perhaps you have menopause or perimenopause-like symptoms, but your gift is behaving like a teenager. It's no wonder you're in conflict."

All the tension our cuddle session had dissolved returned, creeping over my shoulders and claiming me. The old Simone whispered from within. To sleep it off. To hide in a dingy office, not that I still had one, to let things happen the way they were meant to. Maybe Julia taking over as Supreme wasn't a bad idea. After all, she clearly had a hold on her magic, and I could focus on developing mine without the added pressure of leadership.

A new fire, one I didn't recognize, burned, reminding me I'd healed my own burns that very day.

I wasn't that person anymore.

"Can you help me, Gumbo?"

Gumbo's eyes dipped with a sadness I didn't expect. His whiskers quivered.

"Unfortunately, no. Not at the moment."

"What?" I couldn't believe what I was hearing. Had he just said he couldn't help me? "I thought you were my Mystical PAWWtector." I drew out the last word, making it sound cutesy like he sometimes did. "First Lauren betrays me, then Brianne, and now you?"

I hadn't realized I'd come out of my chair. I stalked to the window, and as I watched, a storm raged in the swamps. The clouds darkened to an ugly black. Lightning flashed in them, ready to strike. "This isn't fair."

"Poor baby." His words laced in sarcasm. Gumbo disappeared from the table and popped onto the windowsill beside me. "Poor pathetic Simone. Really, woman, this is tiresome."

I opened my mouth, found nothing to say, and closed it. It wasn't that I couldn't think straight. I couldn't feel straight. I didn't need Gumbo to tell me I was acting like a child.

Or, like a petulant teenager.

"Technically, Simone, I am the house's Mystical PAWtector." I ignored the jab. "While there is a battle for Supreme, my job is to ensure the house is not pulled into the competition until the allotted time."

"What does that mean?" I tilted my head. Something had happened when he mentioned the house. It was almost like it whimpered. "What competition?"

"Of course, you know someone cannot just say they are Supreme?" Gumbo dipped his head forward, beckoning me to pay attention. "There are trials, Simone. A claim must be acknowledged, as detailed in *The Magnolia Codex*."

"There's a codex?" Holy handbook Batman! There was actually a guide out there somewhere that I could read? "That feels like information I should know already."

"Oh dear, I've said too much." Gumbo didn't sound contrite at all. In fact, he sounded the opposite. Cat sarcasm, it turned out, sounded very much like human sarcasm. "If you found out about the trials detailed in *The Magnolia Codex*, you could challenge a natural birth right."

Gumbo gave me a long, pointed stare. I'm not sure how intelligent Gumbo thought I was, but I got it. Somewhere was a book that detailed Supreme trials.

For the first time, a glimmer of hope soothed the fire in my belly.

"Of course, as House's protector, I couldn't possibly interfere and give you that knowledge." Gumbo rubbed his body against my arm. "As your friend, of course, I'm rooting for you. But I remain impartial."

He purred against me, and I scratched his neck and jaw. I didn't fully understand, but I got the gist. There was a way for me to fight. I just had to find it.

"Thank you for being a friend, Gumbo." The moment the words were out of my mouth, I knew the Golden Girls theme song was going to be stuck in my brain for the rest of the day.

Oh well, there are less catchy tunes to hum.

Apparently satisfied with our interaction, Gumbo hopped off the windowsill and sauntered toward the office door.

"By the way, the full phrase is happy as a clam at high tide. Because at high tide, they can't be dug up and eaten. Clams are happy at high tide because it's safe." He looked at the clock, and the second hand resumed. "How safe are you, though, if you never see the sun?"

CHAPTER

SIXTEEN

By Thursday, I'd convinced myself the solution to the problem was to bake a cake. Never in the course of my forty-eight years on this planet, had I attempted to bake a cake before. When Gabe had birthday parties, I relied on the local bakery to supply treats. To be honest, I wasn't much of a cake person.

I know. But give me a big ole plate of spaghetti over a tray of pastries any day.

Maybe I was grasping for a magic bullet. And maybe that bullet had icing on it. Packed days of nonstop sessions were both a blessing and a curse. I wasn't able to obsess over what to do about Julia, or how to find a codex I'd only just learned about.

The lunches that used to be the highlight of my day weren't happening. Lauren never left her side of the Magnolia. Maybe she wasn't there, or maybe she was avoiding me. I didn't know, and my initial attempts to learn more about the business from Brianne had halted.

She and I were barely speaking—and man, did that make

me want to drown myself in pasta. Each morning, her red-rimmed eyes darted toward me from her desk. But she hadn't said much more than a terse good morning.

I should have sat with her and had a conversation. After all, we were adults. But this newly adolescent-behaving side of me was being a coward, so I ate lunch at my desk and avoided the breakroom.

It seemed safer than confronting them. Or dealing with the gnawing fear in my gut that I might lose the one thing I'd claimed for myself in the past month.

And, underneath that fear, the secret sigh of relief that life could be easier. What if I just let Julia take over? What if this was an answer and not a problem? Gumbo had made it very clear there was a way to fight back. Some codex I would have to seek out.

There were ways to find it. I'd start with Ana, the town librarian who now owned the book shop. Last I'd heard, she had a back room full of special editions and rare manuscripts. She might have it in stock, or at the very least know how to obtain it.

Then again, if it belonged to the Magnolia, perhaps it was here in the house? Maybe I just had to ask for it or earn it. I bet if I asked House right now, it would arrive on the countertop.

Or maybe Julia had changed her mind. Since Monday, I hadn't seen hide nor hair of her in the building. Maybe she'd seen how much work it was and decided she'd rather be beautiful and carefree.

But where had she come from? And where was she now? Was she letting me stew or working against me in the background, slowly convincing the other department heads she was best for the Magnolia? Not that she had to. They all believed the claim was hers to stake.

Ethan had been useless in that area. He confirmed her

bloodline, but nothing more. *It's a magic problem, not a legal one.* He'd sent that in a text. And from Ray? Nada. Zip. Zilch. This really was feeling like high school.

Ultimately, this was my problem to solve. And mine alone.

But not tonight. On this long evening in the house that I'd begun to consider home, I was going to bake a cake. Not with magic. But because I needed to do something maternal.

Gabe would be here in the morning. My son was coming to visit, and for the first time in way too long, we were going to have time together and an honest chat.

I headed to the kitchen, googling welcome home cakes on my way. On the counter was a cake tray, adorned with exactly what I'd pictured for Gabe. If he was eight.

Fun blue icing, certain to dye tongues and taint poop, swirled around the three layers. Little candy pieces of paint brushes and easels coated the sides like confetti. On the top was a picture of his first guitar, with the ragged shoulder strap and scratched surface. A boy version of Gabe held the instrument like it was a trophy, his hair mussed from sleep and his holiday pajamas two sizes too small.

Oof. House had plucked that image straight from my memory. Gabe and his two great loves: music and art.

"House, this is awesome. Really. But Gabe is an adult now. I was thinking something more grownup." The cake wavered a little before shifting shapes. The icing was darkening. His boyhood image disappeared.

"Also, I want to make it." The cake stopped moving midshift. Now it looked like a thrown-up cake.

I felt a strange twinge of disappointment, but it wasn't mine. It was like I was eating someone else's emotions. Damn. I'd hurt its feelings. House was so helpful, and always eager to give me everything I needed. And it had been through a lot this week, too.

"I appreciate this, House, I really do. It's just ... I need to create something. To tell him I did it." The cake didn't move, and it was making me a bit sick to look at, so I tried a different tactic. "This is—was—too pretty. Gabe would know I didn't do it."

After another moment, the gross blob disappeared. In its place was a bright red apron with the words *This Witch Runs on Butter and Avoidance Spells.*

"Haa haa," I said, putting the apron on.

I scrolled the endless cake images on my phone. Gabe was still an artist—it was his major in college—but did he still play guitar?

I had to admit, I didn't know anymore. Shame landed like a cold stone in my stomach. My shoulders rolled forward, and I bit back the self-hate that caused a bitter taste in my mouth.

Of all the things I'd messed up, Gabe was by far my biggest mistake.

Sure, I'd been a good mom while he was growing up. As a therapist, I was hyper-aware of his emotions. I'd helped him recognize and process them, giving validation and being present. Sometimes, the only thing that mattered was showing up.

And boy, did I show up. Any extracurricular he wanted to explore, I made sure was available to him. I'd driven countless hours to hobby after hobby after hobby. He'd been a swimmer before deciding he didn't want to do athletics. Then he'd gotten way into chess. And running, because maybe he just wanted to be a different *kind* of athlete.

Art was the only thing that stuck, though he'd transitioned through different mediums like a hummingbird to flowers before landing on graphic design. For all his quirks—and my own neurosis—Gabe and I had maintained a pretty solid relationship.

Until I screwed the pooch after catching his father cheating and hexed my own son while feeling sorry for myself, telling him to forget all about me.

Top notch parenting right there.

I slammed my phone to the counter. Rehashing the past wasn't going to get me anywhere. I'd reached out, undid the hex—but not the pain—and we'd had tenuous texts for weeks. And I'd get to see him in person very, very soon.

I just needed to bake a damn cake first.

Thinking back to the cake House made, I considered what I would change. I'd been tempted to cut into it, to see if it was red velvet, his go-to. Even if it was, the cake was like Ray's old T-shirt. It was familiar and a little nostalgic, but it didn't fit anymore.

No, I needed to make something completely different. Something that didn't come from a Pinterest board. Something from the heart.

A new fear piled itself onto my anxiety. What if Gabe would prefer cupcakes? Or worse, what if he was gluten free now, or vegan, or had some other super passionate but likely only to last a few weeks type of special dietary restrictions that I didn't know about because we weren't as close as we used to be?

Or what if this cake couldn't solve all our problems with a single bite?

I nibbled on my lip, which also didn't solve problems, and took a deep breath.

Sure, we had too many problems for one cake to solve, but I had to make the effort. That's what I would tell my clients.

Sometimes, it's the ingredients you select and the work you put into it that matters. Not the cake itself. It could be dry and misshapen and maybe too sweet or not sweet enough.

"Okay, Simone." I slammed my palms together and rubbed. "Let's bake a cake."

A second later, a score of ingredients, each in measuring cups and bowls and that tube thing you use for sticky stuff, were neatly distributed around a massive stand mixer. One of those bougie ones where the head lifts to make space to pour things in. It even had attachments.

Beside the ingredients sat a set of spatulas, an icing bag I'd probably never use, and every other utensil I might need.

"I meant it, House." I tried to keep my voice firm and yet appreciative. I probably failed. "I want to do it all myself."

Something warm and fuzzy weaved around my legs. I screeched, looking down. Gumbo, with cute *I Can Haz* eyes, mewled like a kitten.

"House, if you want to help, can you get Gumbo some cream?"

Gumbo sat with his tail curled around him, licking a blue toenail that matched the magic cake. His giant bow was the same shade and freckled with paint brushes and easels, just like the cake.

The ingredients disappeared. The counter was clean.

"Okay. I get it, you're mad at me."

I knew nothing about House. Add it to the list. How old was it, what was the source of its magic, how did it connect to me and know what I was thinking and feeling? Why did I sometimes have to say words and other times not? Was that about me?

I went to the refrigerator for Gumbo's cream, found it already in a saucer, and placed it on the floor for his regal adorableness to enjoy. While he lapped at it, I watched, marvelling at how he was somehow still a kitten despite being, as far as I knew, at least forty years old. And, while he could talk and work magic and alter time, he was still, at the heart of it, kitten.

"Gumbo, I have questions about House."

Gumbo lifted his adorable head to meet my eyes. Cream dripped from his kewpie doll mouth and formed a mustache below his nose. Unable to resist, I reached down and booped it.

"That was uncivilized," Gumbo said. With his little kitty voice and big kitty eyes, it was adorable, and I didn't bother to pretend I felt bad about the boop. Had his toe beans been on display, I would have poked those, too.

"As Mystical PAWtector, given the current situation, I am unable to answer questions about House." He returned to his cream. "Particularly given its involvement in the trials."

He'd muttered the last sentence, just low enough I caught it, but in a way that told me he was trying to send me messages again. Right. *The Magnolia Codex* might tell me more about House, or even about my own magic.

Gumbo finished his cream then popped out without saying goodbye. I cleaned his bowl and went back to the fridge.

I had work to do.

CHAPTER
SEVENTEEN

Considering I now lived in my hometown, it felt like a strange switch to drive through New Orleans and feel like I was visiting the past. Gabe's flight was delayed, because of course it was, giving me time to visit some of my old haunts. There weren't many I wanted to see. But there were two places at the top of my list.

The disappearing signature on my divorce papers was still bugging me. As eager as I was to put the past behind me, it continued to creep back in small ways that told me I wasn't as finished with it as I was pretending to be. Maybe there was something here I needed to dig up first.

My first stop was the little corner therapy clinic where I'd not-so-bravely decided to open my own practice after Gabe was born. Located in a mostly franchised shopping center, it was a dull square office with a generic neon sign. It was where I'd lived, literally, after catching Jeff cheating.

Now housing an insurance agency, a white-toothed man in a suit claimed he'd save me money from the new sign. But the windows still held a tint of grunge, and I vaguely wondered how much cleaning they'd done after I left.

I couldn't remember exactly when I'd let it go to ruins. I'd been eager and ambitious about the venture at first. I could set my own hours, which worked around Jeff's schedule, and still feel like I was contributing to society while raising Gabe.

Plus, I didn't want my certifications to lapse. I'd been determined to remain an active member of the social work community.

And I'd wanted to feel like I was more than just a mother. Or a wife—though, looking back, I couldn't remember when that had lapsed, either.

Now, it was just another building with just another business. In the few minutes I sat in the parking lot, no one came in or out. Maybe I'd return in six months and see if yet another young entrepreneur had taken over.

But probably not. I drove away, smiling at the sight of it in my rearview mirror.

My old neighborhood—and I laughed that I remembered it that way when I'd lived there no less than two months ago—looked the same. I'd lived a lifetime in six weeks, but the rest of the world hadn't. Still, as I drove through, it felt foreign. Like I was visiting a town I'd read about, and not the very place where I'd lived. None of this felt like digging up my own past.

It was almost as if I was touring someone else's life.

Jeff's car wasn't in the parking lot, though it hadn't been there when I'd caught him screwing his physical therapist a few weeks earlier so that could mean anything. Not that I was going to go inside.

Now that we were officially divorced, or trying to be, I shouldn't even have a key. House had transported most of what I wanted—or needed—from here without me even having to ask. I'd given Jeff the house and everything left in it.

What would I do with faded furniture and old curtains anyway? The Magnolia was perfect and designed for me.

There was no reason to visit the building I'd once called home ever again.

A car pulled into the driveway, and a pretty blond with a ponytail higher than the sun hopped out. His physical therapist. The one he'd cheated on me with.

Did she live there now?

I twisted my lips, trying to assess how I felt about that. There was a hint of sadness I couldn't deny. Jeff and I had been together too long for me to feel nothing. And though our ending had been volatile, the beginnings hadn't. In fact, they'd been pleasant.

Too pleasant. Like a movie you enjoy while watching but forget about as soon as you leave the theater.

More vivid was the memory of catching them together. I'd thrown up on her shoes. Had she, as the current resident of the home, been the one to clean that up? A little bit of Petty Betty peaked out. I hoped so.

It was then I realized I hadn't been nauseous in weeks. My panic attacks were at a minimum. In fact, aside from being mildly out of shape, I felt good. Was it because of how well House fed me? My daily salad lunches and restful nights were reviving parts of me that had long been dormant.

That was part of it. But a bigger part of it was that I'd gone home. This house, despite its cute gray shutters and pale blue color, had never felt right to me. I'd tried. Desperately at times, I'd painted walls and made dinners and convinced myself I was where I was meant to be.

But it was never true.

She could have the house and everything in it.

I was meant to be at the Magnolia.

I was meant to bake cakes there, and treat clients on my

own terms, and build friendships with people who didn't yet trust me because I hadn't fully let them know me. I was meant to embrace my magic.

"And dammit, I'm meant to be Supreme."

The air around me stirred the moment I said it out loud. Word magic. I wasn't nauseous because my stomach was settled. I wasn't having panic attacks because I felt safe.

"The Magnolia is mine." I liked it, the way my voice was deeper and stronger, as if I had an invisible bullhorn. "I'm going to fight to keep it."

This house, and anything and everyone inside, was my past. I had a new future. I dashed across the street and dropped my key in the mailbox, scampering back before anyone inside saw or heard me.

Maybe I tripped on my way back to the car. And maybe I'd have a bruised knee in the morning. And almost definitely all of that had been caught on their door cam.

I didn't care. My past-life tour was over, as far as I was concerned.

I found easy parking at the airport and waited by baggage claim, bouncing on the balls of my feet like a kid. No matter how much I told myself to act cool, there was absolutely zero cool happening. I wanted to see my baby boy.

Of course, he no longer looked like a baby boy. A full-grown man emerged from security. Shaggy, dark brown hair covered his brows and the tips of his ears. Stubble coated his jaw. His T-shirt, a colorful depiction of some anime show I'd never heard of, was wrinkled over jeans he'd long outgrown.

He looked around until his eyes, a version of mine, found me. The grin that spread wide across his pale face was all little boy.

Everything inside me melted. I knew that look. I was still his momma.

I ran to him, damn near leaping into his arms. My "boy" had me by at least a foot, and the deep laugh that rumbled out of his chest was ten shades deeper than I remembered. He swung me around, and for a moment, it felt like flying. So what if he kind of smelled like he hadn't showered in a few days. I breathed him in.

"It's going to be okay." I was talking to myself, stating the truth I felt buried under all this anxiety and pain.

"Of course it is," Gabe whispered back.

He kept my hand in his as we walked to retrieve his luggage —three old, battered suitcases I didn't recognize. On the drive home, he chattered nonstop, telling me all about his classes and his friends. Gabe had always been a talker, even when I'd expected him to become a sullen teen, he'd told me all about his days on the way home from school. It was nice that it hadn't changed.

The only difference now was the subjects he talked about. Instead of regaling me with the inane details of how he'd achieved some super ultra rare gem thing in a game I couldn't remember the name of, he spoke about future plans and career paths.

The internship had been a great opportunity—arranged by his father, though I didn't begrudge him that.

"I think I'm going to focus on animation, Ma." He said it casually, his long legs stuffed into the jeep I'd borrowed from Misty over on Bridge Island. "You know, making movies? Or maybe graphic novels."

"You've always been a good storyteller." The conversation was so normal. So easy. I almost forgot I'd broken his heart and damaged us. There were harder conversations to be had. But maybe not yet.

We crossed North Bridge to return Misty's car. His luggage

had barely fit and getting it out had us both laughing and sweaty.

"Leave it there," I finally said. "I'll make sure it gets to the Magnolia."

"Sure." He looped his arm around my shoulders and pulled me close. "Whoa! Look at that fat gator. Man, something smells delicious."

"That's Norbert, and the smell is coming from the cafe. They have great food there."

"Oh good, I'm starving!"

With a giddy laugh, I pulled Gabe away from Bridge House. I couldn't match his energy, but I loved every second of the trying.

"Later," I told him. "Let's go to the Magnolia first. I made a cake."

That stopped him in his tracks. For the first time, he stood still and really looked at me.

"You ... baked?"

"Uh-huh." I had zero confidence in the end result, but I wasn't about to tell him that. "It doesn't look great, but it tastes ... fine. Probably."

I tugged at his hand, leading him toward South Bridge and beyond to Treater's Way. As we walked, I pointed out landmarks and places of interest. I described Illusion Square when we hurried through it. We waved at Ruth, the crazy old lady who sat at the base of the Mighty Oak in the town center.

Of course, knowing what I did now, she wasn't so crazy after all.

His jaw dropped when we reached the Magnolia. I wanted to take him inside, to introduce him to Brianne and my colleagues. But not yet. I didn't want anything to sour our mood, so I led him around back and we took the stairs to my part of the house.

"Welcome to my home." I made a silly grand gesture. "Your bags will be in the guest room, back and to the left."

I said it to make it true. I'd already asked House to convert my office to a temporary guest room. He turned in a circle, nodding his approval.

"This place is cool, Momma."

"Thanks." Now that we were here, and the adrenaline was fading, there was awkward energy between us. I swallowed, my mouth suddenly dry. "Do you, uh, want to settle in?"

"Later," he said with a grin. "I want a piece of that cake!"

Oh well, the bubble was bound to burst. He followed me to the kitchen. The cake was on a grand pedestal, with plates and utensils stacked next to it. So, House wasn't totally mad at me. That was good.

It looked like shit. Literally. The chocolate frosting and my poor attempt to cut it into a Minecraft-style block had combined to create a big square of poop. Gabe's hands were on his knees, his laughter filling all the scared places inside me.

I laughed with him, grateful my poo cake had broken the ice completely. I cut it. And we ate it.

And it was delicious.

CHAPTER

EIGHTEEN

G abe couldn't stop talking about Norbert, and I
guess that's fair. Even in my youth, the giant gator
—older than the swamps themselves and missing
one eye—captured my attention. In fact, Bridge Island seemed
like the perfect place to keep Gabe focused so we could have a
real conversation.

If I hadn't been so eager to eat the cake, we might have
stayed there when we dropped off the Jeep. Not that it was far,
but walking through town presented more opportunity for us
to run into someone I didn't want to interact with at the
moment. Like Julia, who had been oddly silent since her challenge. Or Brianne, who barely looked at me these days.

I'd already decided that the first conversation we had
would be about my witchiness. I couldn't explain the results of
my poor choices without admitting I had magic. Far too much
around here couldn't be explained, like how Gabe's suitcases
beat us home.

It was important for me, too. Embracing who I am meant

not hiding it from the people who mattered most. So far, I hadn't told anyone I was a witch—unless they already knew, either about magic or about me. If I could have that conversation with Gabe, I figured I could have it with anyone.

Including my patients. Gumbo was right. I shouldn't be trying to treat mystical beings with mundane methods. If I could integrate my abilities with studied tools, with their permission, I might be even more effective for them.

The thought gave me a thrill and sparked an idea. Leading Gabe downstairs, we snuck in the back and went directly to my office. It was fun, I had to admit, seeing it from his perspective —though as his mother, I could wish he had more words in his college-level vocabulary than *whoa* or *cool*.

We were facing the far wall and the window depicting the view from my favorite park bench. Sure enough, as if he knew he was needed, Norbert was there.

"Whoa."

"Yep," I said. "Pretty cool, huh?"

"Very." Gabe inched closer, reaching out a hand as if to touch it. "Will the screen mess up if I touch it? Where's the projector?" Forget his hand, his nose was almost poking it. "Ooh, is it one of those digital doodads that projects from behind?"

"It's not a screen, Gabe." My voice was shaky. I'd never tried this before.

"What else would it be?" Gabe glanced at me until movement caught his eye. Then he was nose-to-window again. "Wait, is that a cat? Does that gator eat it? Is that why it's missing an ear?"

Sure enough, Gumbo emerged from a patch of trees. His bow was a moss green that blended with the ground. He sat regally, wrapping his tail around his body. He met my eyes and nodded.

I drew in a breath. Okay, I was on the right track with this.

"Gabe." I pulled on his hand to get his attention. "Can you stand with me here for a moment? I'd like to show you something."

"Yeah, sure." Taking a few steps back, Gabe let me intertwine our fingers, but he couldn't tear his eyes away from the window. "Are you going to change the movie?"

"It's not a movie, Gabe. It's … something I have to show you. Something real." I moved us both closer and touched the pane. "It's more like a window. One that we can walk through."

As my finger hit the glass, it rippled outwards, creating a sound not unlike metal warping. Beside me, Gabe mumbled an expletive that was definitely not *whoa* or *cool*. I chewed on my lip. No time like the present.

"Let's go," I said. Together, we walked through, exiting with a bit of a jolt behind my favorite park bench.

"Hello, Simone." Norbert's grin was probably supposed to be welcoming, but even though I knew better, it terrified me. He shifted his fat body to face my son. "And you must be Gabe."

"I—what?" Gabe plopped onto the bench, his mouth so far open a line of drool formed in the corner.

Well, it was a good sign he didn't run. I think.

"Hey, Norbert," I said, taking the seat next to Gabe. "Gumbo."

"Simone." Gumbo was full *I Can Haz*. Did he use that to keep people at ease? I always felt more comfortable when he spoke with authority. "I'm glad you found your way here. That was very wise."

Gabe's open mouth snapped shut. He made a sound in the back of his throat. HIs mouth dropped open again.

"Thanks, Gumbo. Gabe and I have a lot to talk about, and

this seemed like a great place to do it." My mouth was bone dry. "House, would you deliver some refreshments for us, please?"

A small patio table appeared in front of us. It wasn't one I recognized from the house. A white tablecloth blanketed it, with a tray of assorted sandwiches in the center. Next, two tall glasses of ice water and a pitcher for refills. Finally, a pile of bacon, a bowl of cream, and a small notecard.

The notecard read *Compliments of Bridge Cafe. Enjoy your visit to the island!*

Huh. Was the B&B on Bridge Island connected to House's magic? Or did it have a magic of its own? The answer was probably in the codex, which I'd yet to even look for.

Later. Gabe was my priority right now.

"These things are always easier over food and drink. I wanted to discuss it with our cake but, well, it was a nice moment." This was a new thing, being totally honest and vulnerable with my son. I wasn't sure how it made me feel yet.

LIke he was on autopilot, Gabe went to the table and sat, drinking from the glass in front of him. I tossed the bacon to Norbert and set the cream in front of Gumbo. Since Gabe's glass was already empty, I refilled it from the pitcher, completely unsurprised that it was full when I set it back down.

"I thought cats were lactose intolerant?" It was the first coherent sentence Gabe had managed in a while.

"I didn't know that." I looked at Gumbo. "Are you?"

Gumbo glanced up at us, cream dripping from his whiskers.

"Worth it."

Oh dear.

"Pretty sure gators shouldn't eat bacon, either." Gabe tilted his head and raised his voice. "Is that how you lost your eye? Norbert?"

Norbert and Gumbo exchanged an uncomfortable glance. I'd always wondered how he'd lost an eye, too. And why Gumbo only had one ear. But I wasn't brave enough to ask.

"That's a tale for another time, lad." Norbert swayed his body, angling into the water. "I do thank you for the treat, Simone. Please don't tell Ruth." With an impressively agile flick of his tail, Norbert swam away.

"Have a good talk, friend." Gumbo dipped his head at me, then at Gabe, before retreating into the forest.

Alone—and I wasn't sure I wanted us to be, but there we were—Gabe chewed on a sandwich. He seemed calmer. At least his mouth was closed, unless he was eating.

"So, yeah," I began." Magic is real, there's a ton of power here in Treater's Way, and I'm a witch."

Gabe didn't speak. He gestured at me to continue, grabbing another sandwich.

"Okay." I drew in a breath, concentrating on the feeling of energy I sometimes got in my stomach. I wanted to do this from a mystical place, if I could. Drawing it up into my throat, I let my voice speak.

"The thing is, I didn't know I was a witch until about six weeks ago. Agatha, who was sort of my grandmother growing up, ran the Magnolia. She left it to me in her will. It was right after your dad and I, uh, separated."

Gabe nodded, shoving another sandwich into his mouth. Where was he keeping all that food? I swear, the boy had a second stomach.

"I'm a word witch, Gabe. That means my words have power."

"Everyone's words have power." He gulped a few sips of water as if he hadn't just blown my mind.

"True. But mine have a different kind of power." I tapped the table. How do I do this? "I can affect the way people feel with my words. I can put them at ease—or even hurt them. Not that I would."

"Everyone can do that, Mom." Another sandwich. Was my boy dense or was I just explaining this very poorly.

"Maybe a demonstration would be better." I opened my hand, palm up, between us. I'd never done this before. I hoped it wouldn't hurt. Channeling the energy, already ready to pounce, I drew air into my lungs. When I spoke, my voice was that deeper, richer tone I'd only heard a few times.

"My hand is purple. And I have pickles for fingers."

It did hurt. It hurt a lot. My skin turned redder and redder, as if being flushed with blood, before deepening into a dark magenta. My fingers didn't morph so much as disappear, briefly freaking me all the way out. Dill pickles replaced the digits. I wiggled them in front of Gabe.

But given how much the boy ate, it seemed dangerous to keep them that way.

"That's enough of that," I said. With considerably less pain, my fingers unpickled and my skin was back to normal.

Gabe had, finally, stopped chewing. He stared at my hand for several minutes, poking me to make sure it was real.

"So, the things you said when you called me that night. The night you caught Dad cheating. They did a magic?"

I choked up. My brilliant boy.

"I'm so sorry I called you at all that night, son. No one deserves to know what their parents are going through. I put you in the middle of a really tough situation." I could barely see his sweet face as tears filled my eyes. "When I told you that you were better off without a mother …"

I let my voice trail. I couldn't finish.

Gabe took my hand in his.

"Momma, it didn't stick. Not really." I blinked at him through tears. "For a while, until I got your letter, I had this thought: I don't have a mom. But it was like a vague, wrong idea, you know? It hurt, don't get me wrong."

He dropped my hand and returned to the sandwiches.

"But not as much as hearing from you felt good."

I was speechless. The hex wasn't strong enough to damage us?

"I suppose it didn't stick well because I didn't really mean it." I rubbed his shoulder, as much to soothe him as myself. "I'd rather be an imperfect mother to you, my brilliant wonderful young man, than no mother at all. I hope you can accept that and forgive me."

"Yeah, that's done." Gabe grabbed another sandwich. Good lord, boy. He held it but didn't eat it, looking at me instead. "When I talked to Dad, and figured out what he did, I knew you were just hurting. It wasn't great but, hey, we all screw up."

"Yes, we do." I couldn't believe how mature he was. More mature than me, if I wanted to be honest with myself. This was a solid, grownup version of the quirky young boy I'd raised. "I love you, son."

"I love you too, Momma." He gestured around him with his sandwich. "This is all pretty wild. It'll take some getting used to."

"Tell me about it." With most of the tension behind us, I grabbed a sandwich for myself. "I'm still getting used to it."

"I bet." He looked out at the swamp, the water still and brown. A slight wind rustled the trees, carrying the strum of a guitar. The groundskeeper enjoying his afternoon no doubt.

Gabe stacked the mini plates and the now-empty platter.

He gathered Gumbo's bowl and brushed crumbs off the table. When he stood up, I took it as a sign he was ready to explore some more, so I rose with him.

"It's pretty weird." He gathered me close, squeezing until I couldn't breathe. Which was just fine with me. "But cool."

CHAPTER
NINETEEN

"I'm starving."

"Dude. How?" Gabe and I strolled Bridge Island for the rest of the afternoon, catching up and settling in. He had more questions for me, about magic and the Magnolia, and I'd answered them as honestly as I could.

I had to admit, he was asking questions I hadn't thought about yet. Like whether he had magic or not, since it was an ancestry thing. The only questions I didn't answer were about his father.

We'd just left Illusion Square after spending an hour or so among Ana's books. The codex was nowhere to be found, even in her most ancient and mystical section. If it belonged to the Magnolia, it made sense it would be at the Magnolia. Still, it never hurts to try.

A mouthwatering smell greeted us in town, and I was as shocked as Gabe when my stomach grumbled in response.

"Geez, Mom, how many sandwiches did *you* eat?" I poked his rib, following the smell to Gino's Pizzeria.

"Come on, kid. It's early enough on a Friday, we might just get the prime spot."

The prime spot was a tiny booth in the far corner, known for two things: having the best spot under the A/C vent and putting you and your partner in close contact. Everyone knew it was where you went when you wanted to make out with your date.

But on a Friday night, when the music or a game was blaring, it was also the best place to actually have a conversation. Lauren and I sat in the spot a few times, and it was never because we wanted to smooch. It was just a darn good place to soak up the ambience of a slightly grubby—but delicious—wood-fired pizza joint.

Unfortunately, the spot was taken. Even worse, it was taken by Ray.

And he was there with Julia.

They were angled toward one another, so I knew their knees—and who knows what else—were touching under the table. He had his head propped on one hand and a look I could only describe as moony on his stupidly handsome face.

Julia said something, and he laughed. She ran a finger along his jawline. Dammit. I wanted to run my finger there.

My chest was hot. Like my heart burned. It spread right up into my neck and along my cheeks, leaving the back of my head weirdly cold. I knew without looking in a mirror I was bright red.

So, that's where she'd been. And why he hadn't reached out since the impulsive kiss he'd laid on me that I was totally not still thinking about.

They spotted us as soon as we stepped in. Such was the blessing and the curse of the special spot. A sly smirk spread wide across Julia's face. She waggled her fingers at me like she was greeting a bestie, but her eyes told another story. One of triumph and malice.

Ray, to his credit, looked guilty as sin. He sat upright, jostling the table and spilling his beer. Good. This was stupid. Ray and I weren't dating. We'd had one near-moment in thirty years. And he and Julia were exes. Of course, they would hook up again when she came into town.

To stay. Because she believed she'd take control of the Magnolia.

Well, she could have Ray as far as I was concerned. I was keeping the rest.

I could feel Gabe's eyes boring into the side of my face.

"Momma, everything okay?"

"Yep." I turned to him, plastering on a fake smile. "The best spot is taken. But there's a table over there."

We took it, and I only cursed a little that it put Ray and Julia in my eyeline. They were still watching me, so I waved and turned my attention to Gabe.

"So," he said, unfolding his napkin and putting it across his lap. "Which one do we hate, the dude or the chick?"

Despite the bitterness coating my tongue, I laughed.

"Let's say a little bit of both," I replied after the waitress took our drink orders. "And hate is a strong word. Well, for him it's strong. For her ..." Gabe was watching me, one eyebrow lifted so high it disappeared under layers of fringe. "You need a haircut."

"Uh-huh. And jeans that don't stop at my ankles. You told me already." He opened the menu, so wide it filled the table. "Spill it, Ma."

"The man is Ray Chase. He and I had a very brief thing before I met your father." There. That was enough of a truth to feel comfortable about. It was all I had to say. "But there's some residual feelings we haven't addressed."

Damn, I hadn't expected it to come out. Maybe that was all it was: residuals. Between him, Ethan, and my new foray into adolescent emotions, I couldn't see straight. But if I was honest, seeing him with Julia felt more like betrayal than I wanted to admit. Not just because he'd been so supportive the other night, or because of our past, but because she wanted to take something very important away from me.

And he was over there ogling her like she was the last beer at the crawfish boil.

"I hope his beer is flat," I murmured. "I hope every beer he drinks is flat."

"Mom." Gabe's voice held a warning note I hadn't heard from him before.

Oh, shoot.

"I did it again, didn't I?" I'd hexed Ray out of spite, letting my emotions take control. "I'll fix it. I promise."

And I would. But maybe not while he was on his date.

We ordered pizzas, and I begrudgingly included a salad as an ode to Lauren. Gino, the man himself, came over to hug me close, wrapping me in his beefy but sweaty embrace.

"Your momma worked here when she was a teen," he told Gabe by way of introduction. "Best damn waitress ever."

With a smile, I returned to my seat and introduced them. With Gino's attention on Gabe, I was able to wipe off the flour he'd accidentally smeared on my arm without him noticing. We chatted until the salad arrived.

"Salad, huh?" Gino chuckled. "I'll never see the appeal."

"Me either," I admitted, dividing it between two plates. "But I'm trying to take care of myself."

Someone else walked in, and Gino rushed off to greet them.

"Okay, so the guy I get." Gabe moved lettuce around, bypassing it in favor of cheese or a crouton. He was definitely my kid. "But what about the woman?"

"Well, that's my cousin Julia." Saying her name was sour like vinegar. "Which I guess makes her your first cousin. Or second."

"First.," Gabe said, gesturing with his fork. "Once removed. Why do we hate her?"

"I don't hate her." I sighed. It was true. I didn't hate her. There was nothing to hate. Sure, she was conniving and power hungry. But she'd never been directly cruel. "My mom always told me that she'd had a rough childhood. She spent a lot of time with me growing up, then disappeared when Mom died."

It pinched, the way it always did, that Gabe never got to meet his grandmother. To know how wonderful and nurturing she was. If I hadn't hexed myself, he would have been raised here, at least knowing Agatha.

What a different world it would be.

"Earth to Mom." Gabe waved his hand in front of me.

"Sorry." I stacked the plates and pushed them aside. I'd done my penance. It was pizza time. "I get in my head a lot."

"Well, get out of it and tell me why a cousin I've never met is shooting daggers at our table while pretending she's a nice person."

"You're an astute kid, you know that?" The pizza arrived, and I slid a slice onto each of our plates. "Blunt as hell, but really wise."

"I know." He dove in, undoubtedly burning the roof of his mouth. "And I'm not a kid."

Huh. He had me there.

"You're right. I'm sorry." I risked a glance at the make-out table. They were still chatting, but without the same air of romance. Seeing me must have broken the spell a bit. Good.

"She claims she is the rightful heir to be Supreme of the Magnolia. She wants to control the business and the house."

Julia's eyes caught mine. I held hers without blinking.

"But I'm not going to let that happen."

She was the first to turn away, with a nervous flick of her movie star hair. Holy cow! I'd shaken her with just a look and a few words.

Gabe grabbed another slice. I looked away from her to enjoy my pizza and my son. But I felt her eyes on me, and I ate with a smile on my face.

"Cool," Gabe said

Yes. Yes, it was. I took a sip of my cold, not-at-all-flat, beer. "Cool."

CHAPTER
TWENTY

Someone was banging on my door before seven a.m. On a Saturday.

Someone was itching for a good hexing.

I stumbled to fling it open, barely stepping aside before Ethan charged in. He was in bright red basketball shorts and a wrinkled gray shirt. The faint linger of sweat followed him through the door.

Why was that working for me?

"I did not expect my morning run to be interrupted by yet another call about your divorce papers, Simone." He waved them at me like a madman. "It's good luck for you that I have good friends who aren't making this more difficult."

"Sorry." But I was grinning. He was so cute, all befuddled and angry and wrinkled. My grin only made him glare harder.

"I've had enough of this, Simone. Either sign the papers or don't, but I'm not doing this again. It's not just you affected by this, you know. My reputation is at stake." He stepped close, his brow furrowed. "If they don't stick this time, you're staying married."

His voice was a low growl I hadn't heard from him before. This was a new side of Ethan. The wolf side, I realized, as I could see it brewing just under the surface.

Steadfast, loyal, reliable Ethan had a growly side. He wasn't just the soft-spoken—but strong—man who'd been my friend through all of this. Maybe Ray wasn't the only passionate one.

My core coiled, ready to spring. Well, hell. I was gonna try to kiss him again.

"Yes, sir," I said. My voice was low and raw. I licked my lips.

"Simone." His voice held a warning, but his eyes flashed, dark and dangerous. There was the wolf. I could have howled.

I grabbed his shirt and pulled him close. He didn't hesitate, pressing his body to mine. I angled my head to stare up at him, giving him a nod. Silent assent. He lowered his lips toward mine, and my heart thudded into my throat.

"Mom?"

At the sound of Gabe's voice, Ethan stepped away. To his credit, he didn't jump like we were doing something forbidden. It was a controlled, conscious movement that made every inch of my body whimper.

Forget magic adolescence. I had the hormones of a teenage boy.

"Everything's fine." I managed. "This is Ethan. He's an old friend from high school. And my, uh, attorney."

"Attorney, huh?" Gabe didn't bother to hide the humor in his voice, or the mischievous grin. "That's pretty great service for a Saturday morning."

He didn't seem upset that he'd caught me almost jumping a man that wasn't his father, so that was something. Not jumping, Simone. You were just going in for a kiss.

Right.

"I'm going to make a pot of coffee." It seemed like a good time to conveniently forget that House could prepare it. "Ethan, if you'll bring the papers to the table, I can explain."

"You must be Gabe." Ethan crossed the room to shake his hand. I stopped short.

"You knew I had a son?"

"Well, yeah." He twisted his mouth like I was missing something obvious. "When we collected your information for the will, it came up."

"That makes sense." I should have known. After all, he found me in New Orleans to deliver the news about Agatha's passing. It did make sense that he would know I was married and had a child, but it felt invasive. Like he'd delved into my personal life without me knowing about it.

What else did he know?

I filled the coffee pot with water and put it on to brew. If he'd known Gabe and I were estranged, he'd been classy enough not to mention it. It seemed Ethan was always waiting for me. It was touching. Very sweet.

But I had to admit, I wished the wolf would come out more often.

When I returned to the breakfast area, the guys were chatting over a tray of blueberry muffins. My divorce papers were still in their folder, sitting to the side. I checked the outside of the folder. There was no label or writing to indicate what they were.

Good. I wanted to be able to explain it to Gabe.

I poured coffee for both of them, then for myself, and joined them. Gabe dumped even more sugar and milk into his mug. It was barely coffee colored. Definitely my kid.

"Gabe." I swallowed to get the too-big bite of muffin down, and to cover my nerves. "These are your father's and my divorce papers. Every time I've signed them, my signature has disappeared. I want you to know that because it's not going to happen again."

I didn't have to hear the deep rumble of my voice to know it was true. And no matter how lackadaisical Gabe appeared on the surface, he had to have some kind of feelings about his parents separating.

"Should I go?" Ethan swept crumbs off the table and deposited them on his plate. "I can come back and get them if you'd rather—"

"No," I said, not letting him finish. "Secrets and hedging and ignoring my gut haven't gotten me very far. And you're my friend."

He might have flinched a bit at the word, but it fit. Were we more? Almost definitely there was something brewing. But despite what my body wanted, my mind and my heart weren't fully on board yet.

"Gabe, part of me needed to go see our old house, to see that your dad has moved on. But I realized as well that I need *you* to be okay with this as well. The last few months, I've been selfish. But to truly fight Julia, and to make the Magnolia the best she can be, I have to stop thinking about myself all the time."

I tapped the papers.

"That starts here. How do you feel about your father and I getting a divorce?"

Ethan shifted in his chair. I knew he probably wanted to get up and pace. It was how he rolled. He was nice enough to sit still. Gabe, on the other hand, did rise. He cleared the table, leaving Ethan and I staring at each other, wondering what would come next.

When he returned, he took his chair and held my hand.

"So here's the thing. I love you, and I love Dad. He and I still talk about once a week, and we're in a decent place."

Decent. I wanted to delve into that but opted not to. I had to let Gabe speak his piece.

"But what he did to you? And the way he moved on?" Ethan grunted like he couldn't keep it in. "Yeah, that," Gabe said.

He squeezed my hands harder. His eyes shimmered with unshed tears.

"I'm not okay with it. And Dad knows that." He released my hands to open the folder, turning to the signature page. "Sign it. Then let's talk about how you're going to beat this Julia woman."

Ethan handed me a pen. I took it.

"Our marriage is officially over." I signed each page, my voice and my heart strong. "I mean it."

I had to admit, it was a relief. It felt right this time. For the first time since I'd walked in on Jeff, I knew I was saying goodbye to my past life. It truly was behind me. But I was taking the best and most important part of it with me.

I hugged Gabe over the table. It was awkward, but then again so was I.

"What is the latest with Julia?" Ethan took the papers and tucked them into his briefcase. Had he been carrying a briefcase when he walked in? Maybe that was what I'd felt against my leg …

"Um."

I cleared my throat and stalled with a cup of coffee. Gabe was grinning at me again. I swear if that boy was magic and his gift was mind reading, I was in for a world of trouble. "Gumbo has been somewhat distant since Julia made her claim. As protector of House, he said he must remain impartial."

Ethan's lip lifted a little, but no snarl escaped.

"He did let slip that the Magnolia has a codex, and in that codex there is mention of a series of trials. Do you know anything about it?"

"Agatha never mentioned a codex." Ethan sighed and sat back. "My dad had an inventory of the house, though. I can check to see if it's included."

"Thanks. I intend to fight back." I wanted to pat his hand— or squeeze it. But I wasn't being fair to him. Every time I gave him an inch, the man wanted a mile. And I wasn't ready to travel miles. "Even if we find it, Julia is mad powerful. The way she just waved her hands and fixed House was impressive, I have to admit. Even Ray seems to be under her spell again."

I instantly regretted the last comment. If Ethan was hurt, though, he didn't show it.

"Let's start by finding it. We don't have to rush into anything."

There he was, reliable old Ethan. Always wanting to gather data before rushing in. The thing was, now that Gabe and I were on good terms and I felt more sure again, I wanted to rush in. I was ready to face whatever Julia did.

"Momma?" I turned to Gabe. "Can I ask a question?"

"Of course," I said. "Ask away. I can't promise to have an answer."

"Oh, you won't." My breath stilled. I wasn't sure what that meant. I braced myself.

"It's just this thought I keep having." Gabe stood up and paced the floor. I had to laugh. Ethan was probably jealous.

"You keep saying she's super powerful, and you keep saying you're not." Gabe stopped and looked at me. "But you don't see all the ways you use magic without even realizing it. I mean, you turned your fingers to pickles with just a word yesterday."

Ethan chuckled. I wasn't about to explain that one.

"I can't help but feel like you are minimizing what you have and maximizing everyone else around you." He stopped and stared at me. "What if she's not more powerful than you, Mom? What if she just knows her power and you don't?"

CHAPTER

TWENTY-ONE

I was still sobbing the next afternoon, long after Gabe was safely in the airport and I was headed back to Treater's Way. I missed him already. Not just because he was my son and I loved him, but because he was fun to be around.

Gabe saw everything from such an interesting lens. All the little quirky bits he'd had as a kid were still there, and they'd somehow come together to form an interesting and insightful young man. I couldn't take credit, but I sure as shootin' was proud of who he'd become.

Even if that insight was aimed at me. His question about Julia's power vs. mine had dropped my jaw. And he was right. A day later, I still didn't have an answer.

Did Julia have more power than me? Or was I undervaluing myself?

It would be normal for a woman my age, particularly one who'd been a devoted wife and mother, to subtly put themselves down. Right or not, that's what women do. We make a billion subtle sacrifices for our loved ones, all the time telling ourselves we don't need anything.

Then one day we wake up in our forties and realize we need more than we understood, and we have no idea how to ask for it. We need to be seen as whole and complex. We need to be appreciated for the mental load we carry, and we need partners who help carry it without being asked. We need more than a Hallmark-created day that we usually have to plan ourselves, with halfhearted flowers from our spouses.

I loved every moment I'd devoted to my son. I was proud of the sacrifices I made for my husband, even if he didn't appreciate them or respect me. But do I wish I'd asked for more—both from them and for myself? Absolutely.

Women should feel whole and strong and powerful. Women should be honored and revered. Because we run the show.

Every time I started to feel good about myself, either because I made progress with a client or was proud of what I'd overcome, some small part of me held back. Forget what I achieved. I was hyper focused on where I lacked.

Because I wasn't tall, I felt small in public. Because my body was out of shape, I felt misshapen around fit women. Because my husband's cheating had left me feeling undesirable, more so than the years of him paying no attention to me at all.

And despite *two* men making moves on me in just the past week, I still didn't see a sexy middle-aged woman when I looked in the mirror. Had I leaned into their attention a little too hard? Maybe.

Gumbo's explanation of my magic behaving like a teen's made even more sense now. Of course my emotions were over the top. I'd shut them off to cope with a life I didn't want. I'd quieted my inner voice every time it tried to speak up so I didn't have to face choices I knew were wrong.

Now I was taking a straw to a firehose and trying to drink.

I could help a client process these feelings. I was doing that with my new client Sarah already. I'd invite them to be curious about the parts of themselves whispering they are not enough. I'd ask them to keep a success journal. I'd encourage the use of reframing negative thoughts into growth statements.

Julia isn't more powerful than me. She just knows her power and I don't.

Yet.

Okay. So where could I start?

Instead of going up to my living quarters, I decided to head to the office. It was Sunday, but I wanted to restructure my sessions, to give myself more breathing space. I had some 'me' work to do, and burying myself in other people's issues wasn't going to get that done.

I'd asked Brianne to talk with me about it when things slowed down, but nothing was slowing down, and I didn't want to ask for her help until I knew where she stood.

To my surprise, she was standing by her desk.

And she wasn't alone.

Lyra and Julia chatted opposite her—Julia so close to Lyra it looked like they were fused together. They were huddled and whispering, which seemed silly given no one was in the office. The door opened with a loud creak it never had before, no doubt compliments of House announcing my presence.

Lyra's eyes—lovely, but tired-looking—widened when she saw me. She let out a sound I could have sworn was the word *eep*, then scurried to the spa door. The all-powerful fae literally scurried. Away from me. A witch who was just discovering her abilities.

What the what?

"Simone!" Julia's voice oozed like a rancid slime. "What a lovely surprise to see you working on a Sunday. Here I thought you were a 9-to-5 kind of girl."

"Well, it's quite a way to make a livin'." To my mind, there was no situation that a little Dolly couldn't diffuse. I strolled towards them, keeping my tone light. With each step, she sidled closer to Brianne.

Poor Brianne looked guilty as sin. Her eyes were red-rimmed and puffy. Her nose was pink and swollen. Had she been crying nonstop for the past week? We'd been avoiding each other, which hurt more than I wanted to think about.

The woman staring at me was not the ray of sunshine who had greeted me with a hug and an armful of compassion when I'd first arrived. She weaved her fingers together and gnawed on her lip. If it was possible, she seemed even shorter than usual.

Like she was shrinking.

"What's going on here?" I asked. "A little overtime, Bri?"

I wasn't sure what to feel. My heart was thudding so hard I felt it against my shirt. A strange, cold sensation covered my arms and feet. But my head burned hot. It was one thing that Brianne had admitted Julia was the rightful Supreme.

But this was different. Whatever Julia was or wasn't, nothing was official yet. If she was meeting with my people after-hours gathering intel, that was an espionage level of malarkey. And Brianne didn't look okay with it, either. She looked trapped and afraid.

Julia inched further left, attempting to block my view of the desk. With a glare, I stalked to the other side. I read the first few pages, and my heart sank.

"The next board meeting report, huh?" I rifled through them, seeing projected quarterly earnings reports that made my head swim. No wonder Julia wanted to control the Magnolia. We were rolling in dough. "That's this Friday, right?"

"It's supposed to be, yes." Brianne, bless her, met my eyes. "I was running behind this week, so I'd come in to play catchup. That's when I ran into Julia and Lyra." There was a plea to her voice, strong enough I believed her. "I wasn't going to share it with her."

"Oh, nonsense. Of course she was going to share it with me." Julia flipped her hair over her shoulders with a laugh. "I'm the rightful Supreme, after all. I should attend the board meetings. Right, Simone?"

That weird, cold feeling was growing stronger, radiating out through my arms and legs, all the way to my extremities. I had the distinct sensation of floating. A sensation I'd felt once before, when I'd first arrived. Lyra and Lydia had messed with me. Enthralling me.

I was being enthralled. No wonder everyone seemed so dreamy around Julia.

But so what? My shoulders wanted to soften. My hips wanted to relax. Everything felt like bliss.

Sure. Julia was Supreme. I could just hover in the air and be happy. Sounds good. I should just give it to her, let go of this silly challenge idea.

My voice let out a squeak when I opened my mouth.

The air pressure popped so suddenly the backs of my teeth ached. Gumbo materialized in a cloud of smoke, landing on the desk with such force it shook. He hissed—his mouth wider than a cat's should be. My blood ran cold at the sound of it.

Then he swiped at me, his claws barely grazing my forearm. He may as well have dug all the way in. Three angry welts dropped blood onto the papers. My arm burned like it was on fire.

And it snapped me right out of my happy haze.

"What the hell, Gumbo?" I grabbed a tissue from the box on Brianne's desk and blotted at the scratches. Brianne came up next to me, a wet cloth in her hand I hadn't seen her get.

She put it over the wounds and wove her hand in mine. A little part of me unclenched.

"Beg your pardon, madam." Gumbo's voice was old and wise. A mighty lion lording over his subjects. "I received a signal that House was in danger. I'm afraid I reacted before I assessed the situation. Given the events of the past few weeks, I'm sure you understand."

Was he ... winking at me? Gumbo, the Mystical Protector, had stepped in to help me. I had Brianne at my side. I had a cat with a heck of a right hook.

And, I had more power than even I realized.

"You won't be casting any spells on me today, Julia." Ooh, I loved the sound of my voice. It was like it was an instrument being played by a master. "And you won't be taking the position of Supreme without a fight."

"Oh, really?" Julia was trying to sound confident, but her words tremored. "And what do you mean by fight, exactly?"

Damn. I didn't have the codex yet. There was a challenge, and I was almost certain it was ritualistic. There were probably words that had to be said in the right order. I didn't want to screw it up before it began.

My phone dinged in my back pocket. Hooray for stalling.

"That's probably my son, telling me he's landed." I read the screen and let out a silent *whoop*. Everything was falling into place.

"You know what, Julia?" I gave her the same sly smile she loved to flash at me. "Let's have our monthly board meeting right now. You'll be my guest."

I hugged Brianne, because she was my bestie no matter what. Given what I'd just experienced, I was willing to believe she'd been enthralled, too.

Julia was using her power to control others. She was using it to angle into my position. So maybe I should test this cool new theory Gabe had that I was more powerful than I realized. I drew in a deep breath and closed my eyes, tapping into that place in my core where I could most feel the magic.

Latching onto that sensation of light in a dark place, I exhaled, bringing it up into my stomach, through my chest, and into my heart. I let it fill my throat. And I let it speak.

"Attention division heads of the Magnolia, as well as support staff required for our monthly meetings. Stop what you are doing and join me in the boardroom."

My voice echoed through the room, bouncing off the walls and reverberating back. Brianne covered her ears with her hands and squeezed her eyes shut. But she nodded. Like she could hear me in her head.

Lyra had run into the salon, which meant Lydia was in there. If there was passage to their realm from both doors, perhaps they'd gone beyond. It didn't matter. I knew they heard me.

And though I hadn't seen Lauren all week, I was certain wherever she was hiding, she'd come running.

Oh yeah. This was happening. But I was beginning to fatigue, and I'd need my power for the next part. I drew in one more breath and completed my instructions.

"Our meeting starts in ten minutes. Attendance is mandatory."

CHAPTER

TWENTY-TWO

A simple text. Ethan had sent one simple text and changed everything. Sort of. He was a Gen X kind of guy, after all. So, he'd sent four texts that could have been one.

> It took all night, but I found the codex in Dad's inventory. It's in the Magnolia.

> Technically.

> Specifically, the inventory reads: the codex resides in a place beyond time and space, where minds meet and ideas thrive.

> No idea what that means. Hoping you do. ;)

I didn't even care about the cute winky non-emoji at the end of the most important sentence ever typed.

Because I did know. As soon as I read it, the answer was obvious. So obvious that I was a little upset with myself that I didn't think of it sooner.

On my first day at the Magnolia, we had a board meeting. As each division head stated their names and positions, the room around me shifted and changed. It was like the world fell away. The next meeting had the same vibes, and though I'd expected them, it still ripped the rug from underneath me. Literally. I'd floated above the conference table, able to see the whole of the universe above and the Magnolia below.

I'd been beyond time and space. In a place where the caretakers of the Magnolia met, to share ideas and make it thrive.

That had to be where the codex was. It was the safest place for it to exist.

I was pretty confident it was there, but I still wasn't sure where. Rather than frantically search behind every nook and cranny before everyone appeared, I took my position at the head of the table.

And waited.

The chair I'd always thought of as Agatha's was back. It had disappeared when I'd taken my rightful position. On instinct, I gestured for Julia to take it when she stepped in. It put her uncomfortably close to Brianne's seat at the opposite end from me, but I had to believe she wouldn't try anything in this room.

Julia was many things. Dumb wasn't one of them.

Gumbo strolled through the door rather than popping into his designated seat. His tail grazed my leg as he strutted past, a gesture I chose to believe was a silent offer of apology. Which reminded me ...

"My arm is fine." The words were harsh against a quiet room. Julia jolted at the sound of them, watching wide-eyed as the scratches along my forearm faded, then disappeared. The angry red skin surrounding them lasted a moment longer. Then it, too, was gone.

I held myself still, trying to pretend it didn't sting during the process. It was good knowledge for me to have, that my power could heal physical harm.

I wouldn't allow it to. But I needed to be more aware of my impact on others.

Gabe was right. Words really do have power.

One by one, the division heads arrived. Lydia and Lyra floated in as one. With a steady grip on Lyra's arm, Lydia led them behind me and to their regular seats, which put them across from Julia.

Up close, Lyra's appearance was even more disturbing. She was uncomfortably thin. Her ribs poked through the slim dress adorning her long frame. Her cheekbones protruded from a face far too gaunt.

The beautiful tone of her skin—usually so milky—was an almost pasty white. Like spoiled milk. As she stepped past me, a sour odor so sharp it tickled my teeth followed her.

"Lyra, are you well?"

She looked as if she might speak to me, but Lydia clamped a hand over her fingers.

"She'll be fine," Lydia said. Her tone was sharp—the sort of no-nonsense, don't-mess-with-me tone I was accustomed to from her.

But her eyes were on Julia. Not me.

I wanted to know what the dynamic was amongst them. Why Lydia hated Julia so much, and why Lyra seemed afraid of her. Whatever the codex said about the challenges, I might need an ally.

Even though they'd made no efforts to befriend me, we were on the same team. I admired the Twins. Maybe I didn't like them, not yet, but I wanted a chance to.

And it pained me to see Lyra's discomfort.

"Lyra." She didn't respond, and though I hated to, I used my magic. "Lyra, look at me."

When she did, I hit back on the gasp that threatened to escape. Her eyes, that lovely shade of orange that reminded me of fresh sherbet on a summer afternoon, no longer had any color at all.

There was a hint of her iris, a pale circle in a white cloud. They looked like the vortex that had swallowed part of the Magnolia.

And I had to wonder if everything was truly okay behind that door.

"Lyra, if there is anything you need, anything at all, I'm here." I held up a hand to Lydia, already jumping in to speak. "You're welcome in my office or in my home. And I promise, I will do everything in my power to make you well again."

"For now." Julia's half-hearted jab had so little heat to it, I didn't bother to look in her direction. I held Lyra's eyes, ignoring Brianne and Lauren, who'd walked in and taken their seats.

Her lip quivered. She squeezed her sister's hand even harder. Then she nodded, and I nodded back.

It was enough for now. It had to be, because everyone was at the table, and the board meeting of my life was about to begin.

"Please state your name and position. Brianne." I tore my gaze away from poor Lyra. "You start. Everyone, ignore Julia for now."

It was petty, but it felt good.

One by one, with no papers in front of us, each of my division heads performed the ritual I now understood held its own kind of power. It was the forming of our coven, the way we opened our doorway to the magic beyond.

And all this time here I thought we could've done it in an email.

When everyone was done, they turned to me and waited.

"Simone Bardot. Division Head for Magnolia Mental Health and Acting Supreme of Magnolia Therapy and Wellness." That extra word—acting—darn near gutted me. I could do all of this and lose.

Gumbo was right, though. Clams were only happy when they were safe. Meanwhile, I'd been something close to safe for twenty years. And I'd been miserable.

It was time to turn my face to the sun.

"Also in attendance is my cousin and bloodline heir to supremacy, Julia Bardot." I was talking from my gut, having no idea what would come next, but trusting House. I could feel it around me, in that *other* way House had of making itself known.

When I finished, the room groaned. The sound of wooden beams bending and stretching, of pipes expanding beyond their means. The walls warped, bending in then outwards, in rapid succession.

I'd grown used to this so quickly. None of us were phased. Except Julia who gripped the table like she'd float into oblivion if she let go.

Bye, Felicia.

When the commotion settled, the room looked normal. But the air was different. Lighter in a way, and cleaner.

They all stared at me, waiting for me to speak. In the past few board meetings, I'd been the last. I guess things were changing.

"As this is an emergency session, we will forgo profit and loss statements or growth discussions." I surveyed the table, waiting as they nodded assent. Brianne looked relieved, the poor thing. She would have hated us discussing unfinished reports.

"As you all know, a claim has been made by my cousin, Julia." I paused to gesture at her, as if everyone didn't already know who she was. "Julia, as an older bloodline heir to our magic, has made a claim that, unfortunately, I cannot dispute."

Brianne and Lauren shifted in their chairs with uncomfortable murmurs. What were they going to do? Jump up and throw them Springer-style across the room? Lydia's scowl was enough to burn the side of my face.

It was funny. Even though both of them had sided with Julia, I still felt like they were with me. They didn't want her to usurp my throne. I didn't particularly believe I'd proven myself an effective Supreme. I didn't even know what a Supreme did, other than call meetings. Still, they were rooting for me.

Julia sat bolt upright, hope alighting her perfect little face for the first time since I'd walked in. She started to speak, and I lifted a finger. I was keeping the chair as long as possible.

And God, I hoped this worked.

"Julia is older than me by a whopping three months. She also comes directly from the bloodline of not one but two persons of power. While my claim is legally binding, I've found nothing to dispute her hereditary claim as Supreme. The wise thing to do, for the sake of our businesses, is for me to cede my position as Supreme to my cousin."

She folded her hands on the table, eyes triumphant.

"However, no one has ever accused me of being wise." The smile she held fell, and it fell fast. A glare I relished replaced it. "Somewhere in this room, in this place beyond time and space where minds meet and ideas thrive, is *The Magnolia Codex*."

Julia guffawed. I'd never actually heard anyone guffaw before.

"That old book has been lost for decades." She did her favorite hair flip. "Really, Simone, this is getting tiresome."

A soft, cool breeze floated across the floor. My magic, somehow more in tune here than anywhere else, sensed it before it even reached me.

That bitch was trying to cast a spell.

"What's tiresome, Julia, is your petty little magic tricks and not-so-subtle put downs." The breeze halted, tickling my toes before it receded. "We are adults, and this is a serious matter. There are ways to solve this sort of conflict. And the Magnolia itself devised an entire book detailing them."

I wasn't so sure about that last part. Not yet fully versed on the Magnolia's history, I was talking out of my rear. One of our ancestors could have made it up, for all I knew.

But hey, no one needed to know that but me.

"House, Julia and I are both eager and willing to challenge one another for the position. Right?" I lifted one eyebrow at Julia. After a moment's hesitation, she nodded. "Would you please bring forth the Codex, which is safe in this room, so that we might learn how to resolve this?"

It was too long before anything happened. Maybe only a few minutes, but it felt like eternity. I held my breath until I couldn't, released it, and held it again. The air was still, and an eerie quiet settled over us. Apparently, I wasn't the only one holding my breath.

Julia's leer returned. Had she known this was a Hail Mary?

I bit my lip and squeezed my eyes closed. If this didn't work, I had no idea what to do next. Crap. Crap crap crap.

"Simone." Brianne's voice broke the silence, jolting my eyes open. She wore the first real smile I'd seen on her in a long time. She almost looked like her old self.

Then I saw why she was smiling.

With absolutely zero fanfare, a book sat on the table. In front of me.

The Magnolia Codex
Volume Two
The Rites of Bloom

Its dark green binding smelled of the softest leathers. A faint whiff of dust surrounded me. And that beautiful, familiar aroma made my heart go pitter patter.

In my mind, I was transported to the middle of the town library on a hot summer afternoon. Surrounded by books, paper, and the inevitable mold that comes with living in the muggy south.

Reading while Momma worked. Alone, but not lonely.

It was a memory full of joy. The kind of happy nostalgia from my childhood I hadn't carried with me in so long because my life had been divided into before and after. Before I caught Jeff cheating. After I hexed myself.

I recognized the cover. The raised lettering embossed in gold. A magnolia in bloom, held in the gentle embrace of a pair of hands. The phases of the moon arching through the flower's pistil. Had I read this before?

Of course I had. Weren't libraries also a place outside of time and space?

I traced the petals with my finger. At my touch, the book rose from the table, twirling in a graceful arc before landing once more—this time opened.

I held it up, turning it so the room could read.

"The Rites of Bloom," I said, making direct eye contact with Julia. "The trials of the true Supreme."

TWENTY-THREE

T he pages were yellow with age, each of them so flimsy I feared turning them. Not that I needed to. They were predominantly blank. As I read, a few more sentences appeared, as if the book would only share what was absolutely necessary and only when we were ready for it.

Julia rounded the table, reading over my shoulder, bracing her hand on me for support. Petty as it was, I shook her off. The ink was faded, written in a script difficult to make out. But I read aloud for the benefit of everyone in the room.

Let it be known to all who dwell beneath the petals of power: the Rites of Bloom is the sacred path by which the Supreme is not claimed by name but proven by soul. Bloodline grants legacy, not authority. Magic grants ability, not wisdom.

Only through trial shall the truth of supremacy be revealed.

My heart thumped even harder. There was a chance for me to claim authority even if I wasn't the bloodline heir. Julia was so close I felt her breath on my ear. It shuddered with each sentence that appeared.

Good. I wanted her confidence shaken.

Each trial is bound to the moon's phase, as the true Supreme must align not only with her power, but with nature's rhythm. The Rite begins under the full moon and ends before the seventh night wanes. Time, like magic, must remain in motion.

"What does that mean?" Julia pointed at the last sentence. "Time must remain in motion."

"It means Gumbo can't interfere." I didn't mention to her that I'd also stopped time before. It's not like I was going to cheat on something this important. I needed to know, too, if I could pass on my own. This was more than a strategy to remove Julia's threat and keep my new home.

This was the opportunity I needed to prove myself. To the division heads. To my friends. Maybe even to the town.

Most importantly, I was being given a chance to prove to myself that I'd earned this position. The idea landed like a terrified lead brick in my stomach, reminding me just how much I wanted this.

"So, how do we start these Rites?" Julia's bravado was gone, erased by the threat of having to prove she was as powerful as she said. That struck me as odd, given the magic I'd seen her perform. Hadn't she removed the vortex from the Magnolia? And crossed realms?

What did someone that powerful have to be afraid of?

"There are words of invocation." I followed my fingers along the sentences as they appeared. "They have to be spoken in this room. There must be ..."

I trailed off. The words were there, but I didn't want to say them out loud. That lead brick grew about ten sizes. This really was an all or nothing situation.

"What?" Brianne asked, her voice shrill. "What does it say?"

I drew in a shaky breath. Beside me, Julia chuckled.

"You're finished," she whispered. A part of me believed her.

"There must be witnesses with the power to judge their actions. After the final trial, those who've heard the recitation shall bear the burden of declaring a rightful Supreme."

Gumbo. Lyra and Lydia. Brianne. Lauren. Of the group, I only had confidence that two of them would take my side. And that certainty was shaky at best. Gumbo had done what he could to help me, but ultimately his devotion was with the Magnolia. Brianne was my friend. She'd been at my side from the first day.

But when I'd needed her the most, she'd been the one to deliver a painful blow. Lydia hated Julia, that was obvious, but her sister didn't. I was positive her loyalty to Lyra trumped everything. And Lauren? A total wild card.

Maybe that was the way it should be, though. I couldn't ask them to declare me Supreme just because they liked me. Or say I wasn't Supreme because they didn't like me. I had to trust that they would declare a winner based on which of us won.

"What are the trials?" Gumbo crossed the table, pushing his furry body against mine as he pretended to read. Surely, he already knew what they were? My sweet little kitty pal. I scratched behind his ear. "Ah. I see."

"I don't." I peered closer. There were a few more paragraphs, both about how to start the trials. But the rest of the chapter was blank.

"It would appear I am the one to initiate each trial, at the times and places where they are performed."

"We can't start them now?" Julia was still way too close.

She stood upright and flung her hands. Drama queen. "Let's get this over with."

Well, on that we agreed.

"It said they begin on a full moon." I scratched my shoulder. "We each have to say these words. It says the language cannot be altered, softened, or abbreviated."

"Indeed," Gumbo said. He pounced over the book, landing softer than a feather. Standing like the most regal king of kittens, he curled his tail around his toe beans. "We'll hear your recitation now, ladies. Simone, as reigning Supreme, I believe you should go first."

I read directly from the book, ignoring the weird twitching spreading between my shoulder blades and down my spine. Great. Now my nerves were manifesting in my body in an unpleasant new way. I'd have to handle that. Later.

When I was finished, Julia came forward. She wouldn't touch the book, instead putting her hands behind her back and leaning over it.

"By root, bloom, and binding light, I stand before you not in anger, but in truth. I name myself challenger to the title Supreme. Let the Rites of Bloom be witnessed by House and coven, by blood and bond. Let magic choose and may we both yield to the final trials."

She'd spoken the words with an authority I hadn't managed. Like she was running for student council, and the recitation was her stump speech.

"What happens now?" I looked at Gumbo.

Gumbo was silent. He tilted his head, angling first his gold then his green eye at me. After a moment of scanning, he did the same to Julia. She patted her clothes as if she'd been caught with a weapon.

"Right. I will make the arrangements for the trials and send each of you the location at the appointed time." He rubbed his chin against the brittle edges of the book, his deep purr rumbling the table. "Until then, Simone, if you'd be so kind as to adjourn the meeting?"

"Sure." There was a lump bigger than twelve stones in my throat. I didn't want it to end. It meant leaving this safe space and actually facing the trials, whatever they were. I was a clam in here. But I couldn't be a clam forever. "The emergency meeting of the Magnolia is adjourned."

The walls rippled and shook. My ears popped. My stomach lifted then fell as the floor jolted, as if sitting on a plane that had just landed. The clean, thin air we'd enjoyed breathing somehow became heavy with the scent of wood and polish.

We were back in the Magnolia. The Codex disappeared, and Gumbo's cute little face smooshed into the table, his page rub interrupted. He recovered by flipping his body, as if he'd meant to expose his fat cat tummy. Which I willingly scritched.

He rolled again, this time away from me, and sat upright.

"Tomorrow is the full moon, kiddos. Get ready." Then he, too, disappeared.

I waited until Julia left, because I wanted to be sure she did. With a nod to the rest of them, I walked out without a word and headed directly to my office. After all, I'd come in on a Sunday to get some work done.

Nothing was going to stop me from completing it.

TWENTY-FOUR

Three solid hours at my desk turned my brain to mush. It was only by some miracle of physiology that my eyes weren't bleeding from staring at the screen too long. My back and shoulders screamed with pain. My skin was hot to the touch. I thought I'd licked this damn rash. Instead, it was spreading at the worst possible time.

But my week was restructured, and I'd sent notices to all my clients about the new schedule. Some of them would balk, I had no doubt. I could practically hear Doug's grumble before he even read my message. Some flexibility would be good for the man. Even if it meant he stopped mowing my lawn.

As a bonus, I'd managed to tire myself out so much that I wouldn't spend the rest of the evening—and probably the entire night—worrying about the first trial.

Or at least, that was what I was telling myself when I headed upstairs.

And it might have worked, except Ray was at my front door.

He had a box of Gino's pizza in one hand and a bag with

who-knows-what in the other. He wore a Lone Wolf polo over loose fitting jeans.

And the guiltiest smile I'd ever seen.

"Peace offering?" He outstretched the box. "I have a salad too. I know how Lauren gets about eating healthy."

Oh, he was a charmer, that one. A wave of emotions travelled through me at the sight of him. Lust so powerful it was a gut punch. Joy that he'd made an effort, even if it was a few days later, to reach out. And given what I'd just gone through with Julia, a really strong sense of betrayal.

We didn't know each other. Not anymore. And I didn't know if I could trust him. I hated that my first thought was she'd sent him to gather information. Or to mess with my state of mind. Not that I needed Ray for that.

Either way, I wasn't going to let him get to me. I was starving, and the man was holding a pizza. There's only so much I can say no to.

"Peace offering for what?" I lifted the lid to peek inside. "Sausage, huh?"

He had the decency to blush, following me through the door and to the dining table. I set down the box, retreating to the kitchen to gather plates, napkins, and utensils. When I returned, he'd opened the salad and the pizza. He took the plates from me, distributing food onto each and placing them at opposite ends of the table.

He waited to sit until I did. Damn, he was good. We ate in relative silence. Halfway through the meal, an opened bottle of red wine and two glasses appeared. He poured it without speaking.

"House, that is one damn fine wine." I lifted it to cheers the ceiling. "Thank you." Ray propped his elbow on the table and watched me. "What?"

"I've never seen anyone talk to the house like that." He grabbed another slice of pizza. "It's interesting."

"Why's that?" I took another sip. Well, a large gulp. It really was a great wine.

"You treat it like it has feelings." He filled his mouth with pizza, washing it down with wine. "Agatha never did that."

"Really?" That was a surprise. Had Agatha and the house not shared a connection? "It does have emotions, though. I don't know how advanced they are, but I know it feels. When the explosion happened—" I stopped myself. Ray was watching me, eyes intense. "Never mind."

"No, tell me." He stacked our plates. "I'm interested."

"Are you?" I watched the wine swirl in the glass. "Or is Julia?"

He was quiet, and I didn't dare look up. Was he angry? Guilty he'd been found out? I would know if I only looked at him and asked. But I couldn't.

"Simone, will you please look at me?" His voice was quiet. Soft. There was no accusation or anger in his tone. I looked up, shocked to find tears in his eyes.

Wait. Those were my tears. I was the one on the verge of crying. I'd thought my disappointment in him was only surface deep. But here he was in my space, waking up all those dormant parts of me that hoped for him.

No. It wasn't him I wanted. It was the version of him I remembered from thirty years ago. I didn't know this man. And, I had a worse problem.

"I don't trust you, Ray." There. It was out in the open. "You show up on my door and act like you care, but I saw you. I saw the way you looked at her."

With a soft plunk, a box of tissues appeared on the table. I took one and crushed it to my eyes. In the short time we'd spent together, I couldn't recall a time when Ray looked at me the way he had Julia.

"She doesn't know I'm here, Simone." Ray's hand was on my knee. I hadn't seen or felt him move closer. One thumb stroked, softer than cotton. "I'm sorry you saw us together, and I'm sorry I was with her, but I promise you she and I aren't rekindling anything."

"Yet," I mumbled. With a sigh, I gathered myself. "And you can do what you want. We aren't together. We haven't been for a long time."

"That was your choice, not mine." There was an edge to Ray's voice. His thumb stilled. "You left me, Simone."

"No. You crossed the bridge." I needed space. I needed his hand off me. I rose, taking the plates to the kitchen. Washing them, even though House would have done it for me.

He came in, depositing the remaining pizza and salad in the fridge. Helping me clean up like we were a normal couple having a normal conversation.

"You didn't give me a chance to explain that Ethan and I were only friends." I turned to face him, leaning against the counter. He kept his back to me. "And we were. Then."

The muscles of his back pulled taut. His arm moved in slow motion, closing the refrigerator so softly I knew he wanted to slam it. The Ray I remembered never had that self-control. He turned to me and crossed his arms.

"And now?"

"I don't know. I can't tell what's history and what's present. With either of you." I rubbed at the back of my neck. The heat was flaring again, an itch so intense it felt like my bones needed a good scratching. I dug my nails into my skin. "That's not a priority for me right now."

"What are you doing?" He crossed the kitchen and stilled

my hand. Turning me, he yanked the neck of my shirt down with a hiss. "That's one hell of a rash."

"It's the same damn one you saw on my hand two weeks ago." Had it really only been a few weeks and not years? A cool, wet cloth draped itself over the kitchen sink. I handed it to him, breathing a sigh of relief as he pressed it on my back.

"That's not normal, Simone." All the accusations from a few moments ago, all the veiled anger, seemed to disappear in an instant. He was soft again, running fingers along the raised bumps on my skin. "Rashes don't disappear from one part of your body and reappear in another one."

His breath was on my neck. His scent, the lone wolf running through a forest of oaks, was all around me. I took the cloth from him, stepping away. On the opposite counter, a bottle of cooling gel appeared. I picked it up to read the label.

Beware of old flames and fresh regrets.

House back at its jokes.

"How do you know?" I dipped the gel onto the cloth and brought it to my shoulder. At Ray's querying look, I continued. "How do you know what rashes do?"

"Oh, I was an EMT for a while." Ray left the kitchen, and I followed. He topped the wine glasses, handing me one before travelling with the other to the living room. I followed again, sitting on the far end of the couch.

"Tell me more." I curled my feet under me, angling myself into a comfortable staring-at-a-hot-guy position. "What else did you do?"

"Well." Ray paused to take a sip. "I went to an out-of-state college. Colorado."

"College, huh?" I tried to smile. "That wasn't your plan."

"My plans changed." The look he gave me drew fire from

my core. "And I had a … family obligation to attend to. Things to process. So, I went to stay with my grandfather."

I nodded but didn't speak. I knew some of this from Ethan. I knew the family obligation was for Ray to take over as alpha of his pack. If Ray wasn't ready to tell me that, I had to be patient. Maybe this was as close as we would ever get. Casual friends who supported one another but didn't have a true, deeper connection.

I couldn't decide how I felt about that.

"After college I tried medical school," Ray continued. "It was too much pressure for me, so I became an EMT. It was rewarding. For a while."

"What changed that?" I switched the gel cloth to my opposite shoulder. It was working already.

"Embracing my wolf." He stretched his long legs, moving his feet from side to side as if to prove to himself he was a human. "Once the wolf and I learned to live together, it took a lot of my anger away."

I swallowed more wine and waited. A pleasant buzz was making my head heavy. I should have slowed down— tomorrow was a big day. I couldn't seem to stop drinking it.

This was the first time Ray had acknowledged to me that he was a wolf shifter. Even though we both knew I'd seen him in wolf form, and just the thought of it made my fingers want to stroke that fur, we hadn't said it aloud. Until now.

"Accepting all the conflicting parts of yourself helped you to see yourself more clearly," I said mid-sip.

"Spoken like a true therapist." Ray chuckled. "But it's true. I realized I wanted to protect people. Not heal them. So I came home and started Lone Wolf."

"How much security does this town need?" I put the empty glass on the table and wiggled down, resting my head on the couch.

"You'd be surprised." His voice sounded far away. There was a rustle, and something warm and soft landed over me.

"Cozy," I murmured, my voice little more than a slur. "Comfy."

"I don't want Julia, Simone." Had he sounded far away a second ago? He was near my ear again. He took the wet cloth dangling from my fingers. "One minute I was agreeing to dinner, the next we were snuggling in the corner. I don't even know how it happened."

"I do." I pulled the blanket around my neck. My eyes were heavy. "She enthralls people. Especially my people."

There was a sharp intake of breath. I think it was his. I wasn't sure what I'd said, but it didn't matter. The world was falling away.

"Stay away from her, Ray." I let my eyes close. "She's a magical parasite in heels."

If he responded, I didn't hear it.

TWENTY-FIVE

"Hi!" A very different version of the Sarah I'd met a week earlier all but skipped into my office. Water sloshed through the area rug with each step. "Oops. Sorry about that."

When she apologized, her light dimmed. Just a bit.

"You don't have to apologize for a single thing in this space, Sarah." I accepted her warm hug, even though it left damp handprints on my back. "I'm happy to see you looking so vibrant."

And I was happy for the distraction. Tonight was the first of the three trials. I still didn't know what that meant, or what they would look like. And with my week restructured, I didn't have a non-stop barrage of patients to distract me. Darn my decision to give myself breathing room! Couldn't I have done that after the trials?

"I need another one." She tossed the notebook I'd given her a week earlier on my desk. "Please."

"That's a lot of work for one week. May I?" At her enthusiastic nod, I opened the book—its pages warped, the ink smeared. I couldn't have read a single word. Not that the content itself mattered.

The reward was in the doing.

"Here you go." I reached into my drawer and pulled out a stack. "Take your pick, or take them all. I have plenty of them."

"Really?" Her eyes watered, and I had to wonder when someone had given her a gift. She seemed like the kind who always did for others and never asked for herself. I added that note to her file.

"Of course. I see you." I tapped into my magic, adding a touch of oomph to my words. Sarah was a prime candidate for this practice of mixing power with mundane methods.

But it didn't have the effect I wanted. Instead of brightening her mood, she dimmed. Her dress had been a lovely sky blue when she entered the room. Now, it was fading and turning gray. A puddle formed around her chair.

"You're so nice." She yanked a tissue from the box and sobbed into it. "I'm a selfish hag."

I waited a beat, giving her time to gather herself.

"I'm noticing that you're having erratic mood swings, Sarah. Is that accurate?"

She nodded her head. Well, that I could relate to.

"I get them, too." She yanked her head up. "It's true. Lately, I've been feeling like a teenager. That's not an age I wanted to go back to."

A small chuckle escaped her.

"What makes you think you're selfish?"

"I ruined this notebook, and I don't even care. I just want more of them." A sob escaped. "I'll probably ruin those, too"

Ah. Sweet Sarah, who'd always been a mom, wanted something for herself. And that was creating a sense of guilt.

"Sarah, what if I told you I'm glad you ruined the notebook?" She shook her head. "You ruined it by using it, and that's exactly what I wanted. Did it occur to you that you gave me a gift, too?"

"How?" She'd buried herself in a tissue again. Not for the first time, I hoped it was a never-ending box. I had no idea where we stored office supplies.

"Sometimes, a patient and I will do a lot of work in this room. But then they leave, and they forget to do their home-work." I tapped the desk to get her attention. "You did the work, and this ruined notebook—which by the way is not ruined at all, just used—is the result of you actually using the tools we discussed last week."

"So, I made you happy?"

I paused, trying to find a way to word my thoughts carefully.

"I am happy that you are doing the work. But it would have been okay if you hadn't written in the notebook all week, too. We would have explored why. Together. Your job isn't to please me. That's a side benefit. Your job is to tap into the inner Sarah. Get it?"

"I guess so." She didn't, not fully. Doubt etched itself into her eyebrows, creating worrying lines on her forehead.

That was okay. I knew we'd come back to this a thousand more times in our future sessions. As someone who put others ahead of herself, I understood why Sarah wanted to get an A+ in therapy.

"Why don't you tell me more about your week?"

"Sure." After a few more sniffles and a dozen more tissues, Sarah sat upright and folded her hands in her lap. "Well, I started wearing lipstick again."

"I noticed." I had, though I wouldn't have mentioned it. It was wicked dark. "What is that shade?"

"Midnight Allure." She ran her tongue over her lips. "My husband says I look like a vixen."

"How do you feel about that?"

"Naughty." She shifted in her seat, wiggling her hips. "And a little powerful."

"Feeling powerful is a good thing." I tilted my head and closed one eye. She definitely looked different, but it was more than a solid form or a different hue. "Can I ask what you are?"

"What do you mean?"

"What sort of magic do you hold?" Crap. She was looking at me like I'd contracted rabies. "Sorry, I don't mean to be insensitive. I'm fairly new to the magical realm."

Another moment passed, during which I was certain she was contemplating calling the police and having me carted away. The therapist becomes the patient. It was all padded walls for me from here on out.

Then she giggled. A girlish, youthful giggle.

"My mother's mother was a naiad." I blew out a sigh of relief. "Both my parents are human."

I didn't know a lot about naiads. I knew they had something to do with water. I added it to her file. This was definitely going to be on the intake form. I just had to find a less awkward way of wording it.

"I'm a word witch," I told her. "My words can wield power and alter emotions. I've even accidentally hexed a few people." I didn't mention I was one of them.

"Wow. That's kind of cool." I appreciated the awe in her tone, even if I hadn't earned it.

This was what I needed to do. To remain connected to my patients and be open about my abilities. And my flaws. It wasn't a conventional practice for therapists, but I wasn't a conventional therapist. Never had been. Even before I knew about magic.

"I asked about your magical origins because I wanted to

share mine," I said. "But also because that is another piece of your identity. Sometimes I forget that."

"There's a rumor that my great-grandmother was a sea hag." Sarah rubbed a finger along her lip and held it up to inspect the color. "Apparently she was quite the seductress."

At that moment, I envied Sarah. Like me, she was evolving into a different, more powerful version of herself. But she had the benefit of an ancestral line she could tap into. Like Julia knowing she was a full blood heir, Sarah carried the confidence of someone with family.

"What I'm hearing from you, Sarah, is that over the past week you remembered you were more than a mother. That you were also a desirable being." One corner of her mouth lifted. "And you like that realization?"

"Oh yes." She dropped the arm of her dress to expose her shoulder. With an awkward laugh, she lifted it back up. "I don't know what I'm doing."

"You're being curious. That's exactly what we want to do." I needed to be curious, too. "Did you make any other discoveries this week?"

She had, and it was glorious to hear them. She'd learned that baking made her feel solid. The scent of fresh bread in the kitchen. The delighted yums from her children when they tried it.

"And I took some to Illusion Square to share with Ruth. Do you know Ruth?"

I did, and I told her as much. Sweet Ruth Donergan was the elderly woman who sat next to the Mighty Oak every day, carrying on a one-sided conversation with the tree. At least I'd always thought it was one-sided. Who knew in this wacky town?

"What did you and Ruth talk about?"

"Nothing special." But her smile indicated otherwise. "The

weather. Town happenings. I've always wanted a craft fair, and there's a new craft store opening above the art shop."

"You made a friend," I said. "Outside of the home. And you're exploring hobbies that don't revolve around your children."

"Yeah." Her voice faded, like muffled sounds through rippling waves. This was going to be a process. It was going to take work, both on her part and mine. But I could see an end for Sarah, and that was delightful.

She was willing to make an effort. To explore and try new things. I had the feeling that would pay off for her. I wasn't as sure it would pay off for me.

I couldn't lose this. The therapy division. If I lost the trials and Julia became Supreme, I had to find a way to keep this without it breaking my heart. Being a therapist was a part of my identity. An important one.

Maybe I didn't know the witch part of me yet. But I could. With work.

"Sarah, can I send you off with another gift? Besides the notebooks?" I paused and drew in a breath. "A magical one?"

"Like a spell?"

"Yes? I think maybe?" I stopped and tried again, angling for more confidence. "This is something new I'm exploring, weaving magic into my sessions. I won't manipulate you or do anything against your will. Would that be okay?"

"I guess so." She didn't sound any more confident than I did. Oh well, I was diving in.

She'd chosen four notepads but eyed a fifth. I placed it on the stack and hovered my palm over them. I didn't need to use my hands, but I remembered the sensation when Julia had conducted a magical orchestra. It was a cool effect.

"These are waterproof." Her eyes lifted in pure delight.

"They are unbreakable, unbendable, and cannot be ruined. No matter how much you use them."

Sarah squealed. Literally squealed like a little girl.

Her joy stayed with me throughout the day. I latched onto it instead of my nerves.

As soon as Gumbo materialized on my desk, though, the latch broke.

"Simone," the Mystical Protector spoke with reverence.

"Gumbo."

"The first Rite will begin at midnight. Meet me at Nymph Lake."

He was gone before I had a chance to reply.

"Here we go," I said to the space he'd left behind.

TWENTY-SIX

Nymph Lake stood on the outskirts of Treater's Way, enveloped in forestry so tall it shut out the night sky save one small circle. In that circle, the full moon shone overhead, casting a magical glow across the water and the muddy banks that gradually rose to a grassy knoll.

It was a relatively small lake, only the fact that no one knew just how deep the center was kept it from being a pond. According to the founders of Treater's Way, a river nymph created it. She'd staggered here, her heart broken by the notorious pirate Jean Laffitte, and cried tears that filled the land. Tears so heavy with pain the earth refused to absorb them. The rumor continued that, once she'd sobbed herself dry, she used the last of her power to curse a mermaid. Then she'd found her way to town center and let herself die.

In history class, my favorite teacher Mrs. Gregory had sworn the nymph's body gave root to the Mighty Oak. And since people talked to it all the time, and it had the same presence I felt at the Magnolia, I was willing to believe her. They didn't teach history like that back in New Orleans.

The lake was no longer public property, but the children of Treater's Way still played there in the heat of summer. Rumors claimed it was quite the make-out spot. This was the first time I'd seen it.

The owners stood by a nearby tree, waiting to greet us as we arrived.

Amelie Rapport, her blond hair in a thick, messy bun, leaned against her husband Rav. She owned Explore Art, one of the shops at Illusion Square. But to my eye, she didn't look like the talented and mystical artist I knew her to be. With her pregnant stomach protruding over a simple white gown, she looked more like a goddess.

Of course, I was in a fanciful kind of mood. After all, I was about to face my first trial. And the magic of Nymph Lake practically hung in the air. Either that, or my nerves were playing tricks with me.

"Simone." Amelie extended her arms, and I took her hands, offering a kiss to her cheek. I didn't know her well, but she was kind. "We're on your side."

She pulled away, revealing a painting propped against the trunk. I stooped down to have a look, digging my fingers into the wet dirt. It was me. At least I think it was. The 'me' on that painting didn't look the anything like the way I saw myself.

I was standing tall, and there was this vivid glow around me, like a magical silhouette. I peered closer because, like it or not, my eyes were fifty years old, and it was dark out. The glow swirled with colors, mostly shades of greens and blues. My hair swayed from an invisible breeze. I had power in my eyes and determination on my face.

"That's how we see you," Amelie said, helping me up as if I were the pregnant one. "Trust your heart and your voice."

I managed to squeak out a thank you, accepting another hug from Rav. To say I was nervous would be like saying the river bent. It was obvious. But, like the Mississippi didn't bend just once, I wasn't just a little nervous.

The painting helped. Almost as much as seeing Brianne and her husband Nate emerge from the clearing to stand with the small crowd. I risked looking at her, and she gave me a hopeful thumbs up. I missed my friend so much. When the trials ended, whether I won or not, I was going to repair what was cracked between us.

I just had to hope it wasn't broken.

The Twins were there. I hadn't seen them walk to the lake, but Julia followed close behind, her hand low on Lyra's back, as if she were helping her walk. Under the moonlight, Lyra's skin was near translucent. Her minty green hair hung in oily strands. She kept her eyes on the ground, nodding when Lydia whispered in her ear.

Lydia passed Lyra to Brianne as if she were a child. She scanned the lake, finding me on the opposite side and stomping over to me. Lydia and I had stood face-to-face before, and it never failed to intimidate me. Despite our confrontations, part of me had been sure she'd be on my side. Her open distaste for Julia, for one, gave me hope.

But her loyalty to Lyra was stronger than anything we were starting to build. As it should be. And Lyra, for whatever reason, was attached to Julia in a way I still didn't understand.

So I couldn't even feign nonchalance when Lydia leaned in and whispered in my ear.

"Get rid of her for good."

She returned to Lyra as if she hadn't spoken to me at all. I would have stared at her open-mouthed all night, even if she ignored me. But Lauren arrived.

Gumbo emerged from the water. With a single shake, he was bone dry. His nails were not painted, and there was no bow around his neck.

That scared me the most.

"Julia." Gumbo dipped his head towards her. She gripped Lyra's hand in hers, then released it and strode confidently to the lake's edge.

"Simone." I was already walking toward him when he said my name. Such a rule follower.

Gumbo walked a tight figure eight around us, creating a trail of adorably terrifying kitty paws in the mud. His tail brushed my legs, then Julia's. He scanned us with mismatched eyes. He never said what he was searching for, but he gave an approving nod.

"It is time for the first Rite of Bloom." Zero *I Can Haz* in his voice. I'd known it wouldn't be his kitten voice even if I wanted it. "Per *The Magnolia Codex*, the challengers will face The Stillwater Truth Test surrounded by both witnesses and allies."

I breathed a slight sigh of relief. A truth test. All I had to do was tell the truth. I could do that. I'd even been practicing.

"Held under the full moon, when the sky shows its whole face and demands we do the same. The challengers must drown themselves in the sea of forever tears, shining beneath the moon's unwavering gaze. In its light, all illusions dissolve. Only she who faces every hidden scar and sacred truth within may emerge. To be full, one must first be empty."

There was a roaring in my ears, and the ground beneath my feet trembled. Staying within the circle of paws, I turned in awe as the waters of Nymph Lake began to shift. The water rippled, creating massive waves that somehow crashed without a drop of water hitting us. It swirled and swirled, creating a tornado of water in the center.

A face formed in the lake. A beautiful young girl, eyes turned down from sadness, shook her head. Water flicked around her like hair. She turned her hollow expression to me, then to Julia, and finally to Gumbo. He stretched out his front paws, lifting his hind quarters and dipping his head in a regal bow.

The shape of her head dipped in kind. She opened her mouth and wailed. It was a sound beyond description, the wail of a banshee or the cry of the earth taking its last breath. It filled me, as if I were hearing it not with my ears but with my soul. A terrible sadness brought tears to my eyes. They fell to the ground. The lake lapped at them, bringing them into its waters.

With a deafening crash, the water grew still—except for two long paths: one in front of me, the other in front of Julia. They led down, below the surface of the water, far deeper than the lake appeared. The surface, still at eye level, was glassy and smooth. Following that trail meant going far below the bottom of the lake, with the water high on either side, shadows swarming as fish darted about.

"Ladies." Gumbo shook his body from head to tail and sat upright. "Your trial awaits."

My heart thundered like a drum. My throat and mouth were completely drained of saliva. If large drops of sweat weren't rolling down my low back, I would believe the lake had absorbed all the liquid from my body.

Drown herself.

That was the term Gumbo used. If I walked down that path, there was a good chance the water would collapse around me. I had to have faith it wasn't a literal drowning. *Only she who faces every hidden scar and sacred truth within may emerge.*

Whatever was in there, it was dark and ugly. Even the air reeked of it, like fish rotting beside me.

The path extended to a dark place. I couldn't see the end— it might have been miles away despite the lake's small size. The water on either side was easily going to be over my head. I turned nervous eyes to Julia, slightly relieved to see her weaving her fingers together and gnawing on her lip.

At least we were both terrified.

"You've got this," I whispered to myself. "You've faced darkness before."

The words were tight in my throat. I only half-believed them. Not a good sign considering I had to face truths in there. I looked down at my feet, willing them to move forward. My body rooted itself to the mud.

Nope. No way. Nuh-uh. It was dark. And scary.

From the corner of my eyes, I sensed movement. Brianne was walking closer to the water, waving at me. She smiled, her lips trembling, and nodded her head. It didn't alleviate my fear, not one bit. But damn it felt good to know she was still finding a way to be here for me.

"Good luck, Simone." Julia extended her hand to me. Damn my Southern manners. I had to shake it. "And no hard feelings."

With her fakest smile plastered on her face, Julia walked into her path.

Welp. That was that.

To be full, one must first be empty.

Whatever that meant, I had to keep walking. I'd come this far.

Scratching at my palm and the cursed rash I couldn't seem to get rid of, I took my first step forward.

With a shaky breath, I took my second step. My third. My fourth. I was walking. Go me.

I made my way down the path, the water closing in behind me and arching over me. The sky disappeared, the world hid behind the lake, and I was alone inside it.

TWENTY-SEVEN

Whispering voices lived in the water. I couldn't make out their words, but I heard and felt the sounds they made. Urgent whispers. Mischievous whispers. Curious whispers. A voice would say something. Another would giggle.

They were talking about me, that much I knew. Laughing at me. I didn't dare turn my body when the waters closed behind me. I didn't want to see what was whispering. I didn't want to face what I was leaving behind.

My feet squished in the mud. With each step, my toes grew colder as decades old sediment seeped into my tennis shoes. I'd known we would be at the lake. I hadn't expected to go in. Next time the waters parted for me, I was wearing rain boots.

The path was narrow. An occasional splash of water dampened my sleeves. The ground was cold, but the water was warm, most likely heated under the summer sun. Despite water on all sides and overhead, I could see, though not far.

It was strangely serene. Like a wet, smelly cocoon shielding me from the outside stimulants that tended to blur into the background. There was no hum of a power line. No doors opening and closing or heavy footsteps. No harsh lighting.

It was just me in here. Well, me and Julia, wherever she was. Would I face her at the end of this path? Gumbo said we were going to face hidden scars and sacred truths. It didn't sound like we'd be facing each other.

My heart thumped even harder. Most likely, I'd be facing my own hidden scars. My own sacred truths. What if they looked different from what I expected? What scars were waiting for me at the end of this path?

My steps slowed. The water led me around a bend. I curved when the water curved, edging forward as the ground became uneven. It was littered with relics long discarded in Nymph Lake. An old Mardi Gras doubloon. A penny that had lost its shine.

Someone had either lost or thrown a simple diamond ring into the lake. I stepped past it, the jewel still shiny but faded. The simple band was tarnished green and rusted. As I scratched at my hand, I moved to my left finger. Where had my wedding ring gone? I didn't have a memory of taking it off, nor of storing it somewhere safe.

That wasn't my ring. Was it? How long had I followed this path?

The lake and I turned another bend. I paused at the sight of a female silhouette about thirty feet in front of me. She was not tall enough to be Julia, yet there was something familiar about the shape.

"Hello?" My voice was muffled, barely travelling around me.

Then the whispers stopped. The only sounds were my steps as I trudged closer. *Squick squick squick.*

She was no longer a silhouette. There was a woman waiting for me.

"I swear, if that woman is reading a book about me, I'm turning right back around." The childhood trauma that was watching *The Neverending Story* suddenly loomed fresh in my memory. "I'll drain this whole damn lake if I find out there's a dead horse in it."

The woman plastered on a polite smile, as if she'd been expecting me but did not wish to see me. She was my height. She wore my clothes.

She had my face.

I reached out, unable to resist dragging my finger through the water in front of me. It rippled outward from the point I'd touched, temporarily warping the woman's reflection before fading into the edges.

The water no longer swirled. Shadows no longer moved just underneath the surface. It was perfectly still—a mirror in which I could see myself.

I was staring at my reflection. And yet, I didn't recognize the woman in front of me. This woman's shoulders hunched forward. Her arms had no muscle tone. Wrinkles teased the edges of her downturned eyes.

That wasn't what I looked like. Was it?

As a test, I patted the top of my head. She did the same. I rubbed my tummy. She rubbed hers. I stuck out my tongue and wrinkled my nose.

My reflection sighed and shook her head, rolling her eyes like a petulant teen.

Okay, so it was me.

I stared at her. She stared right back—eyebrows raised in expectation. The silence was deafening.

"I don't know what to do," I told her.

"Of course you don't," she said. Her voice gurgled as she spoke. "You never do. You wing it and hope for the best."

The whispers resumed, this time louder and more clear.

Not enough. And also too much. Too short. And yet too big.

I planted my hands over my ears, hoping to drown them out.

"That's not what I do," I said. "You're not what I look like." But I held no certainty in my tone. And the me that was a mirror knew it.

"You're not ready for this." She crossed her arms and glared at me. "I should have known."

The whispers were all around. Behind me, the water crept closer. Chills ran the length of my neck and spine. The air was damp.

"You're going to lose." The reflection waved goodbye, turning to leave.

"Wait," I called out to her retreating back. My body had never felt so uncomfortable. The rash, irritated by dirty water, flamed up my arm. The cold was seeping into my bones. My joints ached.

I felt old.

""I don't want to lose," I said. "I love the Magnolia. Please help me."

She stopped, but the whispering did not. She was talking to them. Arguing. With a sigh, she flung her hands out.

"You want another chance? Fine then."

The woman who turned to me was a younger version of myself. She was heavily pregnant and wearing a shapeless gray dress. Swelling made her cheeks puffy and gave new meaning to the word cankles. Her eyes were sallow and lifeless. Strands of her unwashed hair escaped the loose ponytail held with an ugly yellow scrunchy.

"Why didn't you go home?" There was no accusation in her

words, they were laced with sadness. She ran a hand along her stomach. The baby kicked, lifting the dress. "He could have been raised with magic and love and joy."

"I was hexed," I replied. "I hexed myself." He had grown up with joy, and a small flare of anger temporarily warmed my chest. Even if I hadn't been happy, I'd made sure he was.

But I couldn't say any of that out loud. Was that because I didn't believe it? Or was it because it wasn't true?

"You were powerful enough, even then, to know better." Tears flowed freely down the woman's cheeks. She shook her head. "You'd already given up."

I opened my mouth to defend myself and tasted salt. My hand came away from my cheeks damp—I was crying, too. She was right. I couldn't argue. I'd given up so long ago.

"But that doesn't mean I will give up now." Was that my voice? Was that despair my own? "I'm here and fighting, aren't I?"

Behind me, the water edged closer. Shadows reached out with hands like demons and swiped at me. It was getting harder to breathe. Mildew clung to the mirrored water.

"Are you?" The reflection changed again. Me at eighteen. "Did you fight for your future then? Or did you run away?"

I remembered that girl. Body strong but heart fragile. Her chin lifted in defiance. She stood tall.

"Did you even mourn her?" She jabbed her finger at me, planting the opposite hand on her hip. "I'll answer for you. You didn't. You pushed it aside."

"No." My hands were on my ears again. The water slapped my back. "No, I missed Momma terribly. I ached to see her. I still do."

"Liar." Teenage me sneered. I didn't remember until I saw her. That anger. That rage at the world for taking my mother away. "You hid from your pain. In his bed."

I'd taken solace in Ray, that much was true. But could I say to myself I was just hiding? I didn't know. The voices were everywhere, blocking any clear thought.

"You made yourself forget." College Simone, in Ray's ratty shirt and fuzzy socks, clucked her tongue at me.

"You made selfish choices." Simone, in a forest green graduation cap and gown, shook a job offer letter.

Yes, I'd accepted a big, corporate job after college. An internship while I completed the rest of my training. Had I considered returning to Treater's Way? To train under Agatha?

No. Not even for a moment. Because I knew returning to the past would hurt. I told myself I wanted more than a small town. I wanted prestige and reputation.

"You gave until you had nothing left to give." Briefly, my reflection wore sweats and stood beside a hospital bed. "To a man who never truly loved you."

My reflection changed again. Me, on my first day at the Magnolia, in clothes I'd worn for a week straight.

"You hurt your own son."

She turned to face me. She was wearing my clothes again. The shoulders dropped again.

"You've run and avoided your entire life." Her voice was so soft I strained to hear. Water swirled around us, lifting higher and higher.

They were right. I'd made a lifetime of mistakes. Did that mean I would spend the second half of my life questioning my choices? Was there no path forward that didn't involve constantly berating myself for the past?

I dropped to my knees. The woman in the mirror dropped to her knees. We sobbed together. My body shuddered under the grief I'd carried for thirty years.

This was not what I wanted.

To be defined by my mistakes.

To be the voice that told myself everything I'd done wrong.

To withhold the very grace I extended to others. To deny myself the compassion I gave to my patients.

That was not who I wanted to be.

My tears fell into the mud, but they didn't sink in. They formed a puddle. The puddle became a pond.

The mirror warped. My reflection trembled.

"Do you really think you have what it takes to be the Supreme? You don't even like yourself."

I never got a chance to answer. The pond of my pain lifted to reach the lake surrounding me. With hurricane-like force, the water whipped me side-to-side, dragging me down to depths I didn't think possible only to fling me towards the surface.

Up and down. Side to side. I fought to move my arms, to swim towards a shore I would never be able to find. I opened my mouth to scream. Rancid water filled my lungs until my chest begged to explode.

I landed with a thud at the edge of the lake, soaking wet and chilled to my bones, I retched until my stomach was aching and empty.

Around me, crickets sang a soft night song. Someone extended a hand. I accepted it, hauling myself to my feet. I'd lost my shoes. Left them somewhere in the lake.

"Thanks," I said to the person who helped me stand.

It was Julia. Her hair was perfect. A sleek white dress hugged the curves of her very dry body.

"Wasn't that something?" She flicked her hand to the side, as if touching me was distasteful.

Her smile beamed under the moonlight, triumphant and strong.

A sea of pitying faces was upon me.

Our witnesses.

Deep down in my heart, I knew.

I knew before Gumbo shook his tiny head. I knew before Brianne hid her sobs in her husband's chest. I knew before Lydia's accusatory glare cut through me.

I'd let my past overwhelm me.

I'd failed the first trial.

TWENTY-EIGHT

F ailure is a funny thing. It creates a stain on your soul, forever etching itself into your memories. It forms a haze through which you view every future choice, making even the happiest moments a slightly different color. A darker hue. It was no wonder people avoided it.

I'd always been more afraid of success. Failure, I understood. It was uncomfortable, but at least it was familiar.

So when I awoke the next morning just after dawn, I expected the bitter taste of failure on my tongue. I expected the weight of feeling less than on my shoulders. I expected the nausea of *what if*.

But that's not how I felt. I stretched my arms overhead and opened my chest. I couldn't nail what it was. I was different.

A new pair of sneakers sat on the carpet at the foot of my bed. I laced them up and found workout clothes in one of the dresser drawers. Apparently, I was going to work out.

"Good morning, House." I thought about Ray's comment while I filled a water bottle. I wondered who lived here before Agatha, and whether they'd talked to House like it had feelings. "I'm going for a short run. Can you kindly adjust my office while I'm gone? I'd like to put some free weights and a yoga space up here."

I didn't wait for an answer. I didn't expect House to talk. I just knew it would be there when I returned. In the past few weeks, I'd promised myself I would make use of the top-of-the-line equipment in the physical therapy department. Each time I considered it, I managed to talk myself out of it.

This would be more comfortable. Even though I'd seen first-hand how amazing Lauren's division was, it didn't feel like I belonged there. Maybe that was part of what made us work, though. Each of the divisions had their own look and feel. Each was run autonomously. And yet, they managed to form a cohesive space.

Or maybe I felt that way because I hadn't fully embraced my role as Supreme.

There were two Rites left. I didn't know when the next one would happen. If I failed, mathematically I figured there was no way I could recover. Two out of three would be bad, despite Meat Loaf's claim to the contrary. But if I passed …

If I passed, I was going to understand what being Supreme meant. Not just that *I really should do this* guilt I'd felt a few weeks ago, when Brianne was carrying me and I only had a title.

It was a different sensation, one that made me pause mid-run and rub my chest. I'd changed overnight. During the first Rite, something fundamental inside me had been altered. I felt lighter, my chest less tight.

Unburdened—as if I'd set something very heavy aside. And if I felt this good, Julia must be walking on clouds. Unless that's why I lost. What could she possibly be carrying?

It wasn't a fair assessment. I had no idea where she'd been or what she'd gone through. Just because the Julia facing off against me seemed like the exact same girl from high school didn't make it true. It wasn't fair for me to pass judgment.

Rather than pushing myself until my body was wrung out, I tried a moderate run. When I got home, I headed straight to my office. Sure enough, House had done a phenomenal job. A portion of the floor was now covered in a comfy rubber-looking material. A pair of adjustable weight dumbbells, some kettlebells, and a TV stand lined the wall. Below the television was a stack of workout DVDs.

I chose a short one and hoped I wouldn't be punished too hard.

I carried this newfound sense of freedom into each of my client sessions. It was another area I planned to improve as I got a firmer hold on my magic. But I spoke with each patient about it, gauging their levels of comfort with the supernatural, and talking through some techniques I'd kept in the back of my old noodle brain.

At the end of the day, as I opened the door to House, a wave of sadness hit me. This would be what I missed the most. This space, which I had to assume would become Julia's if she defeated me in the trials.

Walking around, I wondered how she would change it. Did she prefer softer colors and more modern furniture? Probably. It's how I remembered her dressing in high school. Always stylish. Not a hair out of place.

I'd been an unkempt mess half the time. I still was. Fashionable clothes looked great on other people. My torso was too short for most of the cool clothes. Crop tops sat on my hips. Low-cut jeans had no place on my nonexistent waist. The clothes House chose for me were always perfect. Yay magic.

So much of my style was established in high school. That period of awkward hormonal surges and self-discovery really did mold us into the types of adults we'd become. Sure, we were capable of change. If we put in the work. But how many of us put in the work?

My stomach growled and I went to the kitchen. There was still some leftover cake Gabe must have forgotten about. The boy was a human vacuum.

Not a boy. Gabe was an adult now. He'd gone through his own awkward stages and figured out who he was. I took a bite of the cake, already dry, then threw it in the trash.

Being middle-aged wasn't that different from high school, though. Sure, there'd been consistencies in the women I'd faced during the trials. Those versions of me looked like I did and sounded like I had.

But they were points of time. Reflections of different phases of my life.

Not where I was currently. At forty-eight, I was just beginning to discover my powers, literally and figuratively. Maybe it was time to start shedding those old stories I'd told myself, the stories those women had hurled my way, about who I was and what I was capable of.

I still wanted to eat cake.

"House, you want to help me bake another cake?" The thrill ran through me, excited as a puppy. "Why don't we make it together this time?"

I flipped through my phone and found the perfect one. Lemon flavored, with a cream cheese frosting and cute little sugar daisies adorning the top. It was fresh and fun and just a little zesty.

Maybe that's who I was becoming. Someone imperfect, equal parts magical and human. With a hint of zest. I smiled as the ingredients appeared on the counter. I liked that idea of myself.

What would it feel like to embrace my age? I juiced a lemon, careful to strain the pulp and remove the seeds. The vision of the woman in the water, the one with the hunched shoulders and strained eyes, still haunted me. Not because she was old, but because she looked defeated.

I blended dry ingredients. House mixed the wet ones. I hummed a song, some popular number Gabe had on repeat when he was here. I wasn't so set in my ways I couldn't embrace new music. I was embracing a whole lot these days.

The scent of fresh fruit filled the air once the cake was in the oven. Sweet and tangy. I turned on the radio and danced while I washed the dishes. House hated that part, and while I didn't love it, we were in this together. At least for now.

Even if I lost the next trial, I wasn't totally down for the count. I still had my therapy practice. There were plenty of cute places to live in Treater's Way. Would I be able to stay on with Julia as Supreme? Would I be able to face my failure every day?

"I'll still be a part of the Magnolia. No matter what." The wind turned sharp, and a gentle slap landed on my wrist. The house, admonishing me for assuming defeat. "Hey, I'm a realist."

The second slap was less gentle.

"I'm not giving up, House. Don't you worry."

I wasn't giving up. But something inside me had definitely shifted. I was settled in a way I hadn't felt for a good long while. Such a strange sensation, given everything that was at stake.

We'd just finished icing the cake and were assembling the daisies when the air rippled and Gumbo popped into the room.

"Simone." His sweet eyes were serious. His tone somber. Again, he wore no bow.

"Mystical Protector," I replied with a grin he didn't match. Uh-oh. This was even more serious than I realized. "Is it time?"

"Please be at Wanderer's Woods tomorrow at midnight." A bowl of cream appeared next to him. He eyed it with longing but didn't drink. "The second Rite will take place under a waning gibbous."

"What's a waning gibbous? Some kind of monkey?" I ran my finger along the inside of the icing bowl and stuck it in my mouth. Yummy. "Also, by tomorrow at midnight do you mean in, like, five hours or actually tomorrow at midnight, which would technically be Thursday?"

"Simone, do take this seriously." Gumbo hopped onto the counter, meeting my eyes. "The second Rite is no picnic."

"Man, that would be nice." I offered him spare icing from my finger. He declined. "I'm serious, Gumbo. I'm just ... vibing."

"Vibing?"

"It's something Gabe said." I shrugged my shoulders. "I don't totally get it, but I think that's what I've got going on right now. The calm after the storm before the other storm. Peace in the face of my defeat."

Gumbo tilted his head to me, scanning me with his green eye.

"You are well." It wasn't a question, so I didn't answer. "Midnight on the morrow. Don't be late."

"Wait!" Gumbo's form was already fading. He popped back in with a shake of his head. "I have one more question."

"What is it?"

"What the heck are the Wanderer's Woods?"

CHAPTER
TWENTY-NINE

Word of the Supreme trials must have spread. By the time I arrived in Illusion Square a few minutes before midnight, a small crowd of locals had gathered near the base of the Mighty Oak. Doug and a few of my other patients chatted together, as if they all somehow knew they went to the same therapist.

The Eight, comprised of the four women who ran the shops of Illusion Square and their partners, created a krewe of their own, alongside Ana who absolutely refused to age. I still didn't know why they were called The Eight, something about a battle and some treasure.

Pretty cool name, though.

Julia was already there, standing beside the Twins. Same story, different day. I searched for Brianne but couldn't find her. To be fair, she was a shortie in a sea of tall folks. I couldn't spot Nate, though, and I had to admit that gave me pause. As a witness, she was required to be here.

I had to hope my failure during the first Rite hadn't shaken her confidence in me.

It turned out I knew the Wanderer's Woods, and I knew them well. That was the name given to the dense forestry at the edge of Illusion Square. The woods that shielded the entry to South Bridge, a small footbridge that led from Treater's Way to Bridge Island.

I'd walked those woods with Ray dozens of times my last summer here. I knew them like the back of my hand which, blessedly, did not itch. As a hot summer breeze shifted the branches of the Mighty Oak, my confidence bolstered. The wind surrounded me, lifting my hair and warming my skin before diving into the trees we faced.

"I've got this," I said. And every part of me believed it.

At midnight, the crowd moved into complete silence. All eyes were on Gumbo. He stretched his fluffy body and sauntered to the entrance to Wanderer's Woods, where a smaller version of South Bridge protected the narrow creek running alongside Illusion Square.

It really was a beautiful spot. Romantic and secluded. My first kiss with Ray happened right where Gumbo was standing.

"Simone. Julia." Like the first Rite, Gumbo weaved a figure eight around us before settling in the center. "It is time for the second trial for Supremacy over the Magnolia. Rite Two is the Wanderer's Passage."

He strolled to the center of the bridge, turned a circle, and sat upright.

"As the moon begins its slow journey toward the sun, so must each challenger begin her descent into uncertainty. Through the woods where memory slips and time frays, she must walk alone. No path is fixed. No star is loyal."

The other side! I just had to cross the woods and get to Bridge Island?

"The passage tests not the feet, but the heart that guides

them. Only through faith in her inner compass shall she emerge whole on the other side."

Faith in my inner compass? Cool. Cool cool cool. I could manage that. Maybe.

"Your path is not the main path. You must find your own."

The bridge creaked and groaned. Plank by plank, the boards shook loose of their nails. They split into two equal parts, each landing on opposite sides of the bridge's main structure. Gumbo remained still during all of it. With the planks gone, he hovered in mid-air, sitting on space.

"Simone, you will step toward the woods on my left. Julia, you walk right."

"Good luck." Julia stretched out her hand and smiled brighter than a politician kissing babies. She wore the same dress from the first Rite, as if it were a good luck charm. Or a reminder she'd won. "Again, no hard feelings."

I didn't know why that was so important to her. I started to meet her handshake, but my hand paused midway there. I couldn't move it forward.

Don't touch her.

The words flitted through the breeze. If she heard them, she gave no indication. She lifted one eyebrow and tilted her head.

"Simone?" I must have looked ridiculous. My arm was at a weird angle, my fingers outspread. I glanced around, trying to find the source of this magic. Gumbo's face was passive. Neither Lydia nor Lyra looked in my direction. Maybe Julia was doing this to get in my head.

Don't let her touch you.

Welp. Definitely not Julia. Why would she ask to shake my hand then warn me not to shake her hand? Someone, or something, was trying to warn me. If a disembodied force was going to keep me safe, I was willing to go on faith. I clasped my hands behind my back and nodded at her.

"Good luck to you as well, Julia." I gave her a wide berth and stepped to Gumbo's left. Did I sing a Beyonce song as I walked? Maybe. I never passed up an opportunity to Beyonce. When Gumbo dipped his head towards me, I took that as my sign.

I hopped over the creek and approached the edge of the forest. Julia had done the same.

"May the best witch win," Gumbo bellowed.

It didn't have as much fanfare as the first trial. The woods didn't clear. No scary nymph or dryad came out to greet us. The woods were just woods, albeit without a path. At least I'd worn hiking boots this time.

I scanned the row of trees, spotted a clearing I could just slide through, and headed in.

There was no path beyond the bridge. I swayed left, then right, finding space between tree trunks three times as thick as me and twenty times taller. I glanced at the sky, hoping to orient myself with the stars.

Not that I knew what any of the stars were. Or which ones were planets. But hey, maybe I had dormant tracking and survival skills just waiting for this opportunity.

It turned out, that didn't matter. The blanket of branches and leaves blocked out the sky. In fact, as I moved deeper into the woods, darkness became the only constant. Well, that and the really disturbing sounds of animals skittering about.

My eyes adjusted to the night, but it was slow-going. I figured if I didn't turn around, I would eventually find my way through. The forest was dense, but not deep. The entire trek from Illusion Square to Bridge Island was just over a mile.

I just had to keep moving forward.

A twig snapped to my right, startling me. I stumbled left,

tripping over a raised branch and landing on my knees with an *oof*. Bracing myself on ... something ... I stood up, dusting debris from my palms. Something sharp caught my skin and drew blood. My knees burned from the impact. I leaned over to inspect them, but it was getting darker.

My breath came out in ragged gasps. Small clouds pierced the nighttime, the only thing visible. I shivered against the sudden cold as tiny goosebumps travelled up my arms. When had the temperature dropped?

A second twig snapped and the faint rustle of leaves told me I wasn't alone. For the first time in my entire life, I considered that something other than a cute little bunny or squirrel might live in the woods. Duh, Simone. There are probably wolves, or wolf shifters who don't know you. Were shifters feral in their wolf form? Ray hadn't been, but maybe he was the exception or he had special alpha powers.

Awesome. Was the ultimate goal of the second trial just to try not to get eaten or mauled?

"Who's there?" Okay, Little Red Riding Hood, way to make the big bad wolf know where you are. "I'm armed."

A soft laugh responded. A laugh I hadn't heard in thirty years.

"With what, Sweets? A sense of humor and a big heart?"

Sunlight silhouetted the woman who emerged from the trees. The cold—chilling me to the bone only seconds earlier—dissipated. I was warm and safe and all things cozy. My heartbeat slowed. My breath relaxed.

Everything was going to be okay.

"Here." The woman smiled and extended her hand. "Let me help you."

It couldn't be real. And yet it was. She was as solid as the ground beneath my feet. I could even smell the old perfume she wore, the one I'd secretly hated because it reminded me of roses past their bloom.

"Well, what are you waiting for, Sweets?" She jiggled her hand. "Let's go win this thing."

Who knew it was a scent I would miss? Her eyes, always kind and amused unless I was making trouble, met mine. Her hair was the same. I even recognized the dress she wore.

The dress she'd been buried in.

She was solid. The only time she blurred was when tears blocked my view of her. Not that it mattered if I could see her. I knew her.

I reached out, entwining our fingers, and let my mother guide me forward.

CHAPTER
THIRTY

S he didn't speak at first, and I had no words. The walk was easy. I was no longer squeezing between trunks or tripping over knots. We could see. Below my feet, the ground was grassy and plush. In fact, as I glanced around, there were fewer trees than before. I followed her into a grove I'd never seen before. Night flowers bloomed. Though still no stars and no longer full, the moon was bright over our heads.

She turned to me, her smile both dazzling and soothing.

"Let's rest here." She opened her arms, and I sank willingly into her hug.

"Momma." This was home. This was safety.

"I'm here, Sweets." The sound of her nickname for me, coming from her voice, awoke my inner child. I missed her all over again, like she'd died yesterday. I'd experienced this before, when I'd removed the ward I'd placed on myself and my memories returned.

This was different, though. She was here! I could tell her about the ward. I could tell her how much she'd meant to me. I could tell her about the grandson she'd never met.

A single sob erupted from deep within my chest. An avalanche of sobs followed. This was a different cry from the awful tears I'd given to Nymph Lake.

I wasn't crying until I was empty. I was crying because I was full.

My mom lowered us to the ground, damp beneath us as if from a morning dew. I curled into her lap like a child. She stroked my hair and made gentle shushing noises as I released the grief I'd been carrying without realizing.

I guess there are some things you never get over.

I don't know how long I stayed in her lap. Long enough to feel dehydrated and spent. My throat was sore, my eyes raw. Eventually, I sat up and took her in. It was really her, every memory of her as accurate as the woman in front of me.

"You're really here." My voice was odd. Not quite my own, like a younger and more innocent version of me.

"You know, I'm very proud of you." She smiled, tucking a strand of my hair behind one ear.

"You are?" It was a balm over an open wound in my soul. This was the connection I'd missed my entire life. I'd searched for it with Ray. I'd accepted I'd never have it with Jeff. Even when I first arrived here, I'd latched onto Brianne, so hopeful for a soulmate I'd not taken the time to really get to know her.

"Of course." She cupped my face with her hands. They were warm and soft, except for her index finger. The one she'd used for papers and filling. It always had a blister on it. Even now, pressed against my cheek. "Do you know how brave you've been? How strong?"

"I … guess I don't." To my mind, I'd had moments of strength. But being strong through it all? That wasn't the way I viewed myself. "I think I've just been reactive."

"Oh, no, my darling." She was wiping tears from my cheeks. Straightening my sleeves. "You stood up to the challenge. You accepted the unknown. You persevered. You even stood up to wicked old Julia."

A dark thought in the back of my mind began to whisper. My mother would never call someone else wicked. I shoved it down. Maybe she'd been teasing.

"Sure, you've made mistakes and failed a few times." She leaned forward, planting a soft kiss on the bridge of my nose. Had she ever done that before? I couldn't recall. Her lips were dry and scratchy. "But that's to be expected, isn't it? We work with what we've got, after all."

I pulled away. Not far, just a few inches. I tilted my head to look at her. Would Momma expect me to make mistakes? I could rationalize that. Everyone makes them. It's part of being human. She would point that out.

Is that how she would have worded it, though? It was one thing to accept flaws. But to recognize and use your daughter's flaws against her? She would never.

It wasn't just her lips that were dry. With a bit of space and the shock worn off, I could see her more clearly. Cracks lined her skin like pieces of a puzzle. Her movements were stiff. She smiled, but looking closely I saw the smile was flat. It didn't reach her eyes. Dark brown eyes like mine.

Except my mother had blue eyes.

"I have to keep going, Momma." It hurt. It hurt in a way I'd never have words for. It hurt so bad my body held onto the ache even as I stood up. It screamed for me to go back in the form of creaky knees and tense shoulders.

"No, you don't, Sweets." She looked up at me, opening her hand. A tiny branch poked up from her index finger. It hadn't been a blister at all. "Stay with me. You deserve the rest."

It would be a lie to say I didn't want to stay. Even with the illusion shattered, a part of me longed to curl up in her lap and stay there. To bask in her approval another minute. Maybe two. Maybe forever.

But I was no longer a child. The connection I was trying to capture no longer existed.

Maybe that was okay. After all, I was nearing fifty. I had a lifetime of opportunity ahead of me. I was a mother myself. I had a business. I was making friends and settling in.

And those things were true, regardless of whether my mother saw them in me or not. Because, even if she was a phony, she'd been right. I was strong. I kept going, even when it was hard. I was brave. I kept trying, even when I was afraid.

I'd been so busy looking forward, taking stock of what I had yet to accomplish. I'd forgotten to look back at the progress I'd made. I wasn't a failure after all.

I'd just wound up on a different path.

"I'm sorry, Momma." I kissed her palm, resting my head just for a moment in the safety of the past. "But I'm going to keep walking. Even if I'm doing it alone."

She gave a half wave, then the vision of my mother disappeared. In front of me was a tree, small branches jutting out from the trunk. There was no grove. No grass. The sky was no longer visible overhead.

I stepped around the tree, uncertain where to go from here. I wasn't sure if we'd circled back, or if I was heading in the same direction I had been before I ran into her. I turned in a slow circle, hoping for a landmark or clue.

To my left were two rows of trees. It wasn't quite a path, but there was space between them to walk. Hoping it was a sign and not just wishful thinking, I ventured forward. The muggy, still air of Louisiana summer coated me like soup.

I felt like I was treading through soup. Large beads of sweat formed on the edges of my hair and along my brow. They dripped into my eye or down my back. I stopped, pulling my hair into a ponytail with one hand and wringing it out with the other.

"Well, that's hot," a new but familiar voice said.

"Shut your mouth. It is hot." Another familiar voice, this one gruff and masculine. "Everything she does is sexy."

I stepped beyond the trees, already heaving a sigh. I knew where this was going.

Another damn grove. Two passages out. Each one with a man from my past standing in the way.

I turned toward my right first. There stood Ethan in his sexy lawyer suit. His smile was wide. He was always so happy to see me. He held a blueberry muffin in one hand.

"Fancy a run, Little Fox?" My stomach clutched at the playful nickname he'd given me in high school. When had it taken on more meaning? "Maybe we can grab a shower afterwards."

"Oh, come on." I had to laugh at this illusion. "The real Ethan would never say that."

"That you know of." He loosened the green silk tie around his collar and dragged it down. "There are sides to me you've never seen."

Well, he had me there. The patient and loyal version of Ethan I knew was wonderful. But the rugged, intense one who'd burst through my doorway on a Saturday morning? That guy wasn't the kind who sat around and waited.

"But I'm the one you think of at night. Isn't that right, Simone?" Ray's moody green eyes held me in place. "The one who makes your pulse quicken in all the right places."

He'd dragged the word *all* out, managing to make it the sexiest word on the planet. No nickname for me. Not from Ray Chase. Ray was serious. Dedicated.

Passionate as hell.

"You're the one I used to think of at night." It was mostly

true. Sure, there were a few times he'd invaded my dreams. Especially in the past few weeks, as he'd been at my side whenever I needed him. Even if I didn't realize it until I saw him on my doorstep.

"Oh, I'm still in there." He lifted one side of his mouth in a smirk I wanted to kiss off of him. Sure, he was likely an illusion. But it was a damn fine illusion.

"I'll always take care of you, Simone." Ethan took a step forward. "I'll always support you."

"I'll always make you excited, Simone." Ray, with a glare at Ethan, took his own steps. "You'll always have a warm body to hold you."

This was wrong. This was all wrong. They were no more real than my mother had been.

They moved in closer while I stood still. They locked eyes with one another, low growls escaping their fit chests.

"Choose me." Ethan's thumb stroked my hand, tender as a petal brushing my skin.

"Choose me." Ray's strong hands cupped the back of my head, possessive and fierce.

This close, the trick was so much more real. I could smell Ethan's cologne. Ray's boots crushed the twigs under his feet.

Desire ensnared me in a vicious trap and latched on tight. My body was a fire these two men had thrown gasoline upon. A need I'd never felt before rose from deep within.

Hell. I wanted them both.

I wanted the fire only Ray seemed to stoke. Then again, he'd been helpful—someone to bounce ideas off of, as well. He'd shown signs of therapy and growth. He was no longer the impulsive and broken quarterback.

I wanted the stability only Ethan could provide—though there had been a moment where he'd let go of his carefully controlled persona. There were bouts of intensity, and a longing for me that I'd never seen before. He was no longer the good-natured and reliable workout buddy.

They were standing too close. Their shoulders bumped. They locked eyes. Ray's lip lifted in a snarl. Ethan dipped his head forward in challenge.

And there was that. These two still had their own unresolved issues.

Of course, I wasn't the same person either. The lost and longing girl from high school—the one who'd never quite found her place—was gone too. I'd taken on a dozen roles since then. Therapist. Wife. Mother.

This chapter, the one based on what we all knew about one another from the past, had to close before any new chapters could begin.

I was in my own chapter. It was time I figured out who I was when I wasn't being defined by someone else. It was time to create my own labels. Mystical Therapist. Friend. Business Owner.

Supreme.

For the first time, that word meant something to me. There was a power to the idea that beckoned me. I didn't understand what a Supreme was or what they did. But I knew one thing.

I wanted the job.

The growling had stopped. Both men watched me in complete silence.

"Sorry not sorry, guys. It's not time for this yet." I pushed between them. A third opening had emerged in the grove. "I'm choosing me."

I stepped through the opening and forged my own path ahead.

CHAPTER
THIRTY-ONE

I was growing weary. I didn't wear a watch, and with no sky overhead I had no feeling for how long I'd spent in the forest. It could have been minutes. It could have been hours.

My stomach rumbled. My eyes grew heavy. I suppose it could have been days.

The trees were sparser this far in. Either that, or I'd ended up on a far edge. They were still in even rows, with just enough space between them for me to walk forward relatively unscratched. I walked and walked, hoping against hope that I was near the finish line. Hoping there actually was a finish line.

I stopped at the sight of a tiny bud sprouting from a tree trunk. A pretty little flower, pink and pure, blooming against the odds in the dank, dark woods. I touched the petals with a fresh wave of horror.

Because I'd seen that same flower three times. Glancing behind me, I scanned the trees I'd passed. They were all bare. With trembling fingers, I plucked one of the petals and let it fall to the ground. I trudged forward, pushing down my fears, until I reached a tree. At the base of its trunk lay a single petal, and beside it, a tiny pink flower—one petal missing from its stem.

I couldn't be going in circles. I hadn't turned once. I had to be walking toward something.

This was impossible.

I plucked a second petal, this time placing it at the next tree I came upon. The air grew chilly. Then deathly cold. My teeth chattered and my body trembled. After what felt like hours, I approached another tree.

A tree with a flower missing petals. One lay dying over its roots. The second was a few steps forward.

"I'm not making any progress." I said it aloud to comfort myself. To ease the gnawing doubt that I even had a voice any longer.

"I wonder why that is." Agatha emerged from the path ahead of me, a dense fog rolling in around her. The fog scampered towards my feet, already as high as my knees. It stung my legs like acid.

"Agatha." Relief washed over me, despite the fog biting at my pants. I'd seen Agatha before, even after she died. Maybe this was real. The final test before I could emerge. "Thank goodness."

"Glad to see me, CC?" She spoke with humor and depth, her voice rich and full. "I'm so happy to see you, as well. I knew you could do it."

I was so focused on her, I barely noticed the fog creeping higher. It seeped under the hem of my shirt and lashed out. I lifted it, finding blistering welts along my stomach.

"Can you help me?" I held out my hand. She stopped short, just out of my reach.

"Why do you think you're failing, CC?" That little detail that Agatha—one of the few who would still call me by my middle name—clung to me. If this was an illusion, surely she would call me by my first name.

That logic stuck, flawed or not. She had to be real. So this had to be a lesson.

"I didn't think I was failing," I told her. "I mean, yeah, I totally pooped the bed during the first trial. But I thought I was doing okay here."

She merely smiled and folded her arms across her chest.

"Well, I *was* doing okay," I continued. Somehow her silence was more worrying. "I said goodbye to the past. I realized it was time to work on myself and put aside old flames. I was beginning to look to the future, and that was exciting me ..."

"And yet you are stuck in an acid fog after wandering the same path for days."

So many of those words made my heart pound. *Stuck. Acid. Days.*

Pressure clamped like a vise over my head. The muscles of my neck were tense. Heat flooded my veins, battling against the icy sting of the—Lord help me—acid fog. Which was rising. Covering my chest. Making my skin boil.

I hoped I could convey desperation with my eyes because I couldn't speak. I opened my mouth, gasping out a panicked plea for help.

"Come on, CC." Agatha shook her head, her words clipped. "Why do you think you are failing right now?"

I tilted my head up, hoping there was a nearby branch I could grasp onto. Maybe I could lift myself to safety. We hadn't brought supplies into the woods. Not even water. All I had was the shirt on my back, so to speak.

Of course, I could use my shirt as a rope if I needed to. My mind was reeling, latching onto any random thought that flitted through my head.

Don't ruin this shirt, Simone. It's one of your favorites.

A silly thought. Trite, given the pain and panic. Besides, House could find another one for me.

House! That must be the answer. I could ask House to help me. Surely it would hear me, even out here. After all, it had given me a glass of ice water once when I'd broken down near my mother's gravestone.

Man, how I longed for a simple vision of my mother. At least she hadn't tried to kill me.

"You won't die out here, Simone." Agatha was shouting over the din of the fog. Either that, or she was in my head. "Why do you think you are failing right now?"

House wouldn't hear me because I couldn't speak. The fog tapped at my collar bone. It slithered over my back. It wrapped itself around my neck, strangling me. Applying pressure to my vocal cords.

Why do you think you are failing right now?

I had a sudden vision of Gumbo, lounging on my desk while I scratched behind his ears. We'd been discussing my clients and my struggles to treat them properly. I felt like I was failing them.

He asked why I wasn't using magical methods alongside mundane ones. And over the past week, I'd spoken to several of my clients about their comfort level with the supernatural.

Because I had a voice.

Because I was a witch and a woman.

Because I was powerful.

Why do you think you are failing right now?

I was failing because I was telling myself stories. Stories that limited who I truly was and what I was capable of. I was too afraid to ask for more because I'd already told myself no.

I drew in the deepest breath I could manage, tapping into the pool of magic that sat deep within me. It came easier these days, when I actually remembered to use it.

Well, Simone, is there a better time to practice your magic than to escape a magic acid bath?

"No more." My voice was little more than a whisper. It didn't hold the deep timbre of power.

Why do you think you are failing right now?

"Stop." Doubt laced my command, making it more of a question.

If I thought I was failing, then what was I doing here? Why was I fighting to be a Supreme if I couldn't use my abilities? Why didn't I just give up and let fog overtake me?

It reached my jaw. It slapped my cheeks. I closed my eyes.

I don't know why, but the memory of Amelie's painting flitted through my oxygen-deprived brain. I'd had such a profound sense of confidence, the stability that comes with knowing your own power. Light didn't just surround me.

It *was* me. The way she saw me. Maybe even the way others saw me.

But I'd failed the test, hadn't I? I'd nearly drowned in a sea of my own tears, crying until I was empty ...

Why do you think you are failing right now?

And then it hit me. So suddenly I stopped panicking.

"Ho-ly shit."

The lightness I'd felt the day after the trial. The way I was hopeful, always moving forward, willing to face whatever came my way.

I'd fulfilled the requirements of the first Rite. *To be full, one must first be empty.*

"I didn't fail the first trial at all." I couldn't see Agatha, but I sensed her nod of approval.

Why do you think you are failing right now?

Why did I think I was failing? The passage tests not the feet, but the heart that guides them. I may not always be kind to myself, but I knew one thing for certain.

Agatha chose me. Not as a last resort. Not as a favor to my mother. Not because Julia wasn't around.

She chose me because I was the one willing to try. I was the one with heart.

And caring as deeply as I did—so deeply it scared me sometimes—wasn't a hindrance.

If I spoke from the heart, that was my true power. All those voices in my head were a distraction. They were the same illusions I'd seen in the forest.

"Well. I think that's enough of the freaking acid fog." There it was. The voice I wanted. The one filled with confidence. Faith in myself.

It didn't recede. It was gone in an instant, along with every burn and slash on my body. The night was still. Agatha's illusion, if that's what it was, faded. But not before she blew me one last kiss.

Behind her, a narrow sliver of moonlight cut through the darkness.

"Okay." I wouldn't lie to myself. The path towards uncertainty was still terrifying.

But I could handle it. After all, I was a witch.

It only took a few steps to find the next clearing. I braced myself for another challenge.

But the waning gibbous and a sky full of stars greeted me.

I'd made it through the Wanderer's Woods.

CHAPTER

THIRTY-TWO

"Simone." Gumbo weaved himself through my legs. "I am quite glad to see you."

"Are you real?" I reached down to give his ear a good scratch. He purred, that glorious deep sound that vibrated through me and settled my stomach. "Or are you here to teach me another life lesson?"

"It's me." He rolled over, indulging my need to rub his belly. "Accept no substitutions."

"Sure it is." I laughed as he batted at my fingers. "That's what the others said."

"Did they?" As if realizing he'd been undignified, he sat upright. I really missed his bows. I really, really, really missed the adorable voice.

I stopped to think about it, brushing stray leaves off my clothes.

"No," I said. "I suppose you're right. None of them actually said they were real. Felt real though."

"Indeed." He raised his fur, giving his body a shake.

I scanned the area to get my bearings. I was at the

very edge of Treater's Way. South Bridge was on my right. If I didn't know better, I'd think I'd walked in a straight line. And though I couldn't measure time by the sky, the moon was still high, as if no more than an hour had passed.

Even stranger, we were alone. When I'd been thrown out of Nymph Lake, the witnesses were there to watch. But here, it was just Gumbo and me.

"Where is everyone?" I lifted on my toes to see the other side of the bridge. "Where's Julia?"

"Still performing the Rite." Gumbo's voice was laced with pity. "You came out first this time."

"Two down." I rubbed my shoulders. Fatigue was setting in faster than I wanted it to. I still needed to make it home. And I wanted to see everyone. My coven. "Is the third Rite even necessary?"

"Why wouldn't it be?" Gumbo tilted his head, scanning me with his green eye.

"Because I won the first two. Mathematically, Julia can't win. Right?" He tilted again, this time giving me the gold eye scan. "It's creepy when you do that without permission."

"Apologies, Simone. I was merely assessing your aura."

"What's the verdict?" I didn't care if he wanted to be cordial, I wanted kitty love. I crouched beside him, then decided to sit in the cool grass and pet him.

"It is a victory indeed that you recognize you won the first trial. I admit, it concerned me you hadn't caught on." He crawled into my lap. "However, the true Supreme must win all three trials. And the witnesses must confirm."

My heart sank. We were out here alone. That couldn't be a good sign.

"And where are the witnesses?" I curled his tail around my fingers, enjoying the soft fur against my battered skin.

"For this trial, they watched from a distance," he said. "In a place beyond time and space."

"They could see me?" Ugh. My throat dried. "I was so vulnerable."

"As it should be," Gumbo replied. "In order to truly be Supreme, you must be trusted by your coven. A coven that doesn't understand you cannot believe in you."

Well, that was fair. Over the past few weeks, I'd tried so hard to connect with them. But I'd only let them see the parts of me I wasn't completely ashamed of. Sure, it was valid to be concerned about Lydia's judgment given how clearly she disliked me. Lauren and I were working our way towards friendship, but it was clouded by the past we shared.

Did I know—really know—any of them? No. And I'd hidden parts of myself as well.

Gumbo was right. That needed to end. True relationships could only happen if people knew who I was. If they couldn't see my good and bad parts, rather than what I was doing or what I could provide, how could they trust me?

I'd fought through the woods to remove the labels others had placed on me. I couldn't project my insecurities on them, then judge them for labeling me.

"Hop off, kitty." I gave Gumbo a nudge, which he ignored. "Come on, cutie. I want to go home."

"Really, Simone." Gumbo nuzzled closer. "When are you going to remember you're a witch?"

Duh. Hadn't I just gone through the woods to learn that lesson?

"You're right." I closed my eyes and scanned my body. My magic, usually so dim I had to reach for it deep inside of me, was there. Right on the surface. Very cool. "I want to go home."

The sounds of being outdoors were the first to go. Wherever I was, it was quiet. I'd grown accustomed to the scents of the woods. Damp moss. Animal droppings. Earthy trees. When those fell away, I opened my eyes.

I was sitting on the floor in the Magnolia conference room. Lauren, Lydia, Lyra, and Brianne sat at the table, their backs to me. A screen floated in front of them, displaying two sets of video.

The right screen showed Julia, still in the woods. She was on her knees, hands clasped in front of her as she pleaded to the man towering over her. He was impossibly tall and slender, with dark brown hair perfectly styled to swoop over the forehead and land behind his ears. His long fingers jabbed at Julia in accusation, each one ending in a sharply pointed, manicured nail. He wore a black suit and a cape that brushed the ground beneath his shined loafers.

Julia shook her head, tears streaming down her cheeks. Dirt stained her arms. Her hair was coated with mud and sweat. Despite myself, I felt sorry for her. She opened her mouth and wailed before throwing her face to the floor. The man lifted his lip in a sneer.

There was no sound, and I was glad for that. I couldn't imagine what he would say that would reduce Julia to tears like that. But, given what I'd gone through, I knew I wouldn't want to hear it.

The video on the left was me, sitting on the grass near the edge of the water with Gumbo on my lap. We were chatting, and I had a serene smile on my face. Then I closed my eyes, and we disappeared from the screen. It went black.

"Oh," I said aloud. "There must be a delay."

Brianne screeched, hopping up and sending her chair clattering to the floor. She whirled around, her hands clasped in fists. Something fell from her ear and bounced on the floor. A white earbud. So there was sound. Yikes.

Lyra turned slowly in her seat. She propped her head into

her hand, as if even the effort of turning was too much. She was barely there. Her skin had faded far past pale. She was almost translucent. Dark veins ran like webs across her arms and up her neck.

"Holy cow, Lyra." I started to move towards her. "You've gotten even worse."

Lydia slid out of her chair to block my path to her sister.

"Step aside, bulldog." I planted my hands on my hips. After the night I had, I wasn't about to let a judgmental fairy stop me. If my instinct was to help Lyra, I was going to do it. No matter what.

"Let me help her, Lydia." Lydia held my gaze. Brianne rubbed at her heart like it had just attacked her. "I know I can."

She scanned me in a way that was weirdly similar to Gumbo. After a moment, she smiled. She actually smiled!

"I see you finally figured it all out." Lydia stepped to one side. "Took you long enough."

"Yeah." I kneeled in front of Lyra. "Because thirty years of trauma always gets resolved in one week."

She snorted but didn't reply. I took Lyra's hands in mine. She slumped forward.

"Do you need medical attention, or is this purely on a metaphysical plane?" I asked.

"The other one." She licked parched, chapped lips. "The second one."

Got it. Magic stuff. I wasn't sure what I was going to do, or what I could say that might undo this, but I had to try.

"Okay, may I help you?" Beside me, Lydia made a motion, as if she might stop me or speak up. I held one finger up to her. "I got this, sister."

"Let her help," Brianne said, picking up the earbud. "You saw what she went through. She's got this."

"Thanks, friend. It's good to see you again." I smiled at

Brianne, then turned my attention back to Lyra. "Honey, I need your permission. That's important to me. May I help you?"

She closed her eyes, or they closed because she could no longer keep them open. It was hard to say. She nodded assent.

I didn't have to close my eyes, though. I didn't have to reach for the magic inside of me, either just under the surface or deep within. It was there. Waiting.

Waiting alongside a second force. A presence that felt joyful and innocent. House, eager to help.

"House, can we start with whatever that chocolate-looking thing that Lydia gave her is?" I held out my hand, and the pearl-like concoction popped onto it. It looked like candy, but up close the smell was anything but sweet. A foul odor, like the week-old stench of a clogged sewer, made me crinkle my nose.

"I think she needs something to wash it down." I winked at Lyra. "Lord knows I would."

A tumbler of golden-brown liquid landed in her hand, the ice inside clinking softly when she shifted to grip it. That smelled much better.

"Whiskey. Excellent choice, House." Again, that joyful feeling. Apparently, House liked to be recognized. Well sure, who wouldn't. "I think we could all use a drink."

I barely paid attention to the tray that landed on the table. I helped Lyra put the gross not-chocolate thing in her mouth, then guided the whiskey to her lips. She swallowed, her shoulders relaxing with each gulp.

She gave me her signature half-smile. I would take it.

"Thank you." Her voice cracked. "I was almost completely drained."

Lydia pushed me aside with a huff. She cupped her sister's face and turned it side to side, muttering under her breath.

"You said you could handle it." Lydia hopped to her feet, pacing the length of the table. She stopped at the tray of drinks, downed one of them, and resumed pacing. "We should have never agreed to this."

"Agreed to what?" I asked.

Lauren hadn't spoken since they discovered I was here. She'd kept her face transfixed to the live feed, watching poor Julia suffer. But Julia's screen was black, too. She must have finished the Rite.

"We need to find a way to tell her." Lauren slammed her earbuds on the table. I hadn't seen her in a few weeks. Like Lyra, her eyes were sunken and face sallow. Her perky hair was dull and limp. She looked exhausted. And very, very sad. "Julia failed the second Rite anyway."

"It doesn't matter." Lydia lifted her hands to the sky like she was summoning a storm. Her voice rose. "Julia can fail all three rites. She just needs the votes. And we can't tell Simone —" She stopped, her eyes widening as she clutched her throat. She clawed at it then closed her mouth. With a sigh of defeat, she flunked down into the closest chair. "We can't."

"*You* can't. *I* can." Lyra pressed her palms into the table in an attempt to stand. After a moment, she gave up. "Or I could if I had the damn energy."

The fact that Julia failed her test barely registered. My head was hot with anger, my pulse pounding with frustration.

Whatever was going on, I was sick of being on the outside looking in. They were talking about me like I wasn't standing in the same room with them. As if I hadn't just gone through complete emotional and physical turmoil in a bid to earn my place here. Twice.

To hell with that. I was done trying to earn something that was already mine.

"You have the damn energy." My voice spoke before my brain caught up. And it was my big girl voice. Commanding. Potent. Throaty.

Ooh. It felt amazing. I was gonna call it my Big Magic Voice™.

They all turned to me, as if they couldn't look away. Good. It was time they really saw me.

"The essence or energy or whatever you want to call it that was drained from you is yours again, Lyra."

My words didn't feel like enough, and a giddy sensation rushed through me. House. Thrilled that I was finally speaking up. The room began to sway around us, turning in a violent circle.

"You are going to recover. Reclaim everything that was taken from you. And the force that drained you?"

The room spun faster with each word I spoke, though I didn't feel it. The pictures on the walls blurred past in my periphery with blinding speed. A whirring sound grew from a low din to a loud buzz.

We were mostly still, either in chairs or standing. As if we were in the center of it and yet not a part of it. Only Brianne seemed to brace herself, relaxing her silly little fists so she could grip Lauren's hand.

"The force that drained you can't touch you again, Lyra. In fact, it can't hurt any of you. You are under the protection of both me and the Magnolia."

The room stopped spinning with an abrupt halt. I lurched forward, catching myself before I fell into Lyra's lap. Her eyes, already brighter and more orange than I'd seen in a while, shimmered. Her hair's luster was returning. She wrapped her arms around me.

The woman was strong. Fae strong. Those arms were like vise grips, and I wasn't going anywhere. I just had to pray she didn't break my neck with her appreciation. I staggered back when she released me, only to be caught in Lydia's fierce—but brief—hug.

I looked around, half-expecting shattered glass and fallen frames. There was none of that, but the room was different. The walls were a shade brighter, and yet more soothing. The drink cart had gotten a very cool upgrade, including slots for wine and a built-in sink.

And the conference table was painted a different color. No. It wasn't painted. It was a different table.

What used to be a dark, heavy, and super foreboding ebony monstrosity was now a leaner, sleeker walnut beauty. Our chairs were still high-backed, but now they were cushioned and covered in sage green fabric. And there was a skylight, through which I could see ... well ...

It was a place beyond space and time.

THIRTY-THREE

"Oh, that's much better." I took the seat at the head of the table and wriggled my butt. So soft. "This is much, much better."

"Wowie wow wow." Brianne's head was craned back, her mouth open as she peered through the skylight. Swarms of colors, deeper than any I'd seen before, moved like magma through the air. I think it was air. I didn't really know. The colors were alive. Everything was bright but somehow soothing to the eye.

Something cold and wet touched my leg. I let out a yelp.

"Sorry, Simone." Gumbo hopped on the table and turned in a circle before settling in between my arms. He wore a bow that matched the rainbow overhead, and he was full on kitty voice. It made me want to sing. "I get disoriented when I must join the room after the transport."

"We do this every time we have a board meeting?" Gumbo's eyes drifted closed. He seemed so comfortable, more settled than he had in weeks. I poked his toe beans, and he didn't even budge. "Let's have a meeting, then."

Everyone took their regular positions at a new table. Except Gumbo. He snored softly in front of me, his head resting on my hand. That was okay. I had another hand if I needed it.

And Brianne brought me a glass of whiskey before taking her seat opposite me, her grin was nothing short of girlish. She wore the same yellow dress she'd had on when I first arrived at the Magnolia.

I'd missed that smile. That brightness. I'd missed my friend.

"Can I assume all of you were being drained all this time?" At their sea of nods, my throat clogged. I'd assumed I'd done something wrong or was unable to prove myself. I'd missed a more obvious explanation: that it wasn't about me at all. "By what?"

"Not a what." I turned to Lyra, pleased to see she was already looking more like herself. "A person. And not drained, well not all of us. But controlled in some way."

"A person?" I stroked Gumbo's back, eliciting a delightful mid-nap purr. "Who has the power to do that?" Nobody answered, but Lydia looked at me like I was an idiot. And, just like that, I felt like one. "Oh. Well, I feel stupid."

Julia had practically glued herself to Lyra from the moment she came through the vortex. Now that I thought about it, she probably used Lyra's power to get through it.

"So, that's her power, is it?" Ray had looked at her like he was in a spell. Brianne had blurted words that broke her heart. "What kind of witch is she?"

"She's not a witch," Lyra said. "She's a Bloomthief."

"A what now?" I'd never heard of a Bloomthief.

"She's a Bloomthief. Her father is a witch." Lyra sighed, as if the effort of defining this to me was an inconvenience. "A powerful one."

"Right," I replied. "And her mother was a sorceress. She'd

explained very clearly her pure magic lineage was why she'd make a better Supreme." They'd agreed with her, and that still tasted bitter, even if they'd done it against their will.

"That was the lie her family told to maintain their status." Lydia was holding her sister's hand, clasping it tight like she might lose her. Her tone was sharp, but that little thing was enough to soften my view of her. "Her mother was a succubus."

It was my turn to let my jaw drop. I'd heard the term before, but what I knew couldn't apply here.

"I thought succubuses ... succubus ... succubi? Whatever they are. I thought they just had sex with men." I took a sip of whiskey with my free hand. Gumbo still had the other one on lockdown. "And then killed them?"

"Not exactly," Lyra said. "They do have sex with men, but they don't necessarily kill them. In the oldest of times, yes. They absorbed their souls and sucked out the man's energy during climax."

I shuddered. What a way to go.

"But some of the succubi evolved." Lydia picked up where Lyra had left off. "Their powers developed to a point where they were able to control what, and how much, they ... sucked."

"So Julia—with a succubus mother and a witch father—can absorb other people's powers?" Lyra nodded at me in confirmation. "I bet you were a tasty meal."

Lydia shook her head and rolled her eyes.

"I'm just saying." I plowed forward as if I hadn't just said something really awkward. "You're really powerful."

"I have a question?" Brianne raised her hand like a child afraid to ask her teacher something. I was looking forward to getting an opportunity to chat with her one-on-one. She didn't have powers, not magical ones, so why was Julia controlling her?

Unless it was to use her against me. To make me doubt myself. I took Brianne's opinion very seriously. Julia would want Brianne on her side. No wonder she was always whispering to her.

"Oh! Duh!"

A magical voice warning me not to touch her. A rash that always seemed worse in times of stress. Thinking back, I realized she'd been around when they first flared. She'd shaken my hand or laid a palm on my shoulder.

"Sorry," I said to Brianne. "I just realized she'd absorbed my powers, too. She told you to say I was the rightful Supreme, so you did. She used my ability against me to steal you. You—because you're so important to me."

Brianne crumpled. There was no better word for it. Her chin quivered and her lips trembled. Her eyes spouted tears like a geyser erupting. I was around the table in an instant, holding her close.

"I'm so sorry," she sobbed against my shoulder. "I didn't want to say those things to you. I've felt so horrible the past few weeks. You have no idea."

"I have some idea." I held her tight, thinking of the way I'd cried in my mother's lap in the forest. Thinking of the ways Brianne reminded me of her. How foolish I'd been to believe Brianne would ever hurt me on purpose. "I'm sorry, too. I should have confronted you so we could talk it through instead of hiding with my hurt."

"It wouldn't have mattered," Lauren said. "Julia snuck in every day and made sure we knew our roles." She sniffed and wiped at her damp eyes. "I'm sorry, Simone. I couldn't fight it, not completely, but I could avoid you."

I found tissues for Brianne and shared a sweet but somewhat awkward hug with Lauren.

"Oh, and don't be too hard on Ray." She whispered it into

my ear. I guess we were pretending the Twins didn't have supersonic hearing. "He's been asking about you since you came back. She distracted him, just like the rest of us."

A little ache I'd held in my heart softened. Not only was Lauren rooting for me, but she also seemed okay with the idea of Ray and me. Wonder how she'd respond when she found out about Ethan. When I was ready for that path, I'd talk to her first. But for now, it felt easy to push it aside.

"Oh my, so many tears." Disturbed from his nap when I'd gone to Brianne, Gumbo stretched and yawned. "What did I miss?"

"That Julia is a sneaky little succubus and has it in for me for some reason." I squeezed Bri's hand one last time before returning to my place at the head of the table. "And Brianne was about to ask a question before I interrupted her with my eureka moment."

"Yes, so glad that's out in the open. It's been tiresome." Gumbo didn't bother to feign surprise. "What was your question, Brianne?"

"Why you?" She was sipping water and paused to glance at Lyra. "You're the one she targeted the most. Why?"

Neither of the Twins tended to wear their emotions on their sleeves, but occasionally they seeped out. Like now. I'd never seen a magical being look guilty before. Lyra's lips dropped into a deep frown. A furrow grew between her eyes, which she'd cast to the ground.

Uh-oh. Whatever the answer to Brianne's question, it was going to be hard. Time to pull out my Big Magic Voice™.

"Lyra." She looked up at me, and her frown deepened. "I don't want to force you to tell us. But I will."

"It's okay, Lyra. I can do it." Lauren came to Lyra's rescue, like a perky little superhero. She took a deep breath in. "How well did you know Julia in high school, Simone?"

"Not well at all," I said. "Which is weird, given how much time she spent at our house. She kept to herself around me. Hung out with your crowd."

"Did you ever wonder why your mother looked after her?"

"She told me Julia was family. And that everyone needed a friendly face to come home to." My throat bobbed a little. I shrugged my shoulders.

"She was one of the kindest souls I'd ever known." Gumbo was rubbing his chin against my fingers. "A truly compassionate woman."

"Exactly." I gave his neck a scratch. "Momma looked after everyone. I didn't question her."

"Ethan always said she was real nice to him, too." There wasn't any accusation in Lauren's tone, only kindness. If she wondered why Ethan had spent so much time around my mom, other than his dad being Agatha's attorney, she wasn't going to ask. At least not yet.

"The thing is," she continued, "Julia's mom disappeared not long after she was born. And her dad was not a nice man. He was always on her to behave a certain way."

Lauren leaned forward and dropped her voice, as if Julia might suddenly appear and overhear us talking about her.

"She once told me that he was forcing her to stay close to you and your mother. He said you were a threat to her." She sat upright and lifted one shoulder. "We didn't know what that meant at the time."

"You didn't know you were a witch yet, right?" I asked Lauren.

"I didn't know anything about magic." she replied. "Yet."

When they had been watching the second Rite, Julia was on her knees pleading. The man who stood over her was cruel and demanding. He looked like every stereotypical image of a sorcerer I'd ever seen.

"I'd bet good money Julia knew," I said. "And the odds are strong he wanted her to become Supreme."

Poor Julia. I'd seen the pain on her face as that man towered over and berated her. Deep down, I had to wonder if she even wanted to be Supreme. She was borrowing everyone else's abilities and manipulating everyone around her. To please him, no doubt.

What had she faced in the mirror beneath the lake? She'd seemed to come out of it unscathed, while I'd been unceremoniously dumped on the shore like a swamp rat.

"She knew," Lyra said, breaking me from my thoughts. "She found out when she turned eighteen."

My breath froze. Julia turned eighteen around the same time I did. Around the same time my mother died.

And Julia had disappeared, not even making it to her funeral.

"Did she skip town to escape her fate?" My voice was shaky. I'd asked the question, but I didn't want to know the answer.

"Sort of." If I'd been nervous when Lyra started talking, the fact that she got up from the table and came over to me was terrifying. She sat in Gumbo's vacant chair and took one of my hands.

I wanted to stop her. I could use my voice and keep whatever she was about to tell me from destroying what I knew. I never had to hear it.

The desire to run came over me so suddenly I almost let it happen. And a week ago, I would have. Before the trials. But now ...

"Tell me," I said. "It's okay. I can take it."

"Julia confessed to her father that she felt guilty. Your mom was so kind to her, so accepting. And behind her back, Julia was sharing all your family secrets." What secrets? We didn't have secrets growing up. Did we? "She told him she wouldn't do it anymore."

A single tear trailed down her cheek. It glittered like a diamond.

"He did not take it well, Simone. Julia was terrified. She ran to your mom and begged her for help. Your mom had a friend in New Orleans who could take her in. They were on North Bridge when Julia's dad discovered she was running away."

I held up a hand. I didn't want to hear the rest.

"I always wondered why she was going to New Orleans that day. Agatha just said a business matter." Gumbo inched closer to me, pressing his head to my heart as if he could remove the ache. "She was helping Julia escape? Protecting her?"

Lyra's nod almost broke me. I squeezed my eyes as tightly shut as I could manage. Was this better? Was it better that I'd stayed and faced the horrible rather than run away? Maybe tomorrow it would feel that way.

"Simone?" I opened my eyes to meet Brianne's across the table.

"I'm okay," I told her. "I'll be okay." My throat was tight. Fresh nausea rolled in my stomach.

I needed to stand up. To move and let all the tension dissolve away. But it wasn't finished, so I forced myself to remain in my posh new chair and accept the rest of the bad news.

"That still doesn't explain why she targeted you, Lyra."

"She didn't target me, Simone. I let her borrow my power." Lyra sighed. The scent of fresh lilacs floated through the air. "After your mother died, Julia and her father were invited to our realm. Julia and I have been friends ever since. Close friends, until recently."

I did stand up. I was cold all over. I roamed the room as if I'd never seen it before.

"A few months ago, when Agatha told us she was moving on, Julia convinced me it was time to maneuver her into the position of Supreme. She wasn't strong enough to do it on her own. She'd need my power." Lyra had never sounded so human before. "We didn't know about the change in the will, but Julia insisted it didn't matter."

Agatha had come to see me the day she died, and Ethan had told me the will was changed at the last minute. None of them saw me coming.

"Once the plan was in place, Julia insisted we go through with it. Even after you were announced as Supreme."

They were helping a friend. One they'd known for thirty years. I could understand that, maybe, when my emotions settled. I'd known Lyra and Lydia were against me from the beginning. This was not news. Particularly if Julia had spent the last thirty years in their realm, I could see why they would want her to take the position instead of me.

I could even find sympathy for Julia. A frightened girl trying to escape a controlling father. I'd treated many patients with a similar, if less magical story. Being a human in a fae realm must have been difficult. I could empathize with feeling out of place. Particularly since she didn't escape her father.

Which is where I kept getting stuck.

"Why were they both invited to your realm?" I was shouting. I couldn't stop my voice from rising, or the way something horrible and dark rose with it. "Julia I get, but why her dad? Why escape Treater's Way? Unless—"

I choked on a sob. Something ugly was sprouting inside of me. A horrible thought I couldn't suppress. I couldn't breathe. I couldn't stop my feet from moving. Lydia crossed the room, placing one hand on her sister's shoulder.

"He was chasing after them, Simone. Hurling magic and whatever else he could to stop them from leaving Treater's Way."

She stopped my pacing, planting her hands on my shoulders, forcing me to face her. There was so much kindness in her eyes. Sympathy I never expected.

I would have preferred her insults.

"They couldn't prove he caused the accident on purpose. But authorities ..."

A horrible pounding rushed through my ears. Pressure pulled at them, narrowing my vision.

All this time. All the effort I'd put forth. The pain of the trials.

Meanwhile, they'd been working against me. Out of loyalty to the family who took my mother away from me.

She was still talking. I couldn't hear her.

There were only the sounds of my heart beating and my breath stuttering, echoing in my head in strange unison, singing a song of disbelief.

Her lips moved. I think she said my name.

They'd chosen to help her while I struggled. To support Julia out of loyalty.

The room was swaying. The skylight faded from view.

They'd given her everything she lacked so she could beat me. Even as I proved myself.

I was going to pass out. There was no avoiding it. I was almost empty.

And I was pissed.

"That's it. Nobody gets in or goes out."

Patches of red swarmed around my vision. Heat engulfed my neck and cheeks.

"The Magnolia is closed."

CHAPTER
THIRTY-FOUR

*The chains of magic can bind, but the bonds of family can shatter
even the strongest link.*

That phrase repeated itself in my dreams.

I flitted in and out of consciousness for who knows how long. I only woke fully because my stomach would no longer let me sleep. I didn't know when I'd last eaten. Or drank water.

My eyes were crusted over. My nose was rubbed raw. My mouth was dry.

Everything hurt. My trek through the forest—though I'd likely never know how much was real and how much was perceived—had worn my body down to its thinnest threads. The revelations after had done the same to my wounded heart.

My chest ached. My mind was struggling to grasp so much new information. I was trying to process it logically.

No wonder I'd passed out. That much stimulation was enough to overwhelm anyone.

Then, in the wake of the news, I'd closed the Magnolia.

251

It had been a gut reaction at the time. A default instinct I didn't have the effort to question. My Big Magic Voice™ had taken over and made decisions while I flailed. Maybe that was a sign of growth. Maybe it was the proof I needed that my power and I had finally linked.

Now that I'd slept a while, I saw the choice for what it was. I hadn't done it out of spite. I'd done it to *protect* the Magnolia. I didn't have to try and access my magic. It was just ... there. And I'd used it to keep us safe while I sorted things out.

The chains of magic can bind, but the bonds of family can shatter even the strongest link.

It sure could. But there was no way I was going to let anything shatter the links I'd built here.

Here I was, cozy in my bed with no recollection of how I'd gotten here. A soft, cool breeze played with the curtains near my open window. The satin of my pajamas was smooth against my weathered skin.

And the mouthwatering scent of bacon filled the room.

I sat bolt upright. Bacon! And coffee. No wonder my stomach growled.

Voices rose from outside the hall. A clink of a plate. The sound of laughter. I slid out of bed and headed towards the kitchen.

"Good morning, sleepyhead!" Brianne handed me a cup of coffee as soon as I cleared the hallway, as if she'd known I was coming. "Did you sleep well?"

"Uh, I don't know?" I followed her in a daze toward the living room. Blankets and pillows cluttered the usually cozy space. Lyra and Lydia were huddled together on the couch in pajamas that matched mine.

They looked up from the book they shared to greet me. Lyra

offered a smile I could only describe as sheepish. Lydia barely raised an eyebrow before returning to the page. Lyra whispered something, and Lydia nodded.

"Breakfast is ready." I peered into the kitchen, where Lauren was bent over the stove, removing a sheet pan. Bacon.

"Breakfast of champions today, Simone." Brianne giggled as she cut slices of the lemon cake I'd made with House a few days earlier. She separated the slices onto plates, adding spoonfuls of fruit.

I watched in a daze as she carried them to the breakfast area. My cute little table that barely sat four was now comfortably able to accommodate six. I tried to math in my head. Failed. Counted on my fingers.

The four division heads. Brianne. Who was I missing?

Something brushed against my leg. I about jumped out of my skin.

"Good morning, Simone." Gumbo lifted to his hind legs and widened his eyes. "I can haz cream?"

"I've got you over here, furball." Brianne set a bowl of cream on the table. Gumbo, in a bow the same sapphire blue as our pajamas, hopped into a seat.

I was dreaming. I had to be dreaming. Or I'd slipped into the third trial without realizing it. There was no better explanation for this bizarro slumber party. I pinched myself. Why the heck did I think that would work? Now, I was dreaming and my arm hurt.

"You joining us?" Brianne patted the chair beside her.

"Why not?" I said. Why not, indeed. Whatever surreal event was happening, I may as well have bacon.

"This cake is amazing, Simone." Lauren slid her fork out of her mouth with exaggerated slowness. "I need the recipe."

"I found it on Pinterest." I stared at my plate. "House helped me bake it. Actually, House, could I get some water?"

"I'm sure you're thirsty." Lydia shook her head as a glass of ice water formed in my hand. "You've been sawing logs for days."

"Stop it." Brianne batted at her playfully. "She doesn't snore."

"Someone does." Lyra spoke through a mouthful of berries. "Kept me up all night."

"I believe that was me." Gumbo licked a paw, his nails bright blue, and ran it along his ear. Cream dripped from his whiskers. "I haven't slept that well in ages. Your bed is quite comfy, Simone."

"Am I on it right now?" They all stopped eating and chatting and looked at me. "I mean, am I on my bed? Asleep? Did I die?"

Lauren was the first. She snorted. Just a small one punctuated by the silence. She clamped her hand over her mouth to hold it in. And failed. Brianne's joyful giggles came next. Within minutes, the table was laughing. At me. Even Gumbo was making a sound that was something between a meow and a guffaw.

I could go another million years without ever hearing a cat laugh again.

"So I'm not asleep." I let them laugh while I ate cake and drank coffee and inhaled bacon. "Whenever you're ready to tell me what's happening I'm listening."

Despite days of rest, I didn't feel rested. And while matching pajamas and that sense of camaraderie were nice, I was back on the outside looking in. Or so I thought.

"Simone, honey. You're awake." Brianne squeezed my hand. "We're just a little punch drunk. Cabin fever, I suppose."

"Why would you have cabin fever?" I glanced out the window. Had I left us beyond time and space? No. The garden was there, lush and green. Doug was bent low, plucking at a weed. Somehow, he saw me staring and lifted his hand in a wave. "Put sunscreen on, Doug. Your neck is beet red."

Doug nodded and pulled a small bottle out of his pocket. He applied it to his neck.

"You've gotten quite good at accessing your magic, Simone." Gumbo hopped on the table, maneuvering around the plates and utensils to find his favorite spot between my arms. I pushed the cake out of the way and welcomed him in.

"Is that what happened?"

"You've been doing it for two damn days. Making us wear stupid pajamas. Commanding us to build a blanket fort." Lydia sounded annoyed, but her eyes were alight with something close to amusement. "You've been a right boss ever since you locked us in here, shut down the Magnolia, and jeopardized our thriving businesses."

"Nonsense. We will be fine once the doors open." Brianne tsked at Lydia. She smiled at me with the warm and encouraging smile I was used to from her. "But the badass boss part is true. Gumbo's right, you've connected to your magic in a big way."

Try as I might, I couldn't remember much more than sleeping the past few days. But I'd somehow managed to forbid us all from leaving. What could I have said that held so much power?

Oh. Right. *No one gets in or out. The Magnolia is closed.*

I hadn't meant to trap us in the house. Not technically. Poor Brianne. That meant she hadn't seen her family in two days. Yet here she was, defending me despite my behavior.

"Whoopsie doopsie." I lifted my shoulders to my ears and grimaced. "My bad. You're all free to come and go as you choose. But the Magnolia will not be open for business until the trials are complete."

I only had to mention the trials to bring it all back. The part

Julia and her father had played in my mother's death. The undermining and betrayal the Twins had participated in. Even Lauren avoiding me felt a little like cowardice.

Fresh tears filled my eyes. Considering how dehydrated I was, I was surprised I had any left. I was even more surprised when not one of them got up from the table.

"We're here," Lauren said. "And all our secrets have come out. We may as well get on the same page before the third Rite."

"I helped Julia out of displaced loyalty." Lyra sniffed, taking a napkin to her nose. "She took everything I gave her, then came back for more. She didn't care how much it was hurting me."

"*You* did, Simone. You cared." Lydia linked hands with her sister. "I thought you were self-absorbed and weak when you first got here."

"Gee, thanks," I muttered.

"Every time I pointed out one of your mistakes, you'd figure out a way to fix it." Lydia tucked a strand of her lavender locks behind one ear and fidgeted. "I was comparing your magic, which you'd just discovered, to Julia's, which she'd known about for thirty years."

"Hardly fair, is it?" Her head whipped towards me at the harshness in my voice. "You knew more about me than I knew about anything. You all did. And you used that information to form opinions of me."

"To be fair, Brianne didn't." I turned to Lauren. "I filled her in when Julia arrived."

"I didn't know what to think." Brianne's chin trembled. She paused and collected herself. "That vortex thing? It felt like poison to me. Then Julia came through and fixed it with a wave of her hands. I started to believe that maybe the Twins were on to something."

"Except she didn't fix the vortex." Gumbo, who I'd thought was asleep, opened one eye. "She stole Simone's powers and used them against her. I'd have thought that was obvious by now."

He closed his eyes. Seconds later, he was snoring softly, his head resting on my hand. My hand, which had developed a rash when Julia arrived. She'd put on a show, that was for sure. But the magic had come from me.

"Well." I tapped my coffee cup. House refilled it. I freaking loved House. "I guess we've all learned a lesson about letting others steal, or borrow, our magic."

The table was silent again. I started to stack dishes, just to keep my hands busy. No one was leaving, and I wasn't completely sure why. It's as if we were waiting for something to happen.

"Why a slumber party?" Lauren's question jolted me from my thoughts. She handed me a napkin to wipe up fresh coffee. "I was curious why you forced us all into a slumber party. Not that it wasn't fun. But, you know, it's kind of weird."

"It makes total sense to me." I left them all hanging while I cleared the table. Could House have done it? Sure. But House hated cleaning as much as I did. And I'd clearly created extra work for it over the past two days.

I was going to be scrubbing toilets for months.

I wiped the table down, clearing it of crumbs, then returned to my chair.

"For the past few weeks, I've been reliving my high school experience. My emotions and my power were behaving like a hormonal teen. I've felt awkward and like an outcast. And all the prettiest and coolest girls in school were either ignoring me or bullying me." I paused to gesture around the table. I'm not gonna lie, the blush that crept up Lyra's neck was super gratifying.

"I've alternated between these two extremes. Either I wanted to do everything on my own or there was no way I could do it alone. But neither one really fit. Before she moved on, Agatha said something that's really stuck.

"The chains of magic can bind, but the bonds of family can shatter even the strongest link."

I gestured around the table again.

"I'm beginning to see what she meant. We were all bound by magic, in different ways. And the past had a really strong hold on us. On all of us." Lyra nodded softly. "But the bond we could create as a new family? That seems, I don't know, crazy strong."

"I don't get it," Lydia said.

"I used to love sleepovers in high school." Lauren patted Lydia's hand. "We'd giggle about our crushes. Complain about teachers. Bitch about our parents."

"I remember laughing until I couldn't breathe at my first sleepover." Brianne chuckled at the memory. "And trying to stay up all night so no one could put my bra in the freezer."

"If anyone tried to put my bra in the freezer I'd rip them in half."

"It was harmless fun. Junk food and lighthearted pranks." I shuddered at Lyra's threat. "I mean, I think it was. I never went to one. I was kind of a loner. Julia didn't like me. Ethan and I pretended we weren't friends so we didn't upset anyone. I was a bookworm. Most of the time, it was me and my mom."

Both Lyra and Lauren dipped their heads. Lydia was chewing on her lip so hard it was turning purple. But I didn't want their pity. If the trials had taught me anything, it was that holding onto the past was more painful than facing it and letting it go.

"I was half out-of-it when I locked us in here." I continued. "My best guess is that my subconscious needed a connection.

And my teen brain decided to use a slumber party as a team building exercise. Because I will continue the trials, and I plan to remain Supreme of the Magnolia.

"I can do it with or without the support of my coven." They lifted their heads to face me. I didn't blame them. My Big Magic Voice™ was back. "But, if I get to choose, I'd prefer it with."

I took Brianne's hand in mine on one side, and Lauren's on the other. One by one, like a wave of connection, we clasped hands around the table. Blue sparks of light flickered between us, zapping the air like powerful bolts of lightning. The electricity behind it made my teeth tingle. Lyra's hair floated around her.

This time, we all laughed together.

"Okay." Lydia was the first to release hands. She looked at me. "Let's do this."

"Do what?" I asked.

"Sleepover stuff. Tell us all about yourself, Simone." She smiled. A broad smile that lifted her cheeks. "Tell us everything."

And I did. I told them about growing up in Treater's Way and why I left. Lauren interjected, but I didn't let her hold any blame when I explained the hex I'd placed on myself. I offered them every mistake I made, and what I'd done to repair those since.

They hadn't gotten to meet Gabe, but they would. Without fear of judgment, I told them how badly I'd screwed up. And how cool he was when I apologized.

And more. We talked about the trials. I described each of them. What I'd seen and how they made me feel. And how I'd gotten through them. I laid out in detail the plans I had for the Therapy Division. I showed Brianne how I'd restructured my appointments, and she offered notes.

We all laughed until we couldn't breathe. We shared secrets and goals.

We talked all night.

Just before dawn, Gumbo extracted himself from my embrace and sauntered to the center of the table. He sat tall, wrapping his tail around his body. His bow disappeared.

"Simone." The regal cat scanned me with his green eye, then his gold.

"Mystical Protector." I gave him a mock bow from my seat.

"It's time for the third Rite."

THIRTY-FIVE

J ulia, Gumbo, and I stood at the front gate to the Magnolia. Gumbo had already done his figure eight weaving thing. Unlike the other night, no crowd was gathered. Our witnesses were tucked away, presumably in the conference room to watch from their magic screen.

No one from town was peering at us from across the street or peeking out of windows. Was it because of the early hour or something else? Whatever the reason, the perception that it was just the three of us, alone, was hard to shake.

The moon was still visible high overhead in the early light of dawn. Morning dew began to burn off the ground, creating a fog around the house that felt both magical and a little eerie. The porch steps were buried beneath it. The house itself was completely dark.

Standing in front of the Magnolia, I couldn't help but feel as if I'd been transported back to the first day I stepped through this gate. Brianne was waiting by the front door to greet me. At the time, she was the lone shining star in an otherwise dim sky.

Now, the house welcomed you. Fresh paint, properly fastened shutters, and a proper sign made a huge difference. Doug's efforts with the lawn and gardens cultivated lush grounds that screamed of growth and harvest.

This wasn't just a professional building, this was a space with warmth and comfort. It beckoned with open arms.

I'd hesitated that first day. Now, months later, my changes were equally as dramatic. Both the house and I had evolved. Together. While my days were kept busy, my evenings were spent alone inside.

But I'd never been alone. Not really. Because I could feel the house all around me.

Except now. The front gate opened to usher us forward, and I couldn't feel it. My magic was more powerful than ever. But my connection to the presence I always sensed inside the Magnolia had been severed.

It was like missing a piece of myself.

"Is this part of the trial?" We'd been waiting in silence for Gumbo to describe the third Rite, and my question punctuated the quiet surrounding us. Why did it feel so isolated on a busy street in Treater's Way?

"Is what part of the trial?" Gumbo tilted his ear up, as if to hear me better.

"I can't feel House." Julia's head snapped towards me. Surprise cast a shadow in her eyes. If I hadn't been looking, I might have missed it. She replaced it with an expression of boredom so quickly I had to admire it. I could never be that cool with my emotions. "Can you?"

"Of course I can." Julia laced her tone with disdain, as if the mere effort of answering me was beneath her. It wasn't having the effect she'd hoped for. I knew she wore a mask now.

Julia had lost access to Lyra. While I might carry some guilt about taking a friend from her, I didn't care one lick that she hadn't been able to absorb fae magic. And now that I knew just how entwined our pasts were, her bravado didn't faze me. As much.

But none of that meant she couldn't connect to House. Could a Bloomthief absorb inanimate power? If so, and she was able to reach into the very source of the Magnolia, I was in trouble. My lack of connection could mean she'd taken control.

"It's time for the Chains of Devotion. The third trial is ready to begin." Gumbo left his station between us and climbed the steps to the front door. He sat with his back to the house, facing us. It might have been my imagination, but he seemed taller. The doorknob should have been at least a foot above him. Instead, it was barely visible behind his head.

"When the moon is half-lit, it reminds us that no power stands alone." His voice travelled to us. My legs propelled me forward. "The rightful Supreme is not a whole. She is one-half of a sacred link."

We were directly in front of Gumbo.

"In this trial, she who is willing to set aside herself for the greater good must forge a bond with the heart of the Magnolia. No spell may aid her. No charm may shield her. In the silence of separation, her devotion must speak louder than magic."

The silence of separation. So, I was disconnected from the house. Relief flooded through me. And yet ...

I missed my house.

"Only in surrender can true connection form." Gumbo stepped to the side. "You will perform this trial together."

Julia flashed me a triumphant grin. She'd taken time to apply the perfect red lipstick, and I kind of hated her for it. Finding the right shade of red for me took a herculean effort. They were either too pink or too dark. I either looked like a clown or a child putting on her mother's makeup.

Not that I'd bothered to apply makeup this morning. Julia

was lucky I'd brushed my teeth. I was still wearing my pajamas. And fuzzy socks with slide-on sandals.

Lord help me if there was a forest inside. Or a red carpet.

"Before we enter, I want to say something." Julia turned to
me and crossed her arms. This was the same queen bee
behavior she'd shown when she first arrived. Good thing I
wasn't in high school anymore. "You will not touch me or
absorb my magic. Nor anyone, or anything else's. Are we
clear?"

I'd hoped for it to make more of an impact. But my Big
Magic Voice™ didn't come through. I cleared my throat to try
again.

"Simone?" I looked down at Gumbo. "No spell may aid her.
No charm may shield her." At my blank look, Gumbo sighed.
"She can't use magic in there. Neither of you can."

I couldn't access my power. I rubbed at my heart, where a
slow ache was forming. I'd put in all this effort to embrace my
inner witch and learn how to wield it, only to have it stripped
away? What the hell, man?

"In the silence of separation, her devotion must speak
louder than magic." Gumbo repeated the last sentence with his
eyes directly on me.

"Got it," I said. I didn't, not totally. But I would figure it out
as I went along.

Julia and I both reached for the doorknob. Even if she was
disconnected—and I wasn't positive that was true—I didn't
want her touching me. Plus, I'm a Southern girl. I gestured her
forward. No sooner had we both crossed the threshold than
the door slammed behind us.

White light lined the cracked edges between the door and
its frame. So bright I had to shield my eyes, it shot out in rays.
One-by-one, the rays disappeared. The door sealed itself shut,
then faded into the walls.

We were locked inside the Magnolia. Except it *wasn't* the Magnolia.

Not the one I knew. The space was wide and empty, with dirt floors and unadorned walls. Our four division doors were gone, as was the breakroom. Brianne's office area was nowhere to be found.

We were inside a box. Or perhaps a cave, as the walls seeped moisture and reeked of mildew.

Julia stepped towards the center. I followed at a distance. Light crept in from cracks along the foundation, saving us from being completely in the dark. After a few moments, our eyes adjusted.

"I wonder where we go." We were in a large empty space, but there was no echo. My voice was absorbed by the darkness. "Oh, that's weird."

"What's weird?" Julia had wandered to the left, touching a finger to the walls. She wiped it on her pants with a grimace.

"How our voices sound." I twirled a finger in the air as she approached. "We sound muffled. I wonder if we're underground."

I craned my neck to take in the ceiling. In the Magnolia, there was a balcony high above. While I'd assumed it was connected to my living space, I'd yet to find how to access it. Now, only darkness swirled above us. There was no telling how high it was, or how far below we were.

"How did you know?" I could feel Julia's stare on me. I didn't answer. "How did you know I was a Bloomthief?"

"We're doing this now?" There was so much nothing around us. It left me uneasy. I wasn't sure I was ready for a confrontation with Julia just yet. I hadn't had enough time to figure out what I wanted to say—or how to say it. Being careful with my words seemed more important than ever.

"We may as well talk now, Simone." Julia was wearing

perfume. The subtle waft of roses as she moved closer irritated my eyes.

She was trying to use her height against me. Her put-together demeanor. Okay, then.

"Lyra told me. Or Lauren. I can't remember which." I had the gratification of seeing her lips firm. "We had a coven meeting. In the form of a slumber party. You weren't invited."

I couldn't resist adding that last bit, even if it did make me sound like a petty beyotch. I swallowed the lump forming in my throat. There was more I wanted to say. She'd taken the most important person in my life away.

Granted, it wasn't her fault. Not exactly. And maybe, with more time and when I was in a better space, I might understand her choices.

But she was close. And the closest one I could blame.

I wanted to level her with my words, power or not. Here was Julia, perfectly coiffed and pretending to be the big cheese, when I was the one with the real powers. Her father had caused my mother's death, which she knew, yet she'd shown me zero compassion.

Even when it was just the two of us, with no one around, she still played a role. It made me want to strip it on her behalf. To cut her down to size. Magic or no, she had no right to behave as if I was a bug on her shoe. Especially not now.

So what was holding me back from ripping her a new one?

"What else do you know?" Was that actual fear laced in her question? It was too dark to make out her expression, though she was only a few feet from me.

"Everything. I think." I didn't have it in me to recap what I'd learned. Maybe that was what kept me from screaming at her. Or maybe, at my heart, I was just a good Southern girl who couldn't be impolite, even when someone deserved it. "Is there anything you'd like to say to me?"

I don't know what I expected from her. She'd worn arrogance like a cape since she came back to Treater's Way. She'd manipulated and connived her way into my world and was angling for a position of immense power and responsibility. One she hadn't earned. One she wasn't capable of handling.

A stray glimmer of light caught her face, reflecting off the well of tears she'd held in check. The anger threatening to choke hold me faded.

Damn.

Was I such a wimp that just the idea of her crying killed my resolve? Who knew what she'd been doing in the fae realm. She could have thirty years of acting lessons under her belt.

"I want you to know something, Simone." In the darkness, she reached for my hand. I staggered backwards. She held her palms in front of me, a gesture of surrender. "Please. I promise I'm not up to anything."

I didn't trust her. Not one bit. But I wasn't sure she *could* be up to anything, even if she wanted to. She extended her hand again but didn't walk forward.

It was time for me to play my favorite game: what would I tell a patient in this situation?

I'd encourage them to be curious. To wonder why the act of touch was so important to someone like Julia. To question whether it was because of what she gained from it—what she took from others. Or, perhaps, it was the only way she knew how to communicate: through transactions.

When someone has manipulated their friends and spent their lives under the thumb of a controlling, angry man, something as simple as a friendly handshake may well soothe her nervous system.

And that was the doggone part I kept going back to. That flash of video I'd seen of her during the second trial, begging at her father's unforgiving feet. Lyra hadn't mentioned Julia's father beyond their entry into the realm. Was he still alive? Had he made her suffer for trying to run away?

I'd faced many a demon over the past week. I'd looked in the eye of the best and worst versions of myself and questioned my insecurities. I'd bared myself before the past I'd longed for and impossible futures. I'd met headfirst betrayals I didn't know were possible and unearthed the grief that poisoned every choice I made.

She may not have won the trials, but she'd gone through her own. In front of me wasn't a superstar diva or the cousin who ignored me growing up. It was just a woman, just like me, with her own trauma. Her own choices. Playing pretend because she didn't know how to be real.

Confronted with her past, though, was a reality begging to come to the surface.

At the end of the day, it didn't matter what extending some kindness did for her. It was about me. What would put me at ease? What choices would I make to move forward?

Making her feel small wouldn't do that. That need to cut her down to size didn't come from present Simone. Past Simone wanted to be petty.

I just wanted her to go away. More than that, I wanted her to go away without me feeling like crap for sending her off. I was a caretaker. Always had been. Always would be.

I was my mother's daughter, after all. My mother, who'd known exactly who Julia was all along, and still welcomed her into our house.

"What do you want me to know, Julia?" I took her hand, holding still when she wrapped it in both of hers. She stepped closer.

"There hasn't been a day, not a single one in thirty years, when I haven't woken up with shame over what happened to your mother." She chewed on her lip, still trying to control her emotions. In my professional opinion, Julia had a lot of work to do. "She was a wonderful woman, she was always kind to me, and I want you to know that her death broke my heart, too."

She brought my hand to her lips. There was no heat. No instant rash or sudden itching. It was just a woman in pain seeking absolution.

I knew that pain. I knew what carrying guilt did to your body. To your spirit.

And I knew how a single choice could rip out your insides and cause you to question everything you thought you knew about yourself. I'd been given a second chance by Gabe.

A sigh buried deep within my chest rushed out, deflating me. Julia wasn't getting a second chance from me. But I wasn't going to be the one to push the knife in deeper either.

"I've only had a few days to process everything, Julia. I don't know how I feel about it. We're not friends, not that you were asking. We're never going to be friends, and I'm going to fight you in every way the Magnolia asks to remain Supreme." I extracted my hand, softly. "But I don't need to cause you pain in order to heal myself."

She squeezed her fists to her eyes, breathing in sharp through her nose. I caught her nod in the dim light.

"I'll take it."

Tension I hadn't realized I'd held onto drained. I'd never been a huge fan of confrontation. I could do it—if I had to. I wasn't sure there was any benefit to a deep, honest discussion with Julia. Besides, we had a trial to complete.

I think.

Time passed. There was no test. No magic. No sound.

It was too silent in the house. If we were even still in the house. She would occasionally sniff. I'd clear my throat. An unseen drop of water landed in an also unseen puddle.

But nothing was happening.

Just two enemies, standing side-by-side.
In really awkward silence.

THIRTY-SIX

"So!" I clapped my hands, wincing as the sound landed, flat and harsh. "The trials, huh? Doozies, amiright?"

We'd gone at least an hour without speaking, maybe more. I was getting antsy. And a little bored.

"Yeah." I didn't need to see her face to know if she was rolling her eyes. Still, she shuddered. "Wonder what we do here."

"Wish I knew." I scanned the darkness, rubbing my arms. It wasn't cold, not exactly. Just damp.

I wandered to the side and walked along the edges, snapping my fingers and clapping my hands. I tapped the walls in case one of them was false. I looked for stairs or doors or keys under rocks.

The silence was profound. Creepy. Overwhelming.

I hated this. I hated being disconnected from the Magnolia. I hated how quiet and still everything was. I hated that I didn't know what to do or how to win. I hated that I didn't know where everyone else was.

Most of all, I hated that all of this was happening around

someone who made me so uncomfortable. Julia was standing in the center. Waiting, I guess. Just hanging there in case something happened. Not even trying to figure anything out.

I began to hum a song. Our high school fight song. Julia sighed.

"Must you make so much noise?"

"It's better than what you're doing." I clucked my tongue, just to hear the sound. All this nothing was putting me on edge. "Why are you still here, anyway? You failed the first two trials. Your truth is out. Go home, already."

"I made a promise." Julia sat down. On the dirty floor. Those designer pants of hers must be stainproof. "To see it through."

"Who'd you promise?" My curiosity piqued, I met her in the middle and sat opposite her. The stone was cold against my bare legs. Next time I had a slumber party, we were wearing long pants. Just in case.

She didn't answer right away, leaving me to stew in the random thoughts that would not shut up.

"My mother."

Oof. I knew that tone. I knew what grief sounded like.

"I'm sorry," I said. And I meant it. I'd learned so much about her father, but never heard her mother mentioned. "When did you lose her?"

"I was ten. She was sick." Her response was terse and telling. She didn't want to talk about it.

Despite that, I couldn't help but imagine a ten-year-old girl, losing her mother, making such an epic promise. What a heavy weight that must have been to carry. How much of her father's demands were based in his own grief?

The more I poked beneath Julia's perfect facade, the more I understood how her path led her here. But that didn't mean I would step aside and let her steal something I loved for her own selfish benefit. Not when the Magnolia, the coven, and I had plans.

"Can I ask you a question?"

She took another moment then answered with a sigh.

"Go ahead."

"What does Julia want?" I uncrossed my legs and repositioned. My body was not made for hard surfaces. "Do you even want to be Supreme?"

"Right now? I just want you to shut up." Agitation dripped like honey from her words. "Can't you be quiet?"

"Why is silence so important to you?" I was using my therapist voice, partly because her sadness had touched me. But mostly because it annoyed her. "Does my question scare you?"

Another moment. Another long sigh.

"No, Simone." I didn't like the way she said my name, like it was a cuss word. "Silence is important to me because it's part of the trial. Duh."

Okay, so we weren't going to talk. So much for compassion.

"Fine. No more talking." She had a good point—one I was a little aggravated I hadn't picked up on myself. Gumbo had literally told me to be quiet, hadn't he?

In the silence of separation, her devotion must speak louder than magic. Only in surrender can true connection form.

All the stuff that was bothering me was part of the trial. Here I was waiting for it to start, and I'd been in it the whole time. The house wanted my silence. It wanted my stillness. It wanted me to trust it.

I could do that. Probably.

I adjusted again and arched my back. Couldn't I do that in a recliner?! I closed my eyes and touched my fingers to my thumbs creating one of those yoga-looking poses. Maybe I needed to meditate.

Like I'd ever made it more than ten seconds. Or one.

What do you need from me, House? How do I prove my devotion?

No response.

I opened one eye, hoping for a sign. Maybe it was written on the walls again. We were still in the house. Even if I couldn't feel it, it had to be here.

Right?

What had I been fighting for if not connection? We'd had it from the moment I stepped foot on the property. Sure, it wavered a few times, but what good connection didn't? We baked cakes together. We'd redecorated.

House kept me warm at night. It kept me cool during the day.

The Magnolia gave me clothes when I arrived with none.

Even when I was young, I had a connection to House. It made me a Bayou Bliss every day after school and gave me blueberry muffins every morning for my runs with Ethan.

No wonder I hated this emptiness so much. A piece of me was missing.

"I've felt this once before, you know." Silence may be what the trial required, but I was an external processor.

"I don't know what you're talking about." Julia stood and stretched her arms high overhead. She had to be bored, too. "But that's not going to stop you from telling me."

"This feeling of being half of something. Of missing something." I tried to do the same, found my legs were basically bitchy noodles, and extended them instead to wiggle my toes. "I felt it when you came through the vortex thingy."

"What did you do when you felt it?" She asked.

"I fought back." I tilted my head to look up at her, leaning back to rest on my palms. "It felt like having part of me sucked out. I ... sucked it back in."

No one would ever accuse me of being eloquent.

"That's what caused it, then." I didn't like the way Julia hovered over me, or that I'd solved a mystery for her that I didn't even know about it.

"Caused what?" Deal with it, legs, we're doing this. I stood up, trying to be subtle as I shook the pins and needles out of my toes.

"The vortex *thingy*." She flicked her hair behind one shoulder. "I should have been able to enter the realm, reestablish my bond with House, and claim my right as Supreme. But you pulled it away from me."

"Re-establish? What do you mean?" I'd forgotten how tall she was. Even when I stood on my toes, she still hovered. I took a few steps backwards to give myself the illusion we were the same height. All this quiet and darkness was messing with me.

"House and I bonded once. Right after my mom died." She said it softly, her eyes wistful. "It consoled me."

"Yeah, it does that. I still don't understand it completely, but I know it's always been around when I needed it most." I hobbled to the wall for support, putting my back against it. "It's got big mother energy. At least that's what my son called it."

"Your son?" Something was shifting in the air. I couldn't put my finger on what it was. Even though she was only a few feet from me, she felt miles away. Her voice was faint.

"My son Gabe. The one you saw me with at Gino's." The conversation was happening, despite the sensation I was disconnected from it. Like I'd floated outside my body and was observing myself talking to Julia. "He said it had a big mother energy that matched mine."

"The house's energy matches yours?" Julia was staring at the spot on the wall where I'd stood moments earlier. But I wasn't standing there anymore. I was floating above her. "Do you mean you and the house are the same?

"Well, House isn't as clumsy as I am." I'd meant the statement as a self-deprecating joke. But I was soaring through an infinite sky, and I was grace incarnate. It didn't seem clumsy.

This was weird. Nothing had changed. I hadn't had any sudden realizations or done anything that might be considered surrendering. I'd broken the silence every moment I could.

So why was I up here and Julia down there? Was I being sent away?

No. This was not like leaving. This was coming home. And yet ... I'd always been here.

My fingers gripped onto something hard and cool. A wooden banister. I wrapped my hands around it as my feet landed on the floor.

I was on the balcony at the Magnolia. The one I'd never been able to reach before. Below me was still a cave, where Julia talked to a stone wall. Surrounding me were comfortable furnishings and a small lamp centered on a round metal table. I turned it on.

The space was small and angled, with walls that led to a steep point high above me. A triangular stained-glass window cast rainbows of light throughout the room. A plush reading chair in royal purple sat next to a narrow bookshelf. Only enough to hold three books wide and as many high. I sunk into the chair, resting my feet on the matching ottoman, to get a better look at the weathered spines on the shelf.

Not that I needed a better look. I already knew what they were. I knew that deep green leather binding. I recognized the lettering.

The Magnolia Codex, Volumes One through Nine.

So, there were nine volumes. Huh. My fingers ran along them, reading each title aloud.

"*Volume One: The Blooming Root.* Origins and branches of the Magnolia family tree." My heart hammered in my chest.

Were the answers to my family in that book? More about my father?

"*Volume Two: The Rites of Bloom.*" Well, I knew that one already.

"*Volume Three: On Magic and Manifestation.*" I wanted to stop there. Oh, to have all the time in the world to sit and read. The answers to so many of my questions were in these volumes. The temptation to freeze the clock while I had a good read was overwhelming.

Time, like magic, must remain in motion.

It was a tenet of the trials. If I stopped time now, even if I was able to, I'd be violating the rules of the Rites. Seemed like a bad idea.

When I reached volume four, my finger hovered over the title. My hands shook. Time remained in motion, but not for me.

"*Volume Four: The Devoted Heart.*"

I pulled the book from the shelf and held it against my heart like a shield.

She who is willing to set aside herself for the greater good must forge a bond with the heart of the Magnolia.

My breath was ragged. A sliver of hope latched onto me. Was the answer in here? I opened the book to the first page. Like the Rites, the words floated to the surface in a difficult to read script.

The House does not open for command.
It listens to commitment.
She who would bind herself to its heart must not seek glory.
She must seek stillness.
She must be willing to remain when all else moves on.
The Heart of the House cannot be claimed.

Crap. I had to *seek* stillness? I couldn't even sit in silence for a few hours.

"Why won't you answer me?" Julia's voice floated up from below, a touch of shrillness entering her tone.

I rose and peered over the balcony. She was still staring at my previous spot on the wall, her hands planted on her hips.

It was a little funny. Little Miss Super-Controlled was floundering below me, while I sat in a comfy recliner and read the book with all the answers. Part of me wanted to laugh. To let her work herself into a tizzy down there while I secured my right as Supreme up here.

Another, more responsible voice was more logical. Nothing I did or said on the balcony would matter if I was alone. The witnesses were waiting somewhere, and ultimately, they had the final say. Plus, I had to give Julia a chance. If I didn't, I might question myself forever.

I didn't want to question who I was anymore. I didn't want a shred of doubt to ever whisper again, asking myself if I'd truly earned what was given to me. I wanted to be a true Supreme.

"Hey, Julia, I'm up here." I raised the book to one side, hoping she'd be able to see what it was without thinking I was going to pummel her with it. "I found something I think you should see."

Julia's lovely brow furrowed. She craned her head forward, comically turning her body while her head remained facing the wall. Then it, too, rotated, following my voice upwards.

"Oh!" Her eyes widened in horror or shock. She shook her head, as if reliving a horrible nightmare. "No, not again."

Then my ever-poised cousin clamped her hand over her mouth, trying in vain to stop the flow of sobs breaking through. Her shoulders shook. She let out a wail and collapsed to the ground.

I'm not gonna lie. I wanted to enjoy her breakdown a little. Julia was a symbol of the kind of self-righteous arrogance that always bothered me. She'd done me wrong in a myriad of ways.

She'd also lost, over the course of her lifetime, just as much as I had.

I shouldn't feel sorry for her.

But she was a human. In pain.

I dropped the book and leapt over the balcony.

CHAPTER
THIRTY-SEVEN

In retrospect, that was a dumb choice. My foot landed in one direction. My ankle the other. There was a definite cracking sound. Sharp pains shot up my leg, vibrating into my hip like a million tiny jackhammers.

I'd floated up. Why I chose to hop down is beyond me. I crawled to Julia, wincing each time my knees made contact with the ground. This was dumb. This was dumb. This was dumb.

When I reached Julia, I pulled her head into my lap. Whatever she was going through, she needed a mother. Or a friend. I was both, though not to her. I was also a sucker for someone in need of emotional support.

She didn't curl up, not exactly, but she did latch her arms around my waist. It mimicked what I'd done when I saw my momma in the woods. So I stroked her hair and made shushing sounds and held on tight.

This was an ugly cry. A deep, mascara running, throat raw, body aching kind of cry that came deep from the soul.

All I'd done was hold up a book.

When her tears subsided, she started to laugh. A kooky laugh edging on hysterical. She didn't move. Her fingers gripped my skin, and my leg was damp where she'd rubbed her nose on me.

My ankle was throbbing something awful. If I tried to move it, my whole body screamed. I had no choice but to stay still while my archrival had a mental breakdown in my lap.

More time passed. I was getting right sick of this third trial.

"Oh, Simone." Julia sat up and wiped her eyes. "Thank you."

She stood up, dusting her pants off and fixing her hair as if she'd just had a minor stumble. She held her hand out to me. I took it, letting her help me stand.

I couldn't put weight on my left leg. The foot was bent to an unnatural angle. No bones were sticking out—and thank the gods for that because I hated blood—but I'd clearly broken something.

"Can you, uh, help me to the wall?" Maybe if I touched it again, I'd do that floaty thing and end up on the balcony. There was a chair up there. I could just lay on the chair and read until this was over.

"No, I can't do that." She was still chuckling, even as I glared at her. "I can help you to the door, though."

"You ... what?" I could only blink at her with my mouth hanging open.

"I can help you to the door. Because I'm leaving." Her smile was dazzling. "I surrender, Simone."

She wrapped an arm around my waist and put my arm over her shoulders. I was grateful. I probably would have stared at her for days standing on one leg. She guided me towards the place where the front door to the Magnolia used to be. There was still nothing there.

"Do you know what I saw during the Stillwater Truth Test?"

"No, but I know what I saw." I responded. "Different versions of myself. All of them ugly."

"Well, that's close. I saw different versions of myself, too. But they weren't ugly." She ran a hand through her hair, combing down the knotted edges. "They were all beautiful. Perfect."

"That must have been nice." I didn't bother to hide my bitterness. The pain was starting to wear on me. "Thanks for sharing."

"You're not getting it." She kind of laughed, and it wasn't unkind. "They were all perfect because they were fake. I saw myself, over the years, using other people to make myself look better. Every man I dated. Every friend I made. Even Lyra. I love her, don't get me wrong, but at first I latched onto her because she had so much power."

"Then at the end, I saw the ugly thing." She helped me lean against the wall before standing in front of the door. Clasping her hands in front of her, she stared at them as if they held answers.

"Um, thanks?" Dude. I get I'm not a supermodel, but did she have to be so cruel about it?

"I'm screwing this up." She was talking to herself, not me. She twiddled her fingers. "You let yourself be imperfect and emotional in front of people. You let them see your broken bits. You own your mistakes."

She was staring at me again, as if this was obvious. I shrugged my shoulders, wincing as that shrug vibrated all the way through me.

"I saw you high above me, holding a book like a trophy, wearing dumb silk pajamas."

I touched the hem and pouted. I liked my jammies.

"Then you said—the lake you, I mean—said, 'this could be you.' And you, the lake you, changed into me.

"Me. Wearing blue pajamas. Can you imagine?" She laughed again. "Now I get it. The lake offered me a chance to be more like you. I rejected it."

Julia was as calm as I'd ever seen her. I'm pretty sure that's because she'd lost her mind.

"Simone, even in your times of duress, you make yourself available to anyone who needs you. Look what you just did for me. Damn near broke your leg trying to comfort me." I was pretty sure it was more than *near,* but who was I to interrupt her rant? "Hell, you shielded Lyra from me right after the second trial. And I know how harrowing that was. But you took care of her before yourself. I felt it, the moment she went under your protection. I felt all my fake power get ripped away."

She reached for a doorknob that wasn't there and turned it. A door-sized space opened, but there was no passage out. Vines were threaded together, crisscrossing the space, preventing our exit.

"I felt it ripped away, and I was relieved." Julia stepped forward, and the vines parted. She stepped through as if they weren't there.

I pushed off the wall, but the vines were already closing. There was no way I was getting through, not in my condition or without help. Daylight flashed before me.

"You're right. I don't want any of this. Every time the trials tried to show me what it meant to be Supreme, I rejected it." I could just make out her face on the other side of the vines. A silhouette of shadow. "But you and the Magnolia? You're the same, Simone. Two halves of a whole."

The vines weaved a deeper pattern. The door was fading

away, the cave growing dim. Yet Julia's voice reached me loud and clear.

"I'm not willing to be ugly. Not for my mother's dream. Not for my father's power. Not for anyone or anything." Her footsteps retreated down the porch stairs. "I surrender."

The vines were gone. The door disappeared into the wall. All sound receded.

It was just me. Injured, confused, and alone in the silence.

All of a sudden, I missed my enemy.

CHAPTER
THIRTY-EIGHT

I attempted a graceful slide to the ground, but neither leg had escaped injury. Even my "strong" leg, if I could call it that, ached. My knee gave way the moment I tried to bend it, and I sort of toppled sideways. I wiggled myself into a seated position, bracing my head against the wall.

It was like every vein pulsed through my skin. Julia's words had been those of someone who was giving up. But she'd left me alone in here, knowing I was injured. Had her surrender actually been a claim to the Supreme? Surely leaving me for dead wasn't part of the trial.

Like in the forest, and in the lake before that, I had no concept of time. There'd been daylight on the other side of the vine barricade, but whether it was the same day we started or not, I had no way to know. I squeezed my eyes shut, bracing myself, hoping the pain would subside.

It was about that time I forgot about the trials. My throbbing ankle was a pretty solid distraction. I might have slept. My thoughts drifted toward survival.

I didn't ache for food. Yet. But I was parched. I dimly

remembered hearing drops of water somewhere in this massive cave. There was no way I'd be able to find them in this condition. I opened my eyes. Across from me, I could still make out the railing of the balcony. A faded but prominent array of colors streamed over the wood.

I was still in the house. There was magic up there. Maybe it could hear me.

"Hey. House." I licked my lips. When this was over, I was gonna beg Lyra for some sort of moisturizing treatment. "If you're up there, I don't suppose you could get me a glass of water?"

I waited. Nothing happened.

"It doesn't have to be cold. I don't need ice." I swallowed. My throat was tender and raw. There was no Big Magic Voice™ happening. I couldn't force this.

A sliver of frustration bubbled up. I wasn't asking for a lot. I wasn't asking to be healed, or even to leave. I was home, after all. I figured this was where I was supposed to be. House wasn't going to allow me to dehydrate until I turned to dust and became part of its foundation or something.

"The thing is, you've always given me water." I was talking only to hear my voice. To escape the silence. "Remember when I first learned about all this magic and witch stuff? I had a panic attack. I ran to my mother's gravesite to have a good and proper freak out.

"Gumbo found me there. He talked me down. But you ..." The urge to cry rolled forward with the memory. "You sent me a glass of ginger ale. Anytime I was down, you sent me a Bayou Bliss."

I'm going to be honest, House. I never thought of you as a mother." I sighed and let my shoulders sag. "You've always been my friend."

It wasn't totally accurate, though. It felt dishonest to say the house was my friend. We were friendly, which was weird. But it was different from the friendship I was developing with the coven. Or what Brianne and I found right away.

I couldn't put my finger on why. But I needed to. Suddenly more crucial than thirst or pain, I needed to understand what connected me to House.

Why, when Julia came back, I'd felt like my soul was being ripped from my body. Why I'd sensed disappointment when I wanted to bake a cake by myself. Why I knew when it was afraid.

I thought back to what Julia said before she'd abandoned me. Two-halves of a whole.

I missed our connection, even now amidst my more visceral fears.

Because it wasn't a connection to a mystical presence. It was like my power. It was part of me.

"The chains of magic can bind, but the bonds of family can shatter even the strongest link." I sat upright, ignoring the shooting pain I caused myself.

My voice was different.

No, the air around me was different. It was no longer empty.

"But not our link. Right, House?" From a far corner, something giggled. Giddiness washed over me. "Even family can't shatter our link. It's held together by something far stronger than magic."

The rainbow from the balcony window blasted through the cave, lighting the ceiling. As I watched, it transformed into the high ceilings of the Magnolia Wellness and Therapy Center. The light lowered, replacing stone with walls and darkness with light.

It was all that it was supposed to be. The kitchenette table with five cozy chairs. Brianne's lovely little office space. Four wooden doors, each uniquely carved and adorned with a simple yet elegant sign.

I was home.

Our tall front windows formed at my back. The door was restored, its brass knob gleaming. But it didn't open. A sudden rustling, like steps through dry leaves, drew my attention back to the balcony. A series of vines wrapped themselves around the banister.

When they reached the top, they extended out and down. Reaching me, they latched onto my arms and legs. They encircled my wrists and ankles, slithering up my body like happy little snakes, wrapping me in a leafy cocoon.

But they were somehow familiar, and though I was covered head-to-toe in foliage, I could breathe. There was space to move. It was dark and quiet. Once the vines stopped wriggling, there was stillness. It was peaceful. I wasn't even scared.

Well. I was a little scared.

But I wasn't alone. A presence shared the vines with me. It was familiar and friendly. We'd baked together. We'd danced together.

"I know you," I said. The presence giggled, and I giggled right along with it. "You're me."

It moved closer, enveloping me, so I was a cocoon within a cocoon. Then it sank into me, little by little, and I was warm and safe.

We really were half of a whole, the Magnolia and I.

When I'd discovered my new position and accepted it, I'd thought I was doing it to give myself a second chance. Maybe to honor Agatha, and my mother, and everything they were building here. Or because I liked the division heads and Brianne. I even liked the Twins a little.

I'd thought I was being handed a gift. Even if I hadn't earned it.

I'd been willing to try, though—to earn it eventually.

The joke was on me. I didn't have to fight to become Supreme. I didn't have to undergo a dozen challenges or prove myself.

I only had to embrace who I was, flaws and all, and accept my purpose in space and time.

Which, I suppose, is the biggest challenge in the world.

CHAPTER
THIRTY-NINE

The vines had lifted me into the air. When the front door opened, they lowered me slowly onto a chair in the kitchenette. I extended my left leg, trying to bend the ankle. I instantly regretted the attempt.

The division heads and Brianne walked in. They moved slowly, heads on swivels, staring at the walls in awe as if the place were somehow different.

It looked the same to me.

"Hi, guys," I said, my voice falsely chipper. "I don't suppose one of you could give me a ride to the hospital?"

Something cold and wet touched my toes. I yelped, almost jumping out of my seat.

"Sorry, Simone." Gumbo hopped onto the table. He wore a huge bow, suspiciously matching the color of the recliner on the balcony. His toes matched, too. "I was merely assessing the extent of your damage. If it helps, it's just a fracture."

"Cool." A glass of ice water popped onto the table. I'd forgotten I was thirsty. I sucked it down, laughing a bit when it refilled itself. "Thanks, House."

"Are you okay?" Brianne was kneeling at my side, careful not to touch the leg. "You're bruised."

"You couldn't see us?"

"Not this time. We've been outside waiting." Brianne's voice trembled. "Did you and Julia fight?"

"Not exactly." I looked up and pointed at the ceiling overhead. "I was up there. I jumped."

"That was stupid." Lydia rolled her eyes as she sat opposite me.

"Oh, leave her alone. I'm sure it made sense at the time." Well, knock me over with a feather. Lyra was speaking up for me.

One-by-one, they took their seats at our breakroom table. My heart did a little happy dance. This was what I'd envisioned for our daily lunches. I was going to make that a thing.

After we finished all the business.

"Where's Julia?" The front door was still open, but no one was on the other side of it.

"Gone," Lauren answered. "She waved at us and then walked away."

"Walked where?" I turned to Lyra. "Back to your realm?"

"I don't think so," Lyra said. "It seemed like she was walking out of town."

She could have gone anywhere. To wherever she was staying while she was in town. To Ray's house, although I didn't know where he lived. Or to Bridge House.

But I couldn't escape the feeling that she was gone for good. And I hoped, whatever path she took, she found happiness there.

"She's going to be able to put the past behind her." There it was. My Big Magic Voice™. Man, that was a good sound. I looked down at my ankle. It was turning an alarming shade of maroon. My feet looked like sausages. "So, the hospital? Anyone?"

"There's just one matter of business, Simone." Gumbo dropped his *I Can Haz* voice, and the formal kitty came out. "There must be witnesses with the power to judge their actions. After the final trial, those who've heard the recitation shall bear the burden of declaring a rightful Supreme."

"Really?" My chest tightened. "Julia surrendered. Is this part necessary?"

"I'm afraid so." Gumbo butted his tiny head into my arm, a sweet gesture I rewarded with neck rubs.

"This should go fast. I vote for Simone as Supreme." Lauren's bouncy little grin matched her ponytail. She turned a worried glance to Gumbo. "Unless there's some formal language I have to use?"

He batted at my fingers, then sat upright, as if remembering he had an official job to do. Adorable little kitty.

"No formal language. Just an acknowledgement that Simone is the rightful Supreme."

He stretched his front paws, lifting his kitty butt and dipping his head in a regal and downright cute bow.

"Simone, I hereby pledge myself, as Mystical Protector of the Magnolia, to be your protector as well. You have earned the right as our Supreme."

"No way I'm bowing to you." Lydia ran her nails across Gumbo's tail, eliciting a mega-purr. "But you're the Supreme."

"Definitely the Supreme." Lyra smiled, an actual smile, at me. "You earned it. And my gratitude."

For just a moment, her bottom lip trembled. I was grateful for her support, but it had come at a cost. I hoped, when she was ready, I could help her process that.

There was only Brianne left. Brianne, my staunchest defender from day one. Julia's actions had caused a rift between us, but I was confident that time and communication would restore it. I held no ill toward her. I had to assume she held none towards me.

But she didn't look like herself anymore. The smile she'd offered so often and freely was missing. Though her lips curved, there was a shield around her that gave me pause. She was on guard, and I wasn't sure why.

"How'd you do it, Simone?" Her voice wasn't the same either. "How'd you win the third Rite?"

"Didn't you see it?" I was confused. Was she asking if I'd cheated or what lesson I'd learned? Why did she sound afraid? Nerves gripped my throat. "I don't understand the question, Bri."

"I don't either." She squinted for a moment, moving her lips in silence as she reconciled something within herself. Then, she shook her head. "I think I'm asking what you found out. About yourself, I mean."

They'd been restless, but at her clarification the division heads and Gumbo stood still. They watched me, waiting for my answer. And though logically I didn't think they could revoke their claim, I had the sudden feeling that I was back in high school and this was the big exam. If this were a nightmare, I'd be naked.

But I wasn't naked. I was wearing lovely blue silk pajamas. And my friends all had a matching pair.

Besides, this wasn't high school.

"Well, I guess I figured out why I was here." My water glass transformed into a Bayou Bliss. Condensation trickled down the side, creating a pool of water on the table.

"When I first learned about Agatha, and about the role we'd discussed, I felt like I hadn't earned it. After all, she'd made that promise with an eighteen-year-old girl. Even if she believed in me, Agatha didn't know me anymore.

"And I didn't know myself." The condensation continued to run, so I thought about a cute coaster. When it appeared, I slid it under the glass. "The first two trials helped me figure that out. I faced all my imperfections. All my doubts. Every mistake."

My hip ached. My leg throbbed. And I was getting very, very tired.

But there was something in Brianne's eyes that held me in place. A desperation that made me realize she wasn't testing me. She was questioning herself. There was no way I'd let someone as supportive as she is doubt how awesome she is.

"Anyway, the third Rite was pretty much about being alone with myself and realizing I'm not made up of my mistakes or experiences. That's a part of me. Not the whole of me."

I reached across the table and took her hand in mine. A single tear trailed down her cheek and landed on my arm, unchecked.

"I had to see myself as whole. Even if I'm flawed. My magic lies in that wholeness. House and I are connected through that wholeness. House is a part of me, and if I was judging a part of me, I was questioning my power."

I gave her the bravest smile I could manage.

"I guess, if I was going to make it simple, I'd say that I passed the third Rite because I finally understood."

"Understand what?" Her voice just above a whisper, Brianne swiped at the remaining tears.

"I love you. I love the coven. I love myself. And I love the Magnolia." I squeezed her hand, linking our fingers. "And that's a pretty powerful magic."

It was cheesy as hell, and Lydia groaned before I'd even finished saying it. I didn't care. We needed the laugh of a corny sentiment, even if it was true.

"Well then." Brianne stood up, taking a tissue to her eyes. "Let's get our rightful Supreme to the hospital."

"Awesome." Now that I could breathe a sigh of relief, the pain was unrelenting. With nothing to distract me, the true extent of my injuries was super obvious. Just a fracture my butt. And my butt hurt, too.

I'd be lucky if I came out of this without a full-body cast.

Lydia lifted me like I was just a speck of cotton. I grunted because she wasn't exactly soft about it.

"Oh, quit your moaning," she said. But her arms relaxed a little.

My eyes were closing. I couldn't remember hitting my head, so I figure it was fatigue and not a concussion. And since no one was freaking out that I was falling asleep, I decided to go ahead and let that happen.

I was big tired. But super happy.

"By the way." I couldn't resist dropping my head to Lydia's shoulder. "When I get home, the Magnolia is open for business.

"And it's never going to close."

CHAPTER

FORTY

I f Lyra had banged on my door an hour earlier, she would
have caught me half-naked.

Technically, she still caught me without a shirt on.

I was finally home from the hospital, and boy was I happy
about it. Gumbo had been right about my fracture being
simple. But it was still severe enough that I was in a cast for the
next six to eight weeks. I wasn't thrilled about that.

Or about the knee sprain I'd managed on impact. I'd
knocked my spine out of alignment, too—because when I do
something, I go all in. I'd stayed in the hospital overnight,
gotten a nifty IV full of fluids to rehydrate me, and received a
ton of personal attention from a really hot nurse.

It was nice to know at forty-eight I was still turning heads.
Even if I had to bruise my whole damn body to do it.

I was looking forward to a very restful night in my favorite
bed. I'd shooed Brianne away. She'd been at my bedside the
whole time, and I loved her for it.

But I needed some time alone. Not that I was actually
alone.

House helped me wrap the cast so I could take a shower. It even put a little stool thingy in the bathtub. My hair was clean. My body scrubbed.

And I was home.

So when I opened my drawer and took out a fresh pair of underwear, pure bliss overcame me. And not the kind that came from coffee. House blasted spontaneous music. Some Sia song about having stamina and being the greatest.

Sounded good to me. And maybe I couldn't dance, not exactly, but I could hobble a jig.

Which is what I was doing when Lyra banged on my door. House put a shirt in my hand—Ray's old T-shirt—still the most comfortable thing I'd ever worn to bed. And bonus... it covered my butt.

I was still figuring out how to use my crutches, so she banged the whole five minutes it took me to reach the door.

"I'm coming," I shouted. "Relax."

When I opened it, she ran her eyes up and down and shook her head.

"You know you could have asked House to open the door, right? Instead of shoving yourself into clothes that don't fit and hustling over?"

"That's not how we work," I said. Plus, I hadn't thought of it. "Is everything okay?"

"Um. Can I come in?"

This was a new look for Lyra. She'd recovered physically from the Bloomthief's drain, but her eyes were still too dim for my liking. I gestured her in, following her to the living room. All the blankets and throw pillows were still on the floor from our sleepover.

"House can clean up, too." She brushed crumbs off a couch cushion and settled in.

"We like to clean together." I took the chair on the opposite side, so I could extend my leg. When it exposed my underwear, I grabbed one of the blankets and tossed it over my lap. "What's up, Lyra?"

Now that we were seated, Lyra's nerves were on full display. It wasn't just her eyes that dimmed. Her skin wasn't holding its usual glow. She worried her fingers together, shifting in her seat, crossing and uncrossing her legs.

I gave her a few minutes to settle in. Whatever she wanted to talk to me about, she needed to work up the courage to do it. I could have given her the courage. That was a technique I planned to use with some of my patients.

I'd known there was more to my magic than I knew, but I suspected I'd still only broken the surface. Now that the trials were over, I didn't know how to get to the tiny room with *The Magnolia Codex* volumes. I just had to hope they weren't lost to me.

But it struck me that Lyra was having a very human problem. Call it intuition. I sensed that if I used magic to help her uncover it, she'd grow resentful. And maybe she needed to know that.

"Lyra, despite our rocky start, I want you to know I'm here for you." She jerked her eyes to me, gnawing on her lip. "Not just as a division head. Or as Supreme, although both of those are true. I can be a very good friend."

Lyra winced.

"What did I say that struck a nerve?" I asked her.

"The last good friend I had betrayed me." To my complete shock, she started to cry. I couldn't walk over to her, but I did lift a box of tissues.

"House, do you mind?" The tissues floated across the air and landed next to Lyra. She took them with a grateful smile.

"You went through a lot these past few weeks." Lyra blew her nose. She sounded like a foghorn in a rainstorm. "But you seem, I don't know, okay now?"

The hope in her voice was heartbreaking.

"I'm working through it." I didn't want to lie to her. Or to myself. "All my issues were uncovered in really extreme ways, and that takes time to heal from. But I've learned I can handle it. And that's something."

She looked down at the ground and nodded.

"You know, Lyra, you went through a lot these past few weeks as well. It wasn't just my past that got exposed." Her lip trembled. "It's okay if you're struggling right now."

I'd never actually seen anyone square their shoulders before. As if she were grabbing for an internal pocket of bravery, Lyra sat upright and turned to me. With perfect posture, she folded her hands on her lap. Her cheeks and eyes were completely dry.

It was like she'd never shown human emotions. Neat trick.

"I believe you're a good therapist, Simone."

She waited for me to react. I didn't, mostly because I was way in my head. She couldn't know I was a good therapist. Once upon a time, I wouldn't have questioned the statement. But the past few months I'd been adequate, at best.

She was still waiting. I shrugged my shoulders.

"I believe I can be a good therapist." There. That wasn't a lie. Maybe her face fell a bit, maybe I'd disappointed her. But I had to be honest.

"Brianne mentioned you'd restructured your schedule?" At my nod, she continued. "I know you wanted to see fewer patients overall."

"I do. I want time to understand my additional responsibilities. And I want to do better with the patients I've kept."

"Do you have room for one more?"

Her facade broke. Just a speck. It struck me how hard this must be for her. Not only to ask for help, but to do it without her sister by her side. And to ask me, of all people. The person she'd betrayed. We would work through that. Until then, it hung between us.

Most things from the past do that, though. They linger long after they're welcomed. Even the soil we thought we'd dug up and re-tilled tends to carry remnants of the weeds we've cultivated. All the parts of us, good and bad, weave together in a mosaic that forms a picture of us. All the cracks are part of the mosaic, lined with gold, and downright beautiful.

If I could use all my fractured parts to help someone else heal theirs? Well sign me up for that gig.

"Of course I can make room for a friend."

Her relief softened the space between us too. Like a cool breeze on a summer's day. Little acts of kindness. Of acceptance.

Of joy.

Maybe it *was* corny. But it was true. Connections held their own magic.

I walked Lyra to the door, sort of. These doggone crutches were gonna get the best of me. But I managed to get it open, and she managed a quick hug before she stepped out.

"One more thing." She paused with her hand on the doorknob and gave me a very fae grin. "Lydia and I will be joining you for lunch every day, so make sure there's space at the table."

"There's always room at my table," I told her.

She shut the door, and I leaned against it until I could bolster the energy to make it to the bedroom. I did about a dozen little jigs on the way down the hall. I swear, House was dancing, too. Its foundation rumbled, and glass clinked on shelves.

When I reached the bedroom, the door was missing. It was all wall, except for a yellow sign.

You're officially Supreme.
That's hot.
Try not to burn anything.

"Very funny." The sign winked away, and my door reappeared.

I climbed into bed with a happy sigh. Still perfect. A cocoon within a cocoon.

A soft breeze played with the curtains as my eyes drifted closed. Crickets chirped. In the distance, a wolf howled. I wondered what phase of the moon we were in.

But not for long.

"Good night, House." A touch, light as a feather, brushed a strand of hair behind my ear. Safe and snug as a bug in a rug, I drifted off to sleep.

Home at last.

～

THANK you so much for reading *Witchful Linking*! If you loved the book and have a moment, a quick star-rating or review makes a huge difference in helping other readers decide if this is their new favorite series.

～

LIFE at the Magnolia has never been better, or more complicated, for Simone. Proving herself as top dog led to an expansion of magic way beyond her comfort zone, making her habit of talking to herself backfire in the most magical of ways.

Meanwhile, a heck of a hurricane is en route, two very hot wolf shifters are vying for her attention, and her steady-as-they-come new bestie Brianne is losing herself in one doozie of a midlife crisis.

Some things in life can't be controlled. But Simone is ready to embrace the changes that come with age and growth. Probably.

^^^ Scan the code above or click here to preorder book three, *Witchful Sinking.*

A PORTION of The Magnolia Codex escaped its space beyond place and time! Simone *might* have spilled a little bit of coffee on it but hey, I'm sure nothing important was stained...

Download Here

^^^ Scan the code above or click here to download your exclusive bonus scene, free when you join my newsletter.

ACKNOWLEDGMENTS

This book is for all the mommas out there.

For breaking generational cycles, creating future generations, and still managing to be badass humans.

It's damn hard work, and you make it look easy. But that's because you're doing it right.

I see you.

ABOUT THE AUTHOR

Jen Lassalle is a New Orleans writer of empowering women's fiction with a magical midlife twist. She especially loves awkward and compassionate middle-aged females with light romance and found family friendships that empower heroines in inclusive worlds where magic exists and mystical creatures live among us.

When Jen isn't writing, she's hanging with her family and friends at a local park or coffee shop. She likes working out, which is kind of weird, loves yoga, and plays video games. Of course, she reads.

Jen and her husband have two kids. One is an avid competitive swimmer (which sucks up all their weekend time). The other is a daydreamer like Jen who plays Bowie on guitar and anime theme songs on his keyboard.

You can follow Jen's socials using the links below.

f facebook.com/jenlassallewrites

⊙ instagram.com/jenlassalle

a amazon.com/stores/JB-Lassalle/author/B0BFJXP4GC

♪ tiktok.com/@jen.lassalle

www.ingramcontent.com/pod-product-compliance
Lightning Source LLC
Chambersburg PA
CBHW030644020726
47493CB00006B/1856